Taken

Niamh O'Connor

TRANSWORLD IRELAND

TRANSWORLD IRELAND
An imprint of The Random House Group Limited
20 Vauxhall Bridge Road, London SW1V 2SA
www.transworldbooks.co.uk

TAKEN
A TRANSWORLD IRELAND BOOK: 9781848270831

First published in 2011 by Transworld Ireland,
a division of Transworld Publishers
Transworld Ireland paperback edition published 2012

Addresses for Random House Group Ltd companies outside the UK
can be found at: www.randomhouse.co.uk
The Random House Group Ltd Reg. No. 954009

The Random House Group Limited supports The Forest Stewardship
Council (FSC®), the leading international forest certification organisation.
Our books carrying the FSC label are printed on FSC® certified paper. FSC
is the only forest certification scheme endorsed by the leading environmental
organisations, including Greenpeace. Our paper procurement policy can be
found at www.randomhouse.co.uk/environment

Typeset in 11.5/15pt Sabon by Falcon Oast Graphic Art Ltd.
Printed in the UK by CPI Group (UK) Ltd, Croydon, CR0 4YY

2 4 6 8 10 9 7 5 3 1

www.transworldireland.ie

www.**transworldbooks**.co.uk

013669167 8

Also by Niamh O'Connor

Non-fiction

BLOOD TIES

Fiction

IF I NEVER SEE YOU AGAIN

TAKEN

Foreword

Some stories come to newspaper journalists that are impossible to prove. But sometimes you get a sense that a story that does appear in a newspaper is only scratching the surface of something that is far more sinister.

How many times do papers make a splash with an interview with a call girl who has sold the story of her night of passion with a footballer or celebrity? It's almost the norm now for these women to come from privileged, educated, middle-class backgrounds, rather than those of deprivation or desperation, as a reader might expect. It is stories like these that have always made me wonder what it must be like to have the sort of looks that appeal to the very rich, and the brains to make a calculated decision to subjugate the self for cold, hard currency. What are the temptations for very beautiful women who want some of the excesses of the glitzy world for themselves? To whom do the wealthy turn for discretion? And how has the global recession impacted on the sex industry?

This book is an attempt to tease out some of the answers, and it's based on a story that couldn't get into a newspaper; one that keeps coming up through different sources. In essence it's about the model industry in meltdown, and the very real links in the chain between the celebrity circuit, and the gangland horrors – murder, human trafficking, drug importation – that are required to keep the rich and corrupt in their party bubble of excess and decadence. It's the story of the oldest profession in the world.

Because no matter the amount of money that changes hands, or the individuals involved, it's still a story of what happens when sex is for sale.

Niamh O'Connor
April 2011

Prologue

Tara Parker Trench pulled up at the only free pump in the petrol station on Eden Quay, and after a long, hard look through the windscreen wipers, killed Beyoncé's 'Single Ladies' and twisted around.

It was nine o'clock on a Sunday night, and pitch dark, but she wasn't worrying about what might happen if she left her three-year-old son alone in the car near Dublin city centre. Not when she was only going to be gone for sixty seconds maximum, and especially not when it was lashing rain. Her stomach ached as she turned, and she pressed her hand against it.

Presley had nodded off, and was purring like a kitten in the back. The Ray-Bans she'd got him had slid to the tip of his nose, his Tommy Hilfiger jacket collar was turned up and the peak of his New York Yankees trucker cap sloped to the side, skateboarder style.

'Such a cool dude,' she said, giving his Nike runner boot a little squeeze.

Clicking her seatbelt off, she stretched between the seats and tried to tilt his head back into a more comfortable position, wincing as she did so with the exertion. It flopped forward again, and she reached for the Snuggly Puppy on his lap to see if she could use it as a pillow. But even fast asleep, Presley's chubby little fingers tightened their grip.

Tara smiled. She'd only been sixteen when she'd got pregnant, and had had to fight to have, and keep, him. She'd no regrets: she and Presley, they were a team. Despite all the rows with her own mum about the future, she had been able to build a good life for both of them. Tara was never going back to the hardship of just a few years back. Presley deserved the best in life, and so did she.

A sharp beep from the car behind told her to get a move on. Tara glanced in her rear-view mirror, patting the air to say 'calm down'. Little Miss Impatient was a Botoxed brunette in her forties with that puckered look around her lips that collagen always gave. She was driving a brand-new Jag. Catching sight of her own face, Tara wiped away the smudged mascara beneath her eyes. The sooner she got home and into a hot shower the better, she thought.

Stepping out of her black Mini Cooper with white

stripes down the bonnet, she grimaced. The River Liffey stank the way it always did before heavy fog. Screwing off the cap to the car's petrol tank, she gestured to the rest of the bays in the forecourt for the Jag lady's benefit as she began to fill up. They were bumper to bumper and it wouldn't just be this garage that was full, either. Every motorist in the country with an ounce of sense would be filling up tonight. Tomorrow was Budget Day, and the fallout from the bank bailout and the IMF interest rate meant another round of hard-hitting taxes was on the cards.

A wolf whistle rang out, and Tara stiffened. She knew it was for her. Men had been wolf whistling at her since she was twelve years old. Whoever it was had issues with women – it was too drawn-out to be friendly or jokey.

Pushing her long hair out of her eyes, she kept her head down – feeling self-conscious suddenly about the short, glitzy dress she was still wearing and the high heels. She located the man she thought was responsible for the whistle out of the side of her eye. He was parked at pump number three, sitting behind the wheel of a battered HiAce. There was a white Mitsubishi with flashy hubcaps and a spoiler on the boot between her and him. The bay to her right – the one nearest the road – had a white sheet fluttering from the pump which said it was out of service. On Tara's left the boy racer in the white

11

Mitsubishi seat rolled down his tinted window.

'Here, I know you,' he called. 'You're that model, right? I've got your poster on my wall. You know, the one of you posing like Britney Spears in a school uniform?'

Tara sighed. She remembered the shot he was talking about – it was for a campaign against illiteracy to try and encourage older people to go back to school. The message it sent out about what men could look forward to if they returned to the education system was a disgrace, but she didn't object. Money was money, even if a photo call – the bread and butter of a model's trade – was only worth a pittance. She needed every penny at the moment.

'Looking hot, darlin'. Want to go for a drink?'

Tara felt a flash of anger. 'What's your poison?' she called back. 'Lemonade with ice?'

Two of the kid's mates, who had the same chunky silver chains around their necks, came out of the garage forecourt with armfuls of crisps and chocolate, and laughed as they heard Tara's put-down. The boy racer turned red and revved the engine.

Tara angled the nozzle back in the pump. Stooping, she cupped her hands over her eyes to check Presley through the glass, then straightened up to scan the queue at the till inside which snaked right the way down the aisle. It was definitely best to leave him where he was, she decided. She pointed the key fob at the Mini, but changed her mind in case Presley activated the alarm. If he banged his arm or foot against the window and it went off, he would wake, find himself alone and get upset. The last thing she needed now was him bawling all the way home.

The woman in the Jag gave another impatient beep, and Tara reached into the car for her Vivienne Westwood jacket, held it over her head so she wouldn't get wet, and ran towards the entrance, much to the boy racers' delight. They struck up a round of catcalls, and set off after her, a row of flashing blue lights pulsating along their bumper.

Inside, she hurried past a long rack of convenience shelves stocked with the kind of foods that just needed boiling water added. The place was a dive, but at least the queue was moving quickly and there were only three people ahead of her. Then they stopped. Tara strained sideways to see what the problem was. A customer with a shaved head and a Staffordshire bull terrier in tow was pretending he didn't understand the accent of the Chinese man behind the till. 'What?' and 'Can you say it in English?' he kept saying. Tara sighed. At this rate, she'd be here another ten minutes.

She turned to try and peer out the shop front glass to check on Presley, but couldn't see a thing. It was so dark out the fluorescent bulbs overhead had turned the window fronting the forecourt into a virtual mirror.

She focused on the CCTV screen up over the Chinese guy's head, willing it to flash up an image of her car. For a second, she recognized the stripes on the Mini's bonnet but it flashed to another car before she'd had a chance to study it properly.

Shaved head was being asked to stand aside, and was refusing. A man in a suit, standing directly behind him in the queue, pushed his cash in through the sliding hatch in the counter. 'I'm in a hurry,' he said.

Shaved head jerked the dog's leash. The mutt started to growl.

Tara pointed her key fob out the window at where she estimated the Mini was, and pressed the button. Presley's safety was suddenly more important than him getting upset at the alarm going off. When a set of orange indicators blinked back, she exhaled in relief.

The dog had started to bark. Behind her in the queue someone pushed up against her in a way that made her skin crawl. She buttoned her jacket all the way up before turning around. A spotty teenager with a white hoodie pulled over his head nudged her with his shoulder.

'Bet ya he's got a blade,' he said, nodding at the shaved head guy.

He looked like a junkie – his eyes were glazed and he had a nasal tone, but his accent was too posh to be from around there. There was something weird about the way he was staring at her; it was freaking her out. She stepped as far forwards as was possible to get away from him without bumping into the old man in front of her. A car alarm went off outside, and Tara turned, squinting to see through the glass. Was Presley crying? Frantic at the queue stretching behind her, she aimed the remote through the window again and jabbed. The alarm stopped.

Shaved head was dragging his dog towards the exit, still grumbling to himself about the Chinese guy's accent. Hate had made his face tight. His dog was skidding on its paws, every sinew in its body straining to move in the opposite direction. The Chinese guy shouted back through the Perspex protective glass for shaved head to stay where he was until he'd paid, then bent over to reach some button under the counter.

Tara wrung her hands together, and was giving serious consideration to going back out to the car and bringing Presley in with her, when a Muslim guy in a skullcap burst out of a door behind the counter and asked what the problem was.

Shaved head was parallel to Tara now. Picking up a can of Red Bull from the open fridge, he threw it hard at the till. It bounced off the Perspex, and landed on the floor, the contents spraying up in a high arch. The youth behind Tara whooped in delight. The other customers looked either worried or pissed off. The old man was oblivious. Either he'd seen it all before, or was half-blind with cataracts. Tara had to get out.

Shaved head reached for another missile, his arm blocking her exit. Tara ducked under it and bolted as the second can was catapulted to the top of the shop.

Out in the forecourt, she could see that the can of Red Bull had connected with the head of the man in the suit at the top of the queue, who stumbled, then hit the floor with a crash. The dog jumped free of the leash and leapt straight towards him. Tara covered her mouth and ran to her car.

Ducking to look at the back seat, she saw Presley still snoozing his head off. Tara felt weak with relief. 'Sorry, sweetheart,' she whispered, turning the key in the engine, pressing the clutch with her foot and putting the car in first gear. But a hard rapping on the window made her jump, her foot slipped off the clutch and the car did a bunny hop before cutting out.

The Muslim guy was pressed up against the window, and was rubbing his thumb against his first two fingers to signal that she needed to pay for her petrol.

Tara swung the door open, forcing him to step

back. 'I'm only moving it,' she shouted, pointing to the air-and-water area. But the bloke in the HiAce had just swerved out of the bay he was in so hard his tyres screeched. He stalled and blocked her exit, and by the look of things had broken down. His van belched out black smoke. One or more of the plug points had gone, she reckoned. Her ex – Presley's dad, Mick – was a mechanic, and some of what he knew had rubbed off. Tonight, after what she'd been through, she wished they were still together.

The HiAce man was turning the engine over, trying to restart it. It sounded to Tara like he was flooding it, but she wasn't going to get involved. The engine stopped slipping, and he suddenly took off, leaving a trail of dirty exhaust fumes in his wake.

Starting up again, she pulled up twenty yards away, parking alongside the door of a toilet with an 'Out of Order' sign taped to it. She could hear a siren getting steadily louder as she headed back inside the garage to settle the bill.

Miraculously, in spite of all the commotion, she made it to the till within less than five minutes of entering. The dog had been called off, shaved head escorted out of the shop, and by the time the para-medics arrived to tend to the suit, the Muslim manager had mopped up the Red Bull and erected yellow 'Wet Floor' signs around the offending area. As Tara handed over her credit card, she saw the dog being locked in the toilet and a garda pushing the shaved headed guy towards a waiting squad car.

Turning away from the till, Tara nearly collided with the Jag lady, whose mouth was pursed in disapproval. Dressed in a pink cashmere cardigan with stern shoulder pads and gold buttons, and wearing a pair of shades, she looked Tara up and down like she was dirt. Much as Tara wanted to ask what the hell her problem was, she wanted to get back to Presley a whole lot more.

Double-checking her till receipt to make sure she hadn't been short-changed, she pinched open the pack of white chocolate buttons she'd bought along with a packet of painkillers when she'd paid for the petrol, and hurried back to the car. If Presley woke, these would keep him pacified for the rest of the journey home. They weren't good for him, she knew, but she couldn't face any more drama, and anyway she never could resist a chance to spoil him.

Opening the driver's door, she leaned towards Presley, smiling and whispering his name. But Snuggly Puppy was on the floor. And Presley was gone.

Monday

1

Detective Inspector Jo Birmingham was trying to adjust the telly on the wall bracket of her brand-new office so she could see the screen. The glare of the winter sun was making it impossible to watch the DVD which had arrived in the post that morning. Not that the sounds were leaving much to the imagination. It was clearly a sex tape of some description.

She stretched to try and swivel the bracket around. If she'd had the man who'd stuck it up that high in the first place here in front of her now she'd have given him an earful. Even at her height – five foot ten – she could barely reach it. And the bracket was at such an inconvenient angle. She'd enough problems with migraines recently to know that focusing on anything at an awkward position would invite them back.

She was also doing her best not to look through the glass partition that separated her from the rest of the detective unit, where a clock said ten to nine. Jo's darkening mood had more than a little to do with the fact that her ex-husband and present boss, Chief Superintendent Dan Mason, was just back from a weekend in the sun, and was holding court in the open-plan office, recounting some story or other. *He always did have the gift of the gab*, she thought sneaking a quick glance. He looked good, his face and hands were tanned, and his hair had grown a bit, too. There were slashes of grey in the sides. The older he got, the more she thought he looked like Jason Statham in the Guy Ritchie films.

Slipping off her heels, she dragged over a plastic chair which she'd recovered from the storeroom about a quarter of an hour ago, when she'd been trying to find things to furnish her office. Plonking it directly under the TV, she hitched up her skirt and stepped on to it, doing her best to ignore the half-dozen grinning detectives turning to have a good gawk and a laugh. In an ideal world, Jo would have flashed them like in that Maltesers ad, to wipe the smiles off their faces, but there was a newly appointed Human Resources manager in Store Street Station, Daphne, and Jo didn't want the distinction of being the one who finally gave her something to do.

Balancing on the chair, which was beginning to wobble precariously, she lifted the telly from its bracket and on to the corner of the desk she'd snaffled from Dan's secretary Jeanie's office, thanks to the fact that Jeanie was now on maternity leave. She'd taken Jeanie's computer, too.

Jo had sworn to the mules who'd hauled the items down the corridor for her ten minutes ago that, of course, they would go back eventually; but because Jeanie was now living with Dan, and carrying his baby, Jo wasn't planning on keeping her word.

Through the glass, she saw Detective Inspector Gavin Sexton stand up from his desk and start to make his way over. *Bloody men, never around when we need them*, she grumbled to herself, stepping down from the chair, and rubbing a twinge that had struck up in the small of her back.

Dan was watching her – she could feel his eyes on her through the window, but when she turned towards him, he was focused back on his fan club, and was becoming even more animated. Jo hoped her new office wasn't going to make her feel as if she was in a goldfish bowl all the time.

Taking a few steps sideways, she finally made out what was happening on the TV screen. She crossed her arms, and watched as the scene unfolded. A girl with surgically enhanced boobs, wearing only a thong, was standing in the shallow end of an outdoor swimming pool, performing a sex act on a man who was sitting on the ledge, leaning back on his hands.

Within seconds, a group of men burst out of a door just out of camera shot, and started dive-bombing into the water. They were shouting words of encouragement to the first man, who looked up and grinned. The girl carried on regardless. Jo recognized the sound of an Irish accent among the English roars. She reached for the Jiffy bag the disc had arrived in and inspected the postcode. There was no stamp, meaning it had been hand-delivered. It wasn't internal post either, because it didn't have the standard state harp on it.

Her own name was scrawled in capital letters on the outside of the envelope in dodgy green biro under the words 'Private and Confidential'. She had had to borrow scissors from Sergeant John Foxe to get through the multiple layers of Sellotape and staples the Jiffy bag had been sealed with. Foxy had only handed the scissors over on condition that she promised to hand them straight back. His initials were Tipp-Exed on the handle.

As she moved the envelope, a piece of folded paper dropped out. She hadn't spotted it earlier, and she now opened it carefully to view a series of letters and words cut from newspapers and magazines. It read: 'How the other half lives – the justice minister enjoying a night out.'

Jo looked back at the screen, eyebrows raised. The current justice minister was Blaise Stanley, someone she had been dealing with to try and bolster victims' rights in court, but although the party was in full swing in the pool, she couldn't see him. The four men who'd jumped in the water had made a semicircle around the girl, who had stopped what she was doing and was trying to push one of them, who was groping her, away. Jo couldn't see their faces, their backs were all to the camera. The man whose legs the girl had been standing between grabbed her roughly by the hair and forced her head back down in his lap. Jo leaned in closer to the screen. Although the film had been shot at night, she could see palm trees, meaning it had to have been taken abroad. There was a hotel in the background with an onion-shaped roof, and between it and the pool a couple were drinking and chatting. They didn't seem in the least put off by what was going on right under their noses – although the woman looked directly across from time to time.

Jo glanced at the note and back at the screen. *Could that be Blaise Stanley?* She doubted it. It was impossible to tell as his back was to the bloody camera, too. The woman's face was familiar, though. *Who was she?* Jo wondered.

Taking the remote from her desk, she aimed it at the floor where the DVD player had been placed and looked for the 'rewind' button so she could freeze the best shot of the man in the distance, while making a mental note to organize a set of shelves before someone trod on the DVD player.

With a single rap, Detective Inspector Gavin Sexton stuck his head around the door. 'You'll do yourself an injury if you—' He stopped talking as he registered the groans of pleasure coming from the man in the pool. Then, dragging the plastic chair into position in front of the TV, he sat down.

'You could have told me it was starting,' he complained, putting his feet up on the corner of Jo's desk.

Jo slapped his feet down, and went over to the machine to collect the disc. 'Were you born in a barn?' She gave the door a light push to close it.

'Somebody got out of bed on the wrong side,' Sexton said, reaching for the cup of Starbucks Jo had bought on the way to work but hadn't had a chance to drink yet. 'What's eating you, anyway?'

What's wrong with me? Jo thought. *What's eating you, more like?*

It seemed that every day Sexton left work a little earlier than the day before. Come three o'clock he'd be showing signs of getting itchy feet, making a hushed phone call with his hand cupped over his mouth, before announcing he was heading off to meet some anonymous tout whose identity always had to be protected. The next day there was never any information worth relaying when Jo asked him what had come out of it. She thought it a real waste of talent. Without him, she would never have tracked down the Bible fanatic who'd wiped out five people in her last big case.

Just last Friday, she'd come within a hair's breadth of tackling Sexton over his tardiness, because she was knee-deep in trying to find a shred of evidence to link three unsolved rape and murder cases with a rapist currently on trial. But Foxy had stepped in, and had had a quiet word, reminding her it was the second anniversary of Sexton's wife Maura's suicide.

'Do you know what he's carrying around in the inside breast pocket of his jacket, Jo?' Foxy had asked her. 'Maura's suicide note, that's what. He can't bring himself to read it.'

'How do you know that?' Jo had quizzed.

Foxy had tapped the side of his nose twice.

Now, she studied Sexton over the rim of her coffee cup. She was glad to see him take an interest in a case, even if it was only because he was a red-blooded male. His chocolate-coloured eyes needed to get their spark back.

'Where'd it come from anyway?' he asked.

Jo shrugged. 'There was no stamp . . .' She realized she'd got the wrong end of the stick from the way he was looking around. Sexton meant the office.

She grinned at him. 'Great isn't it? Or at least it will be, when I've made it my own.'

The room had previously been designated the station's smoking room because it was the only section of the entire floor with a window that could actually open, the rest being sealed off to facilitate the air con system. A former smoker herself, Jo hated fags with a passion now.

'Did the chief give it to you?' Sexton asked, looking in Dan's direction.

'As if . . .' She scooped up the tape, note and Jiffy envelope, and packed them into the top drawer of the desk, turning the key, which had a spare dangling on its ring. She'd never had a desk with a key still in it, let alone a Formica-topped surface unmarked by a single scorch mark, coffee ring, or set of initials.

'Then it's positive discrimination,' Sexton teased. 'You've got it because you're the only female DI in the Dublin Metropolitan Area.'

'Or, how about . . . I worked bloody hard and I got what I was due?'

'Not a chance,' Sexton said, nudging her elbow, as silver-haired John Foxe stuck his head around the door.

'There's a woman in reception wants to talk to you.'

'Who, Sarge?' Jo asked.

Foxy was the only one she ever addressed by his title. It was a mark of respect. The only reason he hadn't been promoted over the years was because he'd refused it. His daughter, Sal, had Down's syndrome, and he wasn't interested in pursuing a career that would have required any extra hours.

Foxy shrugged. 'She gets an office, she suddenly wants a secretary,' he joked to Sexton, picking up his scissors from the desk.

'Can you ask her to leave her details? I'm on my way out.' Jo zipped up the leather biker jacket she still hadn't had a chance to take off and hang up yet. Not that she had a coat- stand. She added 'hook' to her mental list of furnishings.

'There's a rape trial on in Parkgate Street this morning,' she explained hurriedly. 'I want to stick my nose in on it.' The accused was an ordinary Joe who had abducted a woman in broad daylight, bound her with her bra, and gagged her with her tights. 'I have three unsolved rapes in my filing cabinet with exactly the same modus operandi.'

In the UK, the information would have been entered in a database and would have thrown up an instant alert. In Dublin, Jo had to rely on her gut. 'I want to interview him when the trial ends. Watching him give evidence today, and seeing what presses his buttons, will be a big help in what comes later.' She didn't add that she could also do with a day out of the office now Dan was back.

Foxy looked concerned. 'Please, Jo,' he said, 'can you tell her yourself? She doesn't want to talk to anyone else. She's—'

'What?' Sexton prompted.

'Well, heartbroken,' Foxy said. 'Poor girl looks like she's been sobbing all night.'

Jo glanced at her watch. It was now ten past nine. The trial was due to kick off at half ten. It would take about ten minutes to get there on the Luas tram, which ran right outside the station, as against at least half an hour if she took her car. Even so, she could forget about a seat in court if she didn't leave immediately – according to the papers the public were queuing up to get a glimpse at the defendant. He was accused of raping and trying to murder a teenage Spanish student who was only in Ireland to brush up on her English over the summer. People were appalled by the case, and their morbid curiosity had taken over.

'OK, OK, I'll talk to her,' she said grudgingly, knowing that Foxy's big heart meant he'd be taking a personal interest in this one. She turned and took one last glance round her new office.

'A clock,' she said, ticking a finger.

'What?' Sexton looked puzzled.

She smiled at her colleagues. 'Shelves, a blind, a coat-stand, a wastepaper basket, that bloody bracket lowered two foot – and a clock –– and this place might just be perfect.'

2

The cocaine had travelled across three continents and four oceans to get to Dublin. It started its journey in Colombia as coca leaves picked by peasants in the eastern plains of the Llanos. It had been carried in sacks on the backs of donkeys to drying-out sheds. In paste pits – holes in the ground lined with plastic – it had been treated with chemicals, and stomped on by workers toiling in the scorching sun. The chunky, light-brown putty-like substance that drained off had then been driven in a convoy of 4x4s through the treacherous mountain passes of the Andes, and along the winding road from Cali to the port of Buenaventura, a city of shacks built on stilts on the sea. There, Afro-Colombian slum soldiers had purchased it for the equivalent of four euro a gram, haggling with machine guns, and testing that the produce was untouched by snorting it themselves.

By the time it got to the streets of Dublin – via West Africa, Spain, and Amsterdam – it was supposed to make more than ten times what it had cost Barry 'King Krud' Roberts, the prisoner on remand, to import it. He might not have been able to point out the countries it had passed through on an atlas, but having just received a phone call on one of the four mobiles which he used to run his business from his cell in Portlaoise, and learned that the consignment which had travelled halfway around the world had been intercepted by gardaí the previous night, he was taking it very personally. And consequently, he was going berserk.

The King was trashing his prison cell on the E1 landing, looking for the listening device he was convinced must have given the game away.

The steroids in his bloodstream, which gave him his bulldog neck and spotty skin, meant that when he flew into a rage, a powder keg of hate exploded.

The metal bunks made a deafening clang as he upended them. The contents of the slopping-out bucket sluiced all over the tiled floor as he kicked it in a temper. Even his pet canary was in a flap, trying to fly into the highest corner of its cage. If there was no bug in his cell, he was going to have to work out which rat had betrayed him. That rat would have to die, as had nine others in the last year, as the King secured his stranglehold on the south Dublin drug-distribution ring.

Twenty-four years old, he had got his nickname

from his habit of smearing his face with faeces before every street slaying, and a bloodlust that had catapulted him from small-time street-corner deals to running a gang of killers willing to do anything to hold on to their new-found status in the underworld. The King was not about to let any of that change just because he'd been remanded in custody pending a murder trial. Throughout every one of his court hearings he'd sung the Bob Dylan song about Rubin 'Hurricane' Carter, a black middleweight boxer in the sixties wrongly convicted of multiple murders.

Not that the King was innocent. He'd done the murder he was in for all right. He'd grown up with Joey Lambert, the man he'd knifed in the heart, and had once considered him a mate. But that hadn't stopped him stabbing Joey in a McDonald's in Stillorgan shopping centre full of horrified southside diners. Why? He'd heard a rumour that Joey wanted to oust him as boss. The King had made sure to twist the knife as he'd plunged it in.

No, he hadn't been singing Bob Dylan because he was innocent. He'd sung it because the gardaí hadn't had a shred of evidence against him – all the witnesses who'd been stuffing their faces that night had suffered from a collective lapse of memory. So as far as he was concerned, it was tantamount to being framed. He'd been wrongly incarcerated, just like Rubin.

He also knew the real reason he was inside was because of what had happened after the killing – a twelve-month tit-for-tat street war as his original gang had split. He himself had opened fire on a pub with both barrels of a sawn-off shotgun, hitting a bouncer and a customer.

This was why the state had locked him up – to quell the feuding. And why this particular shipment of cocaine was extremely dear to him. It was supposed to send out a message on the street that, even banged up inside, he was still the King. It wasn't the size of the consignment he'd lost – he'd imported ten times as much in one single deal in the past – it was that he didn't like what the loss said about him: that he was losing control. That was why this one mattered more than any of the others.

When there was nothing left to smash, rip or tear asunder, the King realized there was no bug in his cell. Which meant that someone had betrayed him. Someone who would soon discover there were worse things than death. There was a hard death.

The ringtone on one of his phones started to play the 50 Cent track: 'Many Men (Wish Death)'. The King was all set to throw the phone, too, against the wall until he saw who was calling.

'Who?' he asked, in his pronounced Dublin accent, then nodded, knelt down on his hunkers, reached for some of what had spilled from the bucket, and spread it across his forehead and cheeks.

Slowly a smile spread across his face. Because, as it turned out, the rat was not a him, but a her.

3

There was no doubt the girl in the public lobby was distressed, but what Foxy hadn't mentioned was that she was also very pretty. Jo sighed, and checked her watch. No wonder he'd been so interested. The girl had perfectly chiselled features, striking green eyes and an expensive haircut held off her face with a pair of Gucci sunglasses. She was no more than twenty and dressed in a black blazer, rock-chick T-shirt, a pair of designer jeans and trendy open-toed ankle boots. The studs in her ears sparkled the way only real diamonds can.

'Can you come with me?' Jo asked her, indicating an interview room to the right of the counter. She swiped her card through the pad to open the door, and held it ajar for the girl to enter. Inside, Jo guided the girl by the shoulders into one of the two chairs situated either side of a small square table, noticing as she did so that the girl's toenails had a French pedicure. If Jo had had the time for a pampering, the chances of her squandering it on something like that would have been slim to none.

'You'll think I'm wasting your time,' the girl said.

As she spoke with a cut-glass accent, Jo realized how familiar she was – she had the same sphinx-like quality to her eyes that Kate Moss had. Of course, she'd seen her only the other night on *The Late Late Show*, raising money for charity. Come to think of it, she was a model, and, Jo would bet, one of the country's most well-known ones at that. 'You're Tara Parker Trench, aren't you?' she said.

The girl gave a quick nod.

Why had Foxy not mentioned this, either? Jo wondered. He read every newspaper going, they all came in to the station every day. This girl was one of the It girls of the moment. There was no way her name would have been lost on Foxy. Despite being a stickler for doing things by the book, he loved a bit of gossip. Jo refocused her attention on Tara, who'd begun to weep. She looked unwell; her lips had a bluish tinge.

'Please, it's my little boy, someone's taken him. You have to find him. If anything's happened to him I . . .'

Jo stood, and reached for the phone on the wall. 'We'll have to file a missing persons report. I'll organize the forms we'll need.'

'I've done all that.'

Jo stopped.

'I was in here last night,' Tara explained, wiping her eyes. 'Your lot were right there when he was taken. In the service station around the corner. I told them I wanted you.'

'I don't understand . . .'

Tara sniffed. 'I stopped for petrol on the quays about nine last night, like I already told them. Presley – my son – was in his child seat in the back of the car. I was only gone for a minute, a couple, max . . . he's only three years old. It was lashing . . . he was asleep . . . it was past his bedtime. I didn't want to . . . The gardaí were there because there was trouble . . . There was a squad car parked right beside my car when Presley was taken. I thought he was safe . . .' She fumbled a card out of her pocket. 'That's him, the cop I told everything to. He brought me here last night.'

Jo read Fred Oakley's name on the card. He was a detective sergeant, a great bear of a man with chestnut hair. He was a bit full of himself, but still interested in the job and thorough. Fred was a man's man, he liked swilling the pints and talking about rugby, but as long as he solved crime Jo wasn't about to hold that against him. The fact that this was Fred's case also explained why Foxy had been so scant with details. He'd have known exactly who this girl was, but like the old hand he was, he'd played dumb rather than be accused of muscling in on anyone else's territory. He'd left that to Jo.

'You're in good hands with Fred,' Jo told her.

'But it's you I need,' Tara's voice had risen to a wail. 'I read about what you did in the paper after that reporter's little girl was abducted.'

Jo sighed. Tara was referring to the recent serial killer case she'd worked on, in which the victims had all been connected to the kidnap of a crime reporter's child. She had tracked the killer down by identifying the links between his five victims.

'You have to help me find him. Please. You have to . . .' Tara sounded as though she was about to hyperventilate.

'Is there anything else I should know? Anything about last night? Anything else untoward happen recently? Anyone been giving you bother?'

Tara put her head in her hands. 'Just the row inside the garage shop.'

'What were you driving?'

'My car, it's a Mini Cooper.'

'Colour and reg?' Jo asked.

Tara supplied the details.

Jo made a mental note. 'Did Detective Sergeant Oakley ring someone for you – a friend or partner for you to be with?'

'There's only my mum, and they told her to stay where she was to answer the phone,' Tara answered. 'Please—'

'Look, I'll do what I can, but unless the chief assigns me to the case, I'll only be able to help you on my own time. I'm sorry.'

Tara began to cry again. Feeling a wrench of sympathy, Jo leaned forward and touched her shoulder. Tara flinched.

'The reason why I have to find him . . .' She sobbed. '. . . is because he's got chronic asthma. He takes medication every night. Without it, he'll have an attack. Do you know what that means?' She looked at Jo, fear written all over her face. 'It means he won't be able to breathe.'

Jo asked Tara to wait in the interview room while she headed back out to the public counter. Stretching across the officer on duty, she took the hardback log-book and slid it sideways, flicking the pages backwards till she reached the previous night's reported incidents. Everything had to be logged. She ran her finger up the entries recorded in chrono-logical order. Seconds later, she was tapping the line giving details about a toddler who had been reported snatched from a car in the petrol station a short dis-tance away. The time the information had been received was set at 9.15 p.m., almost exactly twelve hours earlier.

Ordinarily in these circumstances, Jo wouldn't have felt the need to double-check that someone like

Tara Parker Trench was telling her the truth, but it wasn't stacking up. *Why the hell didn't I read about the case in the papers this morning?* she wondered. Putting the child's face in the public eye was policing at its most basic. The station should have been buzzing with it, with every available officer drafted in to a conference and put on the case.

Giving the book back to the officer, she headed upstairs to talk to Dan, glad there was no need to knock on Jeanie's door first. The state of the country's finances meant there wasn't even the budget to get a temp in to cover as Dan's secretary. With no one there, Jeanie's old office looked even more abandoned now that her desk and computer were in Jo's new room.

Jo rapped on the inner door, then stepped inside, not waiting for an answer. Dan was on the phone, talking in that low, sexy tone he had when he was in a good humour. His midnight-blue eyes were dancing with mischief, making Jo think that he had to be talking to Jeanie. Jo felt her insides twist in pain. It wasn't too long ago that he used to talk to her like that.

He continued to ignore her, so she stepped up to his handset and pressed 'hold'. 'Sorry, I know that's offside,' she said, 'but Fred Oakley's missing toddler case – I need to insinuate myself on to it. The little boy has asthma.'

Dan pressed 'hold' again and said, 'I'll ring you

back,' into the handset, before banging the receiver down. 'Forget it,' he said, his eyes cold and hard. 'That's Oakley's case. He's well able to handle it.'

'I agree, but the mother's asking for me, and I can't walk away.'

'It's not her call,' Dan said, still angry. 'You used to want to be transferred out of this station, remember? And anyway, I trust Oakley.' He leaned back. His stomach was tight, but his shirt was in need of a hotter iron, Jo noticed.

'You done something to your hair?' he asked.

Jo touched her head self-consciously. She'd had it cut into shorter layers while he was away, wanting something easier to manage. The front strands were longer, kinking out at the ends, and the stylist had talked her into a scatter of dirty blonde highlights to lift the brown. Jo hadn't expected Dan to notice it. She sat down in the uncomfortable cup chair he kept for visitors.

'How's Jeanie?' she asked.

Dan looked uncomfortable. 'Good, thanks.' He coughed. 'Keeping me on my toes. She had me painting the nursery all last week. Nesting, I believe they call it.'

Jo studied her shoes. She'd thought they'd separated because he couldn't cope with the shock of her second pregnancy, which had come sixteen years after her first. But by the sound of it he was enjoying

Jeanie's. She talked through the lump in her throat. 'I'm worried about last night's missing boy, Dan.'

He exhaled, stood up and walked to the window, turning his back to her. 'Do you know where Oakley should be right now? Home in bed, that's where. He's on nights. Instead, he's out right now looking for the little kid. Knowing him, he'll probably waltz in here any second with the boy in his arms because Little Mizz Up Herself, Tara what's-her-face, has been preventing her ex from seeing his own son.'

Jo swallowed. Tara hadn't told her about her ex. If Dan thought this was a straightforward tug-of-love battle, it was no wonder he'd given the case such a low priority.

'Just give me twenty-four hours on the case, that's all I ask.'

'You know what happened last time you said that? You wanted twenty-four hours on the Bible case after I decided it should go to Sexton. You undermined me.'

'Undermined? I solved it, didn't I?'

He ran a finger inside his shirt collar. 'Oh, you solved it all right, and you made yourself friends in high places in the process.'

'What does that mean?'

'It means while you've been out there lording it over everyone in your own office, I've had to explain to the rest of the team why they're four to a desk. You didn't even have the decency to tell me what was going on. I had a stand-up row with the workmen emptying the room when I got in this morning.'

'But you were on holiday with Jeanie, remember?'

'And you got the minister to organize it behind my back?'

He was referring to Blaise Stanley, who might or might not be on the DVD in Jo's desk. All of a sudden, Jo was glad she hadn't mentioned the sex tape to Dan. 'No! Stanley contacted me to ask if it would help if I had my own office. What should I have said, eh? "No. Wait till I run it by Dan?"'

Dan sighed. 'You could have rung me,' he said gruffly. He crossed the room to stand beside her chair. 'So what did you have to give Blaise Stanley to get it?' he asked, looking down at her.

Jo drew in a long breath. 'Nothing,' she said. 'He's a married man.'

He walked back behind his desk and sat down heavily, reaching for the phone. 'I've made my decision. It's Oakley's case.'

'Please, Dan, just one day. The child is sick, for Christ's sake. Just today, that's all I want.'

But the conversation was over, and Dan had turned back to his phone. Clenching her fists, Jo stood up, and headed for the door.

'And you needn't bother asking your friends in the press to get Tara what's-her-face on the news today, either,' Dan called after her. 'You haven't a hope with the budget. The president could get shot and it would have to be held over till tomorrow.'

Jo didn't turn around to answer him, because she knew if she did she'd bloody well kill him. She'd got an office because she had earned Blaise Stanley's respect for tracking down a cold-blooded murderer. There was no way she was going to let Dan's pride stop her from finding a child.

4

In a café just around the corner from the station, Jo transferred two full Irish breakfasts from a tray and slid a mug of sugary tea in front of Tara, taking the coffee for herself. Circles rippled out through the drinks as a DART trundled by overhead. The café was tucked right under the bridge running into Connolly Station.

Jo watched Tara turn her face away from the smell as she reached for and squirted the plastic ketchup dispenser across her own plate.

'Look,' she said, leaning across the table. 'I need you to stay strong. We've a long day ahead of us, so the sooner you get some food into you, the sooner we get on with it.' Pulling her black-bound pocket notebook and pen from her jacket, she flicked it open on the table, folding a half-slice of toast around a piece of bacon. She took a couple of bites, then checked the pen was working by scribbling on the corner of the blank page.

'Right,' she said looking up in time to see Tara managing some of her fried egg. 'I know you've been through this but I need to go over it again. Where were you coming from last night and where were you going to?'

Tara closed her eyes. 'I'd a shoot at the airport for a holiday brochure. It wrapped at about eight fifteen, and I headed home. I've an apartment in Citywest.'

'Where was Presley all this time, when you were working?'

'With my mum. She takes care of him when I need it.'

'Why didn't you take the M50 from the airport to Citywest?' The ring road bypassed the city centre.

'Mum lives in North Great George's Street.'

Not far from where the boy disappeared, Jo realized. She made a quick note of the word 'mum' and circled it.

'Who's Presley's father?'

'Mick Devlin. We split up about a year ago.'

'Why?'

'He didn't like me earning more than him. He's a mechanic. Everything's black and white in Mick's book. I'd put on a bikini for work, he'd get jealous and think I was doing it to provoke him. He wanted me to stop modelling. When I wouldn't, he walked.'

'You still get along?'

Tara shook her head. 'Not since he applied for sole custody of Presley.'

Jo put her pen down and stared. 'Why would he do that?'

'Because if I want to get a client's product into the paper, I need to be seen out and about at night so as to get the papers to take an interest in me. But Mick wants me home all the time with Presley. He thinks me having a life makes me an unfit mother.' She blew her nose. 'Look, shouldn't we be out there now, looking?'

'Could Mick have taken Presley?'

'To teach me a lesson? Yes. That was the first thing I thought, too. But he's on holiday in Fuerteventura. He's not due back until tonight.'

'Is there a new man in your life?'

'No. And what's that got to do with anything, anyway?'

'I need to know if you're rowing with any other exes.'

Tara shook her head, and started cutting her food up into small pieces.

'Any women got a grudge against you?' Jo pressed on. 'You get on the wrong side of any of the other models lately? It's supposed to be a bitchy industry. A crime like this has a woman's stamp all over it. Anyone's nose put out of joint because of the attention you've been giving their other half?'

'No. And no.' Tara sighed. 'I don't know anybody who'd do something like that.'

'Someone like you gets invited to great parties, and let into nightclubs for free. You must get a lot of attention from men. There must have been a girlfriend along the way who's got the hump.'

'I get offers, sure. But I don't have time for a relationship. Every spare minute I've got, I'm with Presley, or doing my classes.'

'Classes in what?'

'Acting.'

Jo looked up. *Tara does seem genuinely upset*, she thought. 'Are you practising on me now?'

'What do you mean?'

'Are you acting out a role?'

'Of course not.' Tara lifted her hands to push her hair back, and as she did so her T-shirt slid up to reveal a bare midriff and a range of livid bruises surrounding it.

Jo stared, and Tara sat back down again pulling the top down quickly. 'My son's missing. He's sick. What more do I have to do?'

Jo leaned in to Tara. 'Someone been manhandling you recently?'

'No! I had a fall coming down some stairs, that's all.'

Jo sighed, and stood up, reaching for her jacket and bag. 'If I find out you've lied to me, I'm walking away. Now – are you going to finish that?'

Tara shook her head.

'OK, let's make a start.'

Jo could have walked back to the station for a car, but the garage Presley had disappeared from was only a block away, and with traffic it would have taken a quarter of an hour to drive there.

Five minutes later they were there. The Ever Oil garage had a Methadone clinic on one side, a homeless shelter on the other, a dingy pub two doors up, and a sprawling block of council flats behind it. In terms of a place in which to lose a three-year-old, it was your basic nightmare.

It shocked Jo to see it was business as usual so soon after such a serious crime, with no sign of any area having been cordoned off, and not even a road block in place quizzing passing motorists.

She noted six pumps in the forecourt, all of them in use bar one, with queues developing.

Tara groaned, then ran to a corner of the perimeter and emptied the contents of her stomach behind a scrawny bush. Jo went over and put her hand on her back. 'You OK?'

'I'm sorry,' Tara said, 'the petrol fumes reminded me – oh my God, my poor little boy.'

Jo gripped her arm. 'Show me where it happened.'

Tara gulped a few deep breaths, then pointed a shaky hand towards where she'd parked, just round the corner from the CCTV cameras, and the entrance to the garage store.

Jo walked over to the public toilet door and pressed the handle down. It was locked. She walked around to the entrance of the store, and led Tara through the double-glazed glass door, reinforced with a ridged slab of metal at kicking level.

As convenience stores went, there was a depressed feel to the place. The tiles on the ceiling were missing in parts, leaving cable wiring exposed. The stock was sparse, and the whole interior badly in need of a paint and a clean.

'He was here last night,' Tara said, nodding at a Perspex counter.

Jo looked at the Muslim man behind the till. He had a long wiry beard, and was wearing a skullcap. There wasn't a queue yet, and the man was going through the contents of the till from what Jo could make out.

He registered Jo, let his gaze skirt across Tara, then went back to work. Jo didn't like his attitude. If a small boy got snatched from your premises, you'd ask how the mother was doing next time you saw her.

She led Tara towards him, past the shelves of lads' mags. The man kept counting.

Jo held her ID up to the glass. 'Liquor licence, please.'

He snorted.

'And the key to the outside toilet, while you're at it.'

'Customers only.' His accent was inner-city Dublin.

'Did I say I wanted to use it?'

He threw his eyes up to heaven and headed into the back. A few customers started to file in behind Jo, who was scrolling through the contacts on her phone. She chose Fred Oakley's number.

'Oakley?' she asked, as the call connected.

Jo drew a breath. She knew what a voice that was answering from a prostrate position sounded like – so much for Dan's theory that Oakley was out pounding the streets.

'Fred, it's Jo Birmingham.'

He grunted at a pitch that led her to believe Dan must have already briefed him.

'The case of the missing child from last night. Where are we on that?'

He hesitated. 'I'm chasing a few leads. What's it to you?'

'I'm here where it happened with his mother. It's business as usual round at the garage, Fred. Nothing's been sealed off.'

He huffed out a breath, and Jo heard his voice change as he sat up. 'You know who she is, right?'

Jo turned her back to Tara. 'What does that mean, Fred?'

'To put you in the picture, we've had a word with

her boss – I believe the correct term is "agent". She's told us on the q.t. that our Tara's got quite a gift for porkie pies. The word actually used was "Munchausen's". I'm amazed Tara Parker Trench's not plastered all over the papers already, to tell you the truth. I'd bet my mother that's what this is really about. I can see the headline: "How My Boy Was Kidnapped." Papers, publicity, profile. All adds up to money. Look at that Jordan one. She's made a fortune out of a pair of tits.'

Jo sighed.

'You know what Munchausen's is, right?' Oakley said. 'It's where mothers present their children at hospital claiming they're sick, so as to get attention for themselves.'

Jo glanced at Tara. She had both her arms wrapped around her belly, and was carrying the same stuffed toy dog that she'd been holding at the station. Jo lowered her voice. 'Yeah, I know what it is, Fred, but it still leaves me with one question. Where's little Presley?'

Oakley paused. 'With whoever was minding him when her ladyship got back from Marrakesh last night, I presume.'

'You presume? Have you checked?'

'You want to watch it,' Oakley said. 'Are you suggesting I haven't? That's basic policing.'

'OK,' Jo said. She didn't want to provoke him unnecessarily.

'I'm sure she knows where the kid is,' Oakley went on. 'If you need any proof that she's an attention-seeker, you don't have to look any further than the kid's poofter name . . . She did tell you she'd been out of the country?'

Jo moved another few feet away from Tara. 'No, she didn't – but it doesn't change anything, Fred. Especially here in the garage where Presley went missing. First thing I'd have done is make a list of every vehicle recorded on the CCTV driving in, and out, at the crucial times – starting from ten to nine, till ten past and working my way back on either side. I'd have listed the drivers' names in one column, and alongside that I'd have put any previous convictions. But you haven't done any of this, and the question I'm going to be asking back at the station is: why?'

She hung up, and turned back to Tara. 'Why didn't you tell me you'd been on a trip? Why did you give me a cock and bull story about a shoot in the airport?'

Tara had begun to shake. 'I did do the shoot when I got back. I didn't think the trip was relevant.'

'You lied to me about the circumstances leading up to the disappearance of your boy. You think that isn't relevant? I told you if you lied—' She stepped closer to Tara, noticing the tiny bloodspots under her eyes and how thin she was under the expensive designer jacket. She remembered the bruises on her stomach, wondered how they'd got there. 'Even your agent says you're a liar. What's she got against you?'

Tara took a deep breath. 'I'm sleeping with her husband.'

Jo blinked. The teller came back, held the liquor licence paperwork up to the Perspex, and dropped a key through the hatch.

'Open the door,' Jo said, pointing past him to the door into the till area.

He looked as if he intended to say no, then moved slowly in that direction.

'Here, I got a delivery to make,' a pizza guy called from the queue behind Tara and Jo.

'Yeah, get on with it, we've all got dinners to make, and kids to collect and feed,' a woman said.

'Quiet, you lot,' Jo ordered, turning round. 'We're looking for a child who went missing from here last night.'

There was total silence.

'What you got under here?' Jo asked, as she entered the till area. Rows of XXX-rated DVDs were hidden from view under the counter by the teller's leg. 'I don't expect you'll be able to produce a licence for this, now will you?' She took the chits he'd been clipping together from his hand. 'Are they from last night?' The date on the top one gave her the answer. 'I'll be needing these,' she said, putting them in her jacket pocket.

She glanced to his left. 'That the door to the loo?'

He nodded.

'Why don't you let me in this way and save me going the long way around?'

Grumbling to himself, he stepped past her and pressed the door handle down.

Inside, the toilet was pitch dark and the air was dank. Concrete walls gave it a cavernous feel, and the sound of the water glugging in the tank was unnerving. The place also stank to high heaven. Jo reached for a string dangling from the ceiling, pulled it and an exposed bulb threw light around a dirty room measuring about twelve foot by fourteen. On the concrete floor painted over with an industrial red paint, Jo identified the source of the smell as dog faeces smeared all over the floor.

Tara started to wail: a high-pitched keening sound.

'Is the wee child in there?' a woman called from the queue.

'What can you see?' a man said, sounding tense.

On the red concrete floor, a metre out from one of the walls, lay a tiny pair of Ray-Ban sunglasses.

5

Half an hour later Jo had everyone outside the garage, and the whole area cordoned off, as the crime scene examiners arrived carrying their standard black-shell cases. She'd phoned Dan as soon as she'd spotted Presley's shades, demanding that he start taking the case seriously by notifying the Tech Bureau attached to the forensic science lab at HQ. Instead, however, he'd drafted in the local boys attached to the station, which, as far as she was concerned, was the equivalent of giving her the two fingers. It wasn't that the officers weren't highly trained in crime scene preservation – the lads were terrific at what they did, Jo knew that – but they were only ever involved when it was unclear if a crime had been committed in the first place. The green light would only be given to the forensic team at the Tech Bureau after they'd carried out a preliminary examination, all of which was going to add to the delay in finding little Presley.

Jo took a deep breath. She still couldn't understand why first Fred and now Dan were not moving heaven and earth to bring the child to safety. She studied Tara standing on the side of the road, her arms crossed over the toy dog and her whole body shaking. The Muslim manager was shaking too – with anger. His customers were drifting off before he'd had time to collect their payments for fuel.

Jo wasn't having any of it. 'What's your bloody name, bright spark?'

'Hassan,' he answered.

'And what's your problem?'

'She,' he said, jabbing a finger at Tara, 'tried to do a runner last night. That's what I already told your lot. She's the one you want to put under pressure, not me. I'm just trying to make a living.'

Tara had heard what he'd said, and came over. 'How many times do I have to tell you?' she shouted. 'I wasn't going anywhere. I only moved the car because I was freaking out over the shit going on inside; the way that skinhead was throwing stuff left, right and centre. I wanted to check that my son was all right. When I'd moved the car, I was going to come straight back in and pay you.'

'Yeah, well I came out and banged on your window and I didn't see no kid in the back.' He glared at her.

Shocked, Jo turned to face Tara.

'You didn't look in the back!' Tara shouted.

One of the team emerged from the garage and called Jo over. She had met him before. His name was Owen. He was lanky, with an undershot jaw, and he always smelled of soap.

'OK, we're putting the call in to HQ,' Owen said.

'About time, too,' Jo said. She knew none of this was his fault, but she was spitting nails. 'Nothing personal, but we're only about twelve hours late.'

'Yeah, well there's more to this one than meets the eye,' he said.

Jo rubbed the back of her neck. A headache was making itself felt behind her temples. 'What does that mean?'

'Didn't you hear who they found in here last night? Only Tom Burke, that paedophile they've been hunting for the past twelve months.'

Jo exhaled. 'You're joking.' Everyone had been warned to keep an eye out for Burke, a serial child-abuser who'd been released from prison about a year earlier after a long stretch inside. As a registered sex offender, he was supposed to inform the gardaí of his address, but when an incident in a park was reported involving a seven-year-old boy and bearing all the hallmarks of Burke's previous crimes, they'd discovered he'd moved on. The papers had been baying for him to be found ever since.

Jo glanced over at Tara, who was studying some message on her phone and sobbing again.

'The sick bastard's in hospital now,' Owen continued. 'A dog chewed up his leg in here last night. Pity he didn't finish him off, eh? Good thing Fred Oakley was here. He recognized Burke the second he saw him. Turns out that pervert had been lodging around here all along, right under our noses.'

Of course, Jo thought. If the papers found out that a child had been snatched from under officers' noses while a serial paedophile, who'd eluded them for a year, was right there at the time, it would be the worst kind of publicity for the force. No wonder Dan was being so circumspect.

She walked over to Tara and took her arm. 'I want you to go home to your place in Citywest and try and get a couple of hours' rest.'

'But what happens if Presley has an asthma attack? I must stay—'

'Love, I'm going to have to grill you at length later, so I want you at your best. Go home, shower, change, and make sure you have Presley's medication at the ready in case we need it sharpish.'

She flipped open her mobile and started to scroll through for the cab firm the station used, then spotted a cab driving onto the forecourt.

'I want the names of anyone you gave the key to that toilet to last night,' she said to Hassan.

'Impossible.'

'Nothing's impossible. Either you can sift through

your security footage and match the faces up with the times of your credit card transactions to get names for me, or we'll do it for you. And, just so you know, if any harm comes to the missing boy, I'm going to have you charged as an accessory.'

Hassan stepped forward aggressively. 'No, I mean it's impossible. Because the toilet door was open, anyone who wanted could have used it. There's no way I could keep track of everyone.'

'He's lying,' Tara said, over Jo's shoulder. She was about to climb into the taxi Jo had flagged down, and was holding out a scrap of paper in her hand with 'Mum's phone number' scribbled at the top and a mobile listed underneath. 'There was an "Out of Order" sign on the toilet door last night. I saw it. It's gone now. You need to ask him why.'

6

Jeff Cox climbed out of his sleek, black, 7 Series BMW with the morning newspaper tucked under his arm. He jangled a key free from the set as he banged the car door shut, and headed past the fountain feature, towards his imposing mock-Tudor home.

Inside, he cupped his suede loafers off, arranging them neatly at the bottom of the stairs. He knew once his wife, Imogen, realized he was back, she would continue the row they'd had before he'd stormed out and he was going to try and keep that moment at bay for as long as possible. She'd said such horrible things, threatened divorce, told him he wouldn't get a penny. The longer he could put off more abuse, the better. He padded past the giant photograph of her, which dominated the hallway, giving it the customary captain's salute. It had been taken in her modelling days, twenty-odd years ago, when she'd been young and gorgeous. Her dark, kohled eyes smouldered over a scarlet pout. The lipstick ran a couple of millimetres past the outline of her lips. He hadn't been able to keep his hands off her back then. It felt like a million years ago.

Zipping his Abercrombie & Fitch hoodie up as he walked, Jeff headed towards the cold draft of air travelling up the hall, pulling his hands inside the sleeves as he moved. The house was freezing.

He found out why in the kitchen. The sliding patio back door had been left ajar. The wooden slatted blind rattled against it in steady taps.

It didn't make sense to him. Their dog, Molly, always barked at the first sound of his car returning. He'd never have made it from the front door to the back in time to close it before she'd have trundled up to greet him, hips out of sync with the rest of her body, and slavering everywhere.

And if Imogen had taken her for a walk, she wouldn't have left the back door open. Even with a high perimeter hedge around the property and electronic gates at the front, she was still paranoid about security, and guarded their possessions with the zealousness of someone who'd come from nothing. And since the 'burglary', she'd been worse than ever. He couldn't even leave the bedroom window open an inch at night, or she was on his case.

The glass door made a sucking noise as he slid it shut and he stepped awkwardly over the dog's empty wicker basket propped beside it. Molly's sleeping arrangements were an accident waiting to happen, but arthritis was a genetic predisposition of Newfoundlands and he was trying to make her life as easy as possible now she was getting on. The fact that the basket was still where he'd last left it was another indicator that Imogen definitely wasn't around, he realized, though he'd just parked alongside her Land Rover in the driveway, and she hadn't mentioned anything about going anywhere when he'd seen her at breakfast. It occurred to him that she might be in one of her sulks over their row, and be giving him the silent treatment.

Jeff hopped back to clear Molly's basket. But if Imogen had been here she'd have shoved it under the kitchen table and blocked Molly's access with the chairs, he realized. Jeff always kicked it straight back out again, as soon as she'd turned her back.

His eyes skimmed the black marble work surfaces for any sign of a note. Where had she gone at this hour? When would she be back? And was a note letting him know really too much to expect? It was irrelevant, he reminded himself. Imogen didn't do considerate. He cast an eye over the breakfast dishes, which she could never be arsed to move from the kitchen table to the Belfast sink. Their dishwasher wasn't worth a curse because their location on Killiney Hill meant the water pressure was poor. Jeff only ended up making work for himself when he used it.

With a heavy sigh, he began to tidy up, groaning as he realized how long Imogen had left her Rice Krispies to dry in the bowl – they were a bugger to scrape off. He was sure she did it to spite him. He angled the tap over it and turned on the water. The sight of it dripping out didn't help his mood.

He'd be lucky to fit in a trip to the gym, and a swim, at this rate. He was definitely not going into the office, he decided, as he began to put away the breakfast dishes. If Imogen wanted him to be a skivvy at home, she couldn't expect him to show up for work as well. She only wanted him in the office so she could order him around there, too. Well, the mood he was in after everything said between them this morning, he didn't care what threats she made about firing him today. The revenue from the business was down because the world was in recession; it had nothing to do with him not pulling his weight. She could stick her precious modelling business where the sun didn't shine. He'd had enough.

He was still clearing up and putting away things when he spotted her Louis Vuitton handbag under one of the kitchen chairs. He froze. Imogen would never have gone out without her handbag. He stood completely still and listened hard. And then he heard it – what sounded like frenzied barking at the far end of the garden, near the stable block. As he listened, he realized how panicked Molly was.

Heart pounding, Jeff ran to the sliding door and pulled it open again, sprinting to the back of the garden, an acre between him and the pool house. But when he got there, he couldn't believe what he was looking at. Imogen lay face down in the grass, Molly's bark changing to a whimper as she nuzzled his leg.

Jeff's gaze travelled from the blood congealed on the back of Imogen's misshapen head and moved to a bloodstained rock a couple of feet away. He knelt by Imogen and reached for her wrist. She was still warm. He pressed his fingers into her skin and was sure he could feel a pulse. The dark grass around her told him just how much blood she'd lost. His fingers moved to her neck. The pulse was faint, but she was definitely still alive, he realized.

Jeff stood and stared at the house for a second, running his fingers through his hair. 'Come on, girl,' he said, grabbing Molly's collar. If he phoned an ambulance, they might be able to save Imogen. If he gave Molly a feed first, and tinkered about for a bit, perhaps they would not.

7

An hour later, Jo was back in the station and looking for Sexton. He wasn't answering his mobile or the phone on his desk, but one of the guys in the corridor pointed in the direction of the Gents, so this was where Jo headed next. Not bothering to knock, she marched in, shielding her eyes with a hand as she passed two uniforms standing at the urinals.

She called his name. 'Forget it, that's Fred Oakley's case,' Sexton shouted back from behind the only closed cubicle door.

'Well he's making a balls of it,' Jo answered, 'and if you think I'm going to stand idly by when a tot's disappeared from a garage shop where paedophiles were stopping to pick up blue movies, you've another think coming.'

The uniforms glanced at each other, zipped up and made a hasty exit.

Jo heard the toilet flush.

'Where to?' Sexton asked, heading over to the sink,

where he squirted the empty soap dispenser and scrubbed his hands.

'We need to talk to the person who's the reason why nobody's taking what happened seriously,' Jo shouted over the drone of the Dyson dryer. 'Tara Parker Trench's agent. We need to talk to Imogen Cox.'

The car park was in its usual state of chaos, and they lost a good five minutes trying to get a marked car out of it. Cops on their way into the station dumped their cars, leaving the handbrakes off and the doors unlocked for the cops on their way out to worry about. Tara's Mini, with its striped bonnet, was there today, too. Presumably Fred had had it towed there when he'd decided the case was closed, instead of having the forensic team fine-tooth comb it.

Sexton pushed first at the front of the squad car, and then moved to the back while Jo dragged the steering wheel left, then right, her curses growing more explicit by the second. She was about to insist they take the battered Ford she usually drove, and couldn't bring herself to replace because it was a present from Dan, when she finally got enough of a swing to get the squad car out.

Squeezing himself sideways in the passenger door, Sexton read out the address for Tara Parker Trench's boss from a sheet of paper Foxy had handed over on their way out.

'Interesting,' he remarked.

'What?'

'I thought the arse had fallen out of the advertising industry, but judging by where this Imogen Cox lives, she must be minting it,' Sexton added. 'It's Bono and Neil Jordan's neck of the woods – millionaire row.'

He'd barely swung the door shut before Jo was speeding across the Luas tram tracks. Swinging left, she took an immediate right again at the Pig and Heifer, past the green glass and granite IFSC buildings on her left and the city bus terminus on her right, and crossed the Liffey to the south side, turning left on to City Quay at the Matt Talbot Bridge. Only when she had a straight run, in the bus lane on the Rock Road, did Sexton finally speak again.

'You all right?' he asked, gripping the bottom of the seat with one hand, and the overhead handle with the other.

'Fine.' Jo sighed. She wanted to change the subject. 'You're a man about town. Tell me everything you know about Tara Parker Trench.'

'She's a ride.'

'Says you and every red-blooded male in Ireland. What else?'

'She eats macrobiotic food that is inedible, she wears Armani that nobody can afford, and she has a stalker, but we won't hold that against her since that's an accessory in the world she lives in. Oh, and she gave her child a ridiculous name, suggesting she has aspirations of winding up in la-la land.'

'A stalker?' Jo said.

Sexton's knuckles were white from holding on to the overhead handle. 'I'm not saying another word until you watch where you're going.'

Jo clicked her tongue, and slowed down. 'You were saying . . .'

'It's nothing. Stalkers are like accessories in the celeb circuit.'

'Sounds pretty scary to me. What I don't understand is why everyone has got it in for her.'

'Who's everyone?'

'Dan and Fred Oakley for starters, and now you. In other words, all the men she's come into contact with at the station, with the single exception of Foxy.'

Sexton slid his finger under his nose to signal what he was thinking – cocaine. 'They've probably heard the rumours about her fondness for you know what. True or not, mud sticks.'

'And do you believe she has got a drug problem?'

'It goes hand in glove with the social set she prefers to hang out with.'

'She works in the fashion industry,' Jo protested half-heartedly. 'Dan and Fred don't think her boy was taken. Do you? If you don't, now's your chance to tell me. Because if I find out you're not focused on this case, you're no use to me, understand?'

Sexton held his hands up in protest. 'She'd been away in Marrakesh, presumably spoiling herself in a flash hotel without the kid, and she left him alone in the car in a grimy garage at night. It's hardly a glowing reference for motherhood.'

'So you don't believe her?'

'I believe you believe her.'

'I do!'

'Well, I trust your instincts. That'll have to be enough.'

'And what's wrong with your own instincts?'

He turned his face away and stared out the passenger window.

'You went through a lot being cooped up like that in the morgue on our last case,' Jo said, her voice softer. 'Maybe you should get some help. It might be good to talk to someone.'

He didn't answer.

'It doesn't have to be a shrink,' Jo went on. 'Are you dating anyone at the moment?'

'I'm not interested in a relationship,' he snapped.

'I'm not asking you to get married again . . .' Jo stopped abruptly, realizing how insensitive the words sounded. She tried to make light of it. 'What I mean is, when was the last time you had sex?'

Much to her relief, this time Sexton took it in the

laddish spirit she'd meant it. He grinned, relaxing visibly. 'If I asked you that, Daphne would have me up for sexual harassment.'

Jo glanced across. 'Don't get me started. Human Resources translates as management giving itself a licence to poke around in the personal life of staff, in my book.'

'Politically correct you just don't do, do you, Jo? Well, I got news for you. Daphne's all right.'

Jo felt like she was tiptoeing through a minefield trying to have a conversation with him. She decided to cut through the dross and give him a few home truths. 'Sexton, you're the best cop I ever worked with by a mile. But if Daphne's the one advising you to carry Maura's suicide note around with you – it's bad advice and I should know. I wallowed in grief for long enough over the crash that killed my father. The only way you're going to get your head straight is to get on with your life and let go of the past.'

Sexton turned to stare. 'Who told you about the note?'

'Look, if I tell you something that I've never told anyone about the night my old man died, will you open that bloody thing and read it?'

'The only person I told about it was Daphne.'

'My father died because I opened the passenger door while he was driving down the motorway. I needed to puke and I was too bloody drunk to ask him to stop. It was my fault he died. He was reaching over to try and pull the door closed when he hit the . . .'

Jo stopped. She could feel Sexton's eyes still on her. 'Don't you want to know why Maura died?' she asked softly.

'I know why Maura died,' Sexton said, his voice harsh. 'She died because I wasn't there for her when she needed me. Isn't that enough?'

When they reached the salubrious Sea View Road, sporting palm trees, wilting purple-flowered rhododendron bushes and panoramic sea views, Jo slowed down. She was checking out the house names on the right against Foxy's address, with Sexton scanning the ones on the left, when an ambulance overtook them and swerved into a driveway up ahead. Jo jabbed the accelerator and took off after it. Sexton reached for his grips again, as they pulled up outside a set of wooden gates leading to a mock-Tudor pad where another ambulance was waiting. The name of the property carved into the gate pillar was the same one Foxy had given them as being Imogen Cox's address. The back doors of the first vehicle were open and a female paramedic in navy trousers and a shiny bomber jacket was rooting around in the back. She turned around, clearly stressed.

Jo and Sexton stepped out of the car at the

same time. 'I'm DI Birmingham, Store Street,' Jo said.

'That was quick,' the paramedic answered, glancing over Jo's shoulder and giving a thumbs up to the other paramedic. 'Victim's a forty-three-year-old woman, with two serious head injuries.' She moved towards the second unit as the driver stuck his arm out the window handing over a wad of grey plastic. The paramedic grabbed it, and ran towards the house with it tucked under her arm, looking back and waving Jo to follow.

'The victim's husband rang it in,' she told Jo as they neared the front door. 'Said she'd been attacked by an intruder. We've got three no shocks on the defib. She should have been moved to the hospital by now, but we've only got a fixed stretcher, and her husband says they've lost the keys to the gates for the side entrance. We can't get her out through the house on the ordinary stretcher because of the angles. I'm Ann, by the way, station officer in Dún Laoghaire. Why've they sent Store Street, if you don't mind me asking?'

'Long story,' Jo answered, following her down through the hall and then kitchen. If the defib was flat-lining, Imogen Cox was clinically dead, though only a doctor could pronounce it.

A good-looking man with a silver ponytail and dark-brown eyes was sitting at the table holding an oxygen mask to his face while being tended by another paramedic. His eyes followed Jo's as she and

Sexton continued out through some patio doors that led to the garden.

At the back of the landscaped garden, a group of three more paramedics were working on the victim lying on her back beside a pool house. Clear plastic tubes and sterile packaging were strewn in a radius of a few feet around her head. Jo was interested to see what looked like the murder weapon – a bloody rock – lying within easy reach. A clump of hair the same jet-black colour as the victim's was stuck to it. If the killer had grabbed the nearest thing to hand to bludgeon the woman's head in, it suggested to her that this was a crime of passion.

The victim's face did not show her age, Jo reckoned, judging from the wrinkled skin on her neck. Her body looked much younger. Her T-shirt had been cut in a straight line up her breastbone to expose a waist that was tiny. She had scars a couple of inches long at the base of each breast, indicating a boob job. Jo couldn't see her face properly. It was a mask of muck and blood, her hair sticking to places where the blood had congealed into a crust.

Sexton looked away while Jo took it all in. Sticky clear circular pads with metal buds were dotted over the woman's chest. Little red wires with pincers gripped them and led to a machine with several electronic displays. A paramedic with a moustache, wearing the same navy uniform as the girl, was kneeling before the machine. Two more paramedics crouched either side of the victim's head, administering CPR. One, who'd red hair and a red face, was pressing the heel of his joined hands into her chest. After a series of thirty presses, which he counted aloud, he leaned back on his hunkers to allow his bald-headed partner to blow two spurts of air into the woman's mouth, held open at her nose and chin.

'How long has she been here?' Jo asked Ann, who was rolling out the sheet.

'A lot longer than her other half says,' the redhead answered.

Jo glanced at her watch. It was nearing midday. 'She's not dressed for the outdoors, so she must have bolted out here. That's hubby inside, I presume. What's up with him?'

'Shock,' Ann answered.

'Right,' the red-haired paramedic answered, positioning himself at the woman's feet as the bald paramedic moved to her head.

'In three,' said Ann, beginning to count.

After an awkward shuffle, she and the three paramedics managed to heave the woman on to the plastic sheet. Sexton moved to one of the four corners, and together the four men lifted her up and carried her towards the house.

Jo slid the patio door open to full width to help them pass through.

The man at the kitchen table didn't stand up. The mask was gone from his face, but he still looked grey and sick. A big black dog – old by the looks of it – was stretched out by his side, dozing.

'Will she b-b-be OK?' he asked, in a high-pitched voice.

'We're doing everything we can,' Ann answered.

Jo noticed that, along with the newspaper open at the sports pages on the table, there were fliers about adopting an orphan from Africa, and a stack of bank statements, as if someone had been doing accounting.

The men manoeuvred the body through the doorways of the house with difficulty. Some of the victim's hair was pushed off her face with the movement.

Jo gasped.

'You recognize her?' Ann asked, as they walked back towards the ambulance. 'I did, too, when I heard her name. She's always in the VIP mags. It's Imogen Cox.'

But Jo knew the victim as someone else entirely. Imogen Cox was the woman who had been sipping cocktails with an unknown, white-haired male on that morning's sex tape.

8

According to one of the paramedics, the husband claimed to have seen an intruder, so Jo asked Sexton to phone in a request for the air-support unit to scan the fields and coastline from overhead and search for signs of anyone on the run. Then she headed back into the dead woman's kitchen, where Jeff Cox was now alone, sitting on the edge of the table. She looked at him with interest. Despite his grey hair, he was a good ten years younger than Imogen Cox, and, unlike his wife, physically very fit.

'Sir, I understand you're upset, but this house will have to be combed for forensic evidence, and I'd ask you to keep your movements to a minimum. When you leave here in a moment, it may be a week before you're allowed back in.'

'Yes of course, I'm sorry. I'm not t-t-thinking properly,' he said.

His stutter was slight, Jo realized, and he pronounced 'th' like 't', which told Jo that there probably hadn't been as much money in circulation when he'd been growing up. He took a sip and put the mug down. Jo also noticed his teeth were crooked, another sign she was on the right track. Kids with wealthier parents tended to get orthodontic treatment in their teens.

'I'd like to ask you what happened,' Jo said. 'I'm not looking for a formal statement at this point, but I have to caution you that you have the right to remain silent, and anything you do say will be taken down, and may be used against you in a court of law.'

She looked carefully at his black designer T-shirt and denims. Apart from his hair, which needed a cut, he was extremely well groomed, and he smelled of a citrusy aftershave. Interestingly, there didn't seem to be a speck of blood anywhere on him. He'd found his wife, and his natural inclination should have been to touch her. Unless he'd showered since, as she strongly suspected.

'Anything . . . I'll do anything to help. Do you t-t-think she'll be OK?'

Sexton appeared in the doorway. Jo gave him a nod. 'I'm sure they'll let you know as soon as there's any news,' she said, thinking that if he was that concerned about his wife, he'd have asked to accompany the ambulance. 'Now – Jeff, isn't it?' She pulled out her chewed-on biro and a notebook, snapping the elastic off. It opened on the page marked with the word 'mum' from her interview notes with Tara, and she folded it over. 'How did you find her?'

Cox pulled the tip of his nose. 'I, I, I took the dog for a walk, and when I came back I found her lying there, at the back of the garden. She was still conscious, I think – but there was so much blood.'

'Sorry . . . You were coming from where?'

'I went for the newspaper.'

'Where and when?'

'Foley's newsagents, I was b-b-back here about five past ten.'

Jo looked at her watch. 'Really? It's noon now. Why such a long time delay between the time you got home and when the ambulance was called?'

'I t-t-took a shower when I got in.'

'Where was Imogen at this point?'

'Sorry, yes, sh-sh-she was in bed, lying in. I didn't want to wake her, so I went for a wash. I was d-d-due in the office. Business has been slow, we needed to drum up some new clients.'

'What's your business?'

He looked surprised.

'Oh, sorry, I thought everyone knew. We've got a modelling agency – well, Imogen has. She founded it. But I work there, too.'

'What as?'

'S-s-sorry?'

'What do you work as?'

'A photographer. Is this relevant? Shouldn't you be out looking for him, the man who did this?'

'Please answer the questions, Mr Cox.'

He rubbed his eyes. 'I'm a photographer. I'd been working in the field before I met Imogen, but I was let go from a previous company a couple of years ago. T-t-times are tough for everyone. Imogen hired me. She said my experience was an a-a-asset.' He stood up, and the dog stood, too, whining and wagging his tail. 'I was doing the housework when I heard her scream in the garden. I ran out, but I was too late. Her attacker ran, and Imogen was . . . Imogen was—'

The doorbell rang. 'Will you e-e-excuse me?'

'Never trust a man with a ponytail,' Sexton said, once he was out of earshot.

Jo smiled at him, glad to see him taking an interest, and looked around the kind of state-of-the-art kitchen you only ever saw in a *Hello!* magazine spread. Jeff Cox had landed on his feet, but he was now on the verge of losing it all – as prime suspect for the murder of his wife.

9

Tara Parker Trench was in the back of the cab that Jo Birmingham had put her into, but she wasn't heading for her apartment in Citywest. She was going to the five-star Triton Hotel on the south side of Dublin, because that's what the person who had taken Presley had told her to do. A text telling her how to get her son back had beeped into her phone while she'd still been in the garage with Jo. That's why she'd given Jo her mum's number – just in case something bad happened before she got Presley back. Tara rested her forehead against the window. The message had said: 'If you want your boy back, come to the spa at the Triton Hotel and I will be waiting for you. Bring anyone with you, and next time you see Presley he'll be in a white coffin.'

She rubbed her eyes with the balls of her hands. *Who hated her so much they would say that?* The question went round and round her head. It had to be someone she knew, because they had her private number. Her stomach constricted. She didn't know which was worse: the thought of someone she knew wanting to hurt her that much, or the idea of her little boy with a stranger. She wouldn't be able to cope if anything happened to him. He was like her lucky charm. Everything she did in life, she did for him . . .

Tara picked up the phone. She'd texted back the kidnapper that she was on her way, and to take care of Presley, that she'd do anything they wanted, but there'd been no response yet. God – what had happened to her in the last couple of days had been bad enough, but to lose Presley on top of everything – she took several deep, calming breaths. No, as long as she kept her cool, and did what the kidnapper said, everything would be all right.

She sat up straight, and tried to see herself in the driver's rear-view mirror. She needed to look good. Taking a tube of lipgloss from her jacket pocket, she opened it and applied it liberally. The Triton was the top hotel in the city for visiting celebrities and dignitaries. Anyone who was anyone stayed there, and the manager made sure the papers got tipped off so they could pap the VIPs going in and out. Tara had all the snappers' mobile numbers in her phone anyway. She usually buzzed them herself to let them know what time she'd be heading out, and with whom. She knew each edition time by heart, and had perfected the 'taken by surprise' look for them. It was the way to keep them onside. Press interest meant work. The ad agencies only ever booked girls whose faces were guaranteed to get their product some free publicity.

Combing the ends of her extensions with her fingers, she caught the driver's eye in the mirror. He had that smug look on his face that told her he thought her preening was for his benefit. It reminded her of the way the men had looked at her yesterday in Marrakesh. Like she was irrelevant. *Don't go there*, she told herself. *You haven't got time to think about this now. Presley needs you.*

She lowered the window and tried to take a big gulp of air, but her mouth was too dry for her to swallow. She bit hard on the inside of her cheek to try and control the feelings overwhelming her, tasting coppery blood. If she could just turn back the clock to those two minutes in the garage, and unstrap Presley and carry him inside to pay for the damn petrol! Or if she could just turn the clock forwards till he was back with her again . . .

She covered her face. If something had happened to him, she'd feel it in that sixth-sense way a mother knows. *Wouldn't I?* she asked herself. There were things in her life that she had done that were going to haunt her to the grave, but she could live through anything, as long as she had Presley. In her own mind, he made what she was willing to do to better their situation honourable. Without him, she was something else entirely.

If it turns out Mick has something to do with this, I won't be responsible, she thought, thinking of her ex. Maybe he was trying to teach her a lesson about him needing to see Presley more often. Deep down though, she knew Mick was too soft to have had any hand, act, or part in something like this. And even if he had, at this point it would have felt like a godsend. At least then she'd know Presley was with someone who loved him. She'd know her boy was safe. But if she didn't get Presley back soon, she was going to have to tell Mick that he'd been taken, and he could use it to get Presley away from her for good. And if the papers made her look like a bad mother, it would destroy her party-girl brand. Her modelling days would be over. She was only going to tell Mick as a last resort, she decided. *First I'll do everything I can to get Presley back by myself.*

She craned her neck to see the traffic. She could see the hotel in the distance, but the flow had come to a complete standstill. *What happens if the man who has Presley doesn't wait for me?* she thought. *If I jump out and run, I'll get there quicker.*

'Do you have a boyfriend?' the driver asked, suddenly. She could feel his eyes on her again, and sensed what he'd like to do to her.

Tara felt her skin crawl. She wondered if he had

had something to do with Presley's disappearance. He was acting as if he had. He hadn't been flagged down by Jo Birmingham at random, she realized. He had pulled into the service station at exactly the right time. She flicked her hair, about to make conversation just to keep him cool, when her phone beeped with another message.

It was from the same number as the kidnapper's text, but this time it was a multimedia message. She pressed 'open' and saw Presley's beautiful face.

Her head lightened with relief. He was OK. He looked happy. She could kiss him better when she had him back. The main thing was it wasn't too late.

'You think you're something big, but you're a nothing and you're a nobody,' the driver was saying. 'I've seen you parade about in your knickers and bra. You get paid for stripping, and that makes you no better than a slag. I wouldn't pay for a hand job from you.'

Tara looked down at the phone and studied the picture of her little boy, because she knew there was something wrong. Then it dawned on her: Presley wasn't wearing the Tommy Hilfiger jacket he'd had on last night. His shirt was different, too. She pushed the phone closer to her face, and recognized it as one she'd bought him a couple of months ago. It hadn't even lasted a day; she'd had to get rid of it the first time he'd worn it because he'd got sick all over it.

The driver was spewing more bile, but the words didn't register because Tara knew exactly who had taken a picture of Presley that day. And now she was really scared.

10

Jo and Sexton were outside the Coxes' house, their conversation drowned out by the air-support chopper whirring overhead. The fact that it was hovering in one place meant it hadn't found anyone to follow. Jo wasn't surprised: the paramedics had suggested the victim had probably died hours earlier. The ambulance was leaving, and in the front garden a uniformed officer, who'd arrived from the local station minutes earlier, was about to set up a cordon. He'd already informed Jo that his inspector and superintendent were on the way, which she took to mean that he was unimpressed by their presence and, having informed his superiors, they'd taken a dim view, too, and were coming to check it out. The competition between stations to crack cases was immense, and Jo knew that she and Sexton were about to be given their marching orders. Not that Sexton was going to need any encouragement to leave. He was looking depressed again, and his mind seemed to be on something else entirely. Jo felt a pang of concern. He'd had a difficult time coming to terms with what had happened to him during the Bible killer case, and now there was the bloody suicide note. But there was a little boy in serious trouble, and that had to be her priority.

Opening the front door, she stepped back into the warmth of the house. At the other end of the hall she could see Jeff Cox talking to his lawyer. She turned to face a giant image of Imogen Cox.

'I need you to get up there and check every room for any sign of Presley,' Jo told Sexton, pointing to the stairs.

'Why can't you do it?'

Jo sighed. 'Because one of us is going to have to keep whoever appears talking, which someone will any second now – it's bloody well guaranteed. Oh, never mind . . .'

Slipping off her shoes, she ran up the stairs two at a time, moving fast and on the balls of her feet.

Upstairs, the landing branched left and right, with doors on either side.

Jo turned, and opened the only door on the left. It was a large bedroom, and based on the doilies on the locker and the scatter cushions on the bed, probably for guests. After a quick sweep, involving kneeling to look under the bed and opening the empty wardrobe door, she was satisfied the boy was not there. A fine layer of dust everywhere told her that the room had not been in use for some time.

She heard Sexton talking to someone downstairs and moved quickly to the first of four doors on the right-hand side of the stairs. It led to a master bedroom, with a door to an en suite. A giant sleigh bed dominated; the fabrics were pinks and crushed velvets. A giant plasma TV was fixed to the wall opposite the bed, and an extensive wall of wardrobes contained only women's clothes. Jo stepped out on the balcony with its sea views and cocked an ear to see if she could make out what Cox and his solicitor were talking about underneath.

'Just refuse to answer any questions,' the solicitor was saying.

Shaking her head, she carried on into the en suite and put her hand on the shower head. It was cold. There was no sign of Presley, or any of the accoutrements that went with stashing a little boy. Jo slipped out and back into the hall.

She caught a flash of uniform downstairs, heard Sexton telling the cop he'd forgotten his car keys and was heading back into the kitchen to look for them.

The next door along the landing led to what looked like an office, with a desk and computer. She clicked the mouse and the screen burst to life with a list of names, times and numbers. It was impossible to make out what information was contained in the columns, as most of the text was blocked: by a window demanding a memory stick be reinserted. Jo glanced around for one, but thought she heard something, and left the room, running on down the corridor past a giant chandelier. From the hall came the sound of Sexton explaining to the garda why he hadn't realized the keys were in his pocket all along.

The next room was a bedroom, which was sparse and without any flourishes. An Airfix model aeroplane sat on a dresser, along with a one-eyed teddy that looked ancient. A Gibson guitar was lying on the floor in its case. The wardrobe was full of men's clothes, and Jo surmised from them that Jeff Cox liked to dress a lot younger than his years, in designer clobber. He was also clearly sleeping separately from his wife.

She picked up a single page of a bank statement from the locker, which had, as far as she could see, just one cash withdrawal, circled with a biro. Jo made a mental note of the branch address, and ducked into the en suite to test the shower head there, too – it was warm. Jeff had washed all right; not hours ago like he'd told her, but while his wife had been dying outside.

Quickly, she moved to the last room. It was the main bathroom with antique fittings. Pulling open the medicine cabinet, she took a quick look at the labels on the vials – noted the presence of Viagra,

Prozac and sleeping pills among the other regulars – before flushing the toilet and heading back downstairs.

'Speak of the devil,' Sexton was saying, his forehead furrowed.

Cox's solicitor stood on one side of him, along with Jeff, who was looking agitated. The first officer on the scene had been joined by his superiors, who seemed even less pleased. She knew them both. The Dalkey super's name was Reg. He was all right, in Jo's book, though she was wary of the fact that he was dressed in full uniform, cap included. If he'd taken the time to change his clothes, he was more interested in being on telly than in solving the case, as far as she was concerned.

'Here, Jo, apparently there's a bathroom down here you could have used all along,' Sexton said.

Jo gave him a grateful nod. 'I'll know next time then, won't I?' Glancing at Cox she said, 'I'll see you later.'

'Over my dead body,' Reg muttered. 'You're bang out of order, being here at all.'

Jo turned and gave him one of her killer smiles. 'You're acting like the case is solved. Isn't everyone innocent until proven guilty?' She caught Jeff Cox's eye again, and he looked thoughtful.

When they were outside, Jo turned to Sexton. 'Can you head straight to their bank? I need you to get their accounts to me before Jeff and his solicitor reorganize them.'

When she had them, Jo would be able to establish how much Jeff Cox was going to benefit from the death of his wife. She could read the state of an entire relationship from how a couple spent their money: by looking at their day-to-day lifestyle and their haunts. She could understand what made them tick. Did the Coxes have a standing order to feed an orphan in Malawi, or were they trying to bring one home? Did they eat out? If so, were the meals for one or two? Was the business solvent?

If money was keeping Jeff with his wife, the accounts could show that, too. If Imogen Cox had been a control freak and her husband having an affair with one of the country's most desirable women, it must have led to a lot of tension in the house.

'Why can't you go?' Sexton asked.

Jo threw her eyes up to heaven. 'Look, I know you're not in a good place right now, and I'm sorry Maura did what she did. But we've got a little boy out there who could end up in an early grave if we don't get on top of this case. I'm going straight back to the station to give Dan an earful and get the resources we need to find him. I need you to look for any recent life insurance policies or unusual cash withdrawals. That way, if Jeff Cox did murder his wife, we'll know where to start looking. Can you do that?'

He nodded. 'You think he did it?'

'Despite how it looks, my gut tells me he didn't,' Jo said. 'But he's lying through his teeth, and I want to know why.'

1

Barry 'King Krud' Roberts w~~ ~~snorting one gram off the back of the cistern in the john of the gym to top up. Three lines. Not enough to put him in the party mood, but enough to top up the three grams he'd had already today, and make him feel more like himself. His nose started to tingle. Good, they'd cut it with lignocaine, an anaesthetic used by dentists, like he'd told them to. The muppets had tried to cut corners last time by using lactose. He'd gone ballistic when he had found out. If you used lignocaine, the customers thought the buzz was cocaine-induced, enabling King to mask just how much he'd bulked the stuff out to make more profit. He'd got two dentists on board to buy lignocaine for him. It wasn't hard to recruit professionals. People who had been to college seemed to believe not going down the pit every day carrying a canary entitled them to a lavish lifestyle. King's money always did the talking. He had an accountant to cook the books and keep the Criminal Assets Bureau off his back, and a solicitor to

assets. That was why he was still the

uld feel his heart pump harder, and his blood
to race. *Fuck it*, he thought, pulling out another
wrap and sprinkling it on the surface, chopping it up
with a razor blade. That was the thing about feeling
invincible: you always wanted more.

I've earned it, he told himself. He'd been pumping
iron for hours. It was vital he stay fit. The easiest
place in the world for his enemies to take out a hit on
him and have him whacked was in prison. All you
needed was a crooked screw to turn a blind eye for
ten minutes.

He had a couple of screws on the payroll himself,
enabling him to organize phones and the charlie, but
the staff were changed all the time to try and prevent
corruption, and his men weren't rostered to work
today. The only reason he'd managed to get away on
his own was because he'd told them he was going to
the john. Even the ones who couldn't be bought
didn't have the stomach to follow him in there.

He dialled his lawyer, leaving a message when the
answering machine came on that he was expecting a
visit at half past three that afternoon. It was lucky he
was in a good mood, or he'd have phoned one of his
runners to check where the brief was. He hated it
when the phone wasn't picked up.

While he'd been pumping iron he'd worked out

exactly what he was going to tell his lawyer. He wanted to discuss the murder trial, of course – but also tell the brief he held him responsible for the drugs that had disappeared the previous night. That was the way it worked. If you brought someone to the table, as his lawyer had done, you were responsible for recouping any losses and undoing the damage, should they mess up.

The King bent over to hoover up the last of his lines. He'd got the name and address of the woman who'd been making things worse, and was quite enjoying thinking out a way to teach her a lesson; something that would send out a message that he was still the King. It had to be something spectacular to undo the damage of losing his first prison haul.

He sniffed and closed his eyes as the buzz moved to his brain. It was good gear all right. He felt like champion of the world again.

12

In one of the private rooms in the spa of the Triton Hotel, Charles Fitzmaurice was lying on the massage table. The multimillionaire owner of the hotel, he was the man Imogen Cox had turned to for help when the economy had gone into recession. Now that the big money had dried up, and the away gigs that used to be part and parcel of the game had come to an end, the high-escort end of the business was in jeopardy. 'Fitz', as he was known, had been one of Imogen's regular clients, but now that he was bank-rolling her business, he was taking a hands-on interest in every aspect of making it pay. But the recession had hit the hotel industry harder than most, and Fitz was not about to let everything he'd worked for slip out of his hands. As an amateur aviator with a landing strip in the grounds of the hotel, he'd even started flying new VIP clients directly in himself.

'You said you'd tell me where my son was,' Tara said, praying he wouldn't notice the slight quiver in her voice. Fitz got off on fear. He was sixty-odd, over-weight and had a flock of seagulls for a comb-over peeling away from his shining bald head. She'd realized in the taxi that Fitz was behind Presley's disappearance – he was the one who'd taken that photograph of him on a helicopter ride, a trip that had made Presley sick. Now all she had to do was find out where Presley was being kept.

She was going out of her way to keep Fitz happy, her fingertips kneading ever increasing circles across his thick skin. Her hands moved in the same rhythm until they met at his spine. Shifting the pressure to the heel of her hands, she changed direction, rubbing down to the tuft of hair sprouting from the base of his back, where a snow-white terrycloth towel covered his buttocks.

There'd been clients who'd revolted her in the past, lots of them, but with enough coke and booze anything was possible, and she got past the lack of physical attraction by concentrating on how she was going to spend the cash-in-hand fee.

She had been nervous when Imogen had first asked her if she was interested in this line of work, of course. But Imogen had claimed that the kind of money men were prepared to pay was the only thing about it that was obscene. And in truth, Tara hadn't needed much persuading. With one job you could go from being broke to flush in the space of an hour, and as Imogen put such an emphasis on discretion, she'd never had to worry about the truth getting out. Both parties had as much to lose if it did, Imogen had said. The clients were only ever going to be celebrities and the filthy rich, she'd promised. She had even managed to make it sound romantic. Tara would be flown by specially chartered planes – and from time to time private jets – to some of the most exotic locations in the world. She would stay in the best hotels, eat in internationally renowned restaurants, be treated like a superstar. She might even meet the man of her dreams and spend the rest of her days living in luxury.

Imogen had also stressed that if any of the girls were uncomfortable, they had the right to say no at any point in the proceedings, maintaining that this was the crucial difference between a high-class escort and a common prostitute. Anyway, she'd pointed out, just by being models, they were both in the sex industry already.

And for a couple of years, when the money hose had been on, that's exactly what it had been like. Tara had never needed to exercise her discretion. There had been oddball clients with strange perversions along the way, things she was trying to forget, but the excesses had been even more unbelievable. A Russian mining magnate had taken his Rolex off and handed it to her as a tip after celebrating his thirtieth birthday with models from every

European capital in his villa on the French Riviera. An Irish rock star, who had hired a yacht and flown a bunch of the girls to the Greek Islands just because it was the weekend, had handed her a bit part in one of his videos – which had given her the dream of one day becoming an actress. A racing magnate had even organized a diamond-encrusted Tiffany's pendant as a gift after she'd admired it in a magazine on his bedside locker.

Some of the girls had landed on their feet. Olga, a six-foot Ukrainian with the face of Anna Kournikova, had been set up with her own apartment in the Boho Club, a hotel and golf club in Meath owned by a property magnate whose permanent residence was in Jersey, and who divided most of his time between the Czech mistress he kept there, and the Cayman Islands, where his wife and children resided. He only ever came to Ireland to play golf, and according to Olga his back was too bad to manage anything other than lying prone while she worked on top.

Tara had had a couple of offers herself to become exclusive, too. One had involved a five-star suite she could call home – but her son could not. Presley. She caught her breath as she thought of him. She knew that Imogen and Fitz were behind his disappearance – they had to be – but where were they keeping him? This was what she intended to find out.

Fitz gave a low moan of pleasure as her hands slid further down his body. Tara decided there and then that as soon as she got her boy home she was going to get herself straight. She'd been thinking about getting out for ages. The moment the recession had hit, the fees had halved overnight. In the good old days it had been two grand for straight sex, fifty per cent of which went to Imogen. These days Tara was lucky to get five hundred euro per session. Since nobody was giving out free lines of charlie any more, there were expenses incurred that left a girl with barely anything to show at the end of the night.

Anyway, with the business now mainly concentrated in Dublin, it was just too close to home for comfort. She couldn't afford to be caught in any kind of compromising situation. Some of the models had gone on to get careers in the media, others had become actresses. If what really went on ever got out she'd stop being the darling of the press, and that would be the end of her career.

And last, but by no means least, was the fact that the punters' demands were changing. When Tara had started, anal sex had been a big deal. But now most of the clients considered it obligatory. There was so much of it in porn anyway that they presumed it was a matter of course.

But Imogen had made it sound like the old days might be returning when she had told Tara about the

Morocco gig. An Irish-born premiership footballer had wanted to party overnight in the Atlantis, a lavish new hotel in Marrakesh, to celebrate winning a match against his old rivals in Old Trafford. He had specifically requested Tara. The guy was world-famous, married to a pop singer, and had three young children.

A bead of sweat rolled down her back as she remembered the heat of the Moroccan midday sun, and the footballers' harsh faces. Shaking her head, she willed the image away. *Stay focused*, she told herself. *Just get Presley back*.

'Hey!' Fitz grunted. 'Why have you stopped? You give me what I want first, remember? That's the deal.'

Tara closed her eyes – she had to hold it together for Presley's sake. She moved her fingers further down.

He groaned with pleasure. 'You've been a very naughty girl. What were you doing trying to run out on my footballer friends? Who do you think you are?'

'I didn't walk out, Fitz. I did what I was paid to do, and was nearly killed in the process.'

'I don't want to hear about it. A grand you got for that job. Enough to pay for a therapist, and some. Car going well, is it? Apartment nice? Don't forget where they came from, either.'

Tara swallowed. She was not going to cry, was

not going to show him that he was getting to her.

Fitz rolled over, and she was struck, again, by how old and ugly he was. 'Don't try to play the innocent with me. I know exactly how rough you like it. Those footballers' wages are the only thing in the world that is recession-proof at the moment. You nearly blew it for us all last night, you know that? What the hell were you doing in that garage, too? You've cost me a bloody fortune. Well, you'll have to work very hard to clear your debt.'

Tara knew where this was going by the way his tone was changing. He couldn't get an erection until he'd hurt her, usually by landing a few punches to her chest and belly. Once, after knocking her to the ground, he'd put a shoe on so he could kick her properly.

'You're going to have to make it up to them, that's all there is to it. The lads are staying in the hotel the next couple of days.'

Fear flooded through Tara's body. 'Where's my son? Where is he? Where's Presley?'

'I'll tell you later. First, you need reminding who's boss. And that's going to take some time.'

'Please, Fitz, just tell me Presley's OK, and I'll do whatever you want. But I have to see him first.'

Fitz clenched his fist, drew his arm back and landed a blow to her side.

She flinched. 'I've been a bad girl,' she said,

robotically. She moved back to his shoulders and started to massage.

'Harder,' Fitz demanded petulantly. 'Nothing's happening yet.'

Holding back her tears, Tara thought about her boy, and how she was going to spoil him rotten once she got him back. She'd get him all the toys that she'd told him he'd have to wait till Christmas for – Buzz Lightyear, Woody, Slinky Dog, and that bucket of toy soldiers, and that was just for starters. It didn't matter how much it all cost, she'd get the money somehow. There were always ways.

'I'm going to have to teach you a lesson, you know that, don't you?'

Tara felt herself start to tremble. 'Yes, Fitz.' The last time he'd used those exact words, he'd inserted a bottle of beer into her. There had been a nick out of the top of it, and she'd needed stitching up after.

His fleshy left hand extended and clamped her thigh. Tara was wearing the standard-issue suspenders under her white coat, a uniform that she'd put on as soon as she'd arrived at the Triton.

'I saw for myself what happened in Marrakesh, and you were out of order,' he said, snapping the elastic with his fingers.

'Were you there?' she asked, confused.

'No, I wasn't there, you stupid slag. I saw the film.'

Tara's legs felt like they were going to go from under her.

All the promises about discretion, about protecting the girls and the clients: it was all lies if they'd filmed it.

'We'll make a famous actress of you yet!' Fitz chuckled.

She tried to go back to the toy shop with Presley in her imagination, visualizing which toys could be found in the different aisles, but all she could think about was people finding out about her, and her career being over.

She reached down. His pot belly hung over his penis, which was short and erect, and almost hidden in dense pubic hair.

'Climb aboard,' he invited.

Taking off her white coat, she climbed on to the massage table and straddled him.

'Where's Presley?' she asked softly, putting her hands around his throat and squeezing. 'Where's my son?'

13

It was early afternoon, and for what seemed like an age, Foxy had been staring over the public counter of Store Street Station at a woman draped head to toe in a black burka.

She'd arrived at the station with her husband, Hassan, the garage manager Jo Birmingham wanted interviewed. But for the past three-quarters of an hour, the station's three interview rooms had been in use. Until now, that is. Two officers and a mugging victim had just vacated the room off the public lobby, parking a fire extinguisher in the doorway because the swipe cards were always getting mislaid.

Foxy needed to get in there and start interviewing Hassan before someone else took his slot, but he could not bring himself to leave the woman with her frightened eyes alone – because he'd noticed the sneers, scoffs and muffled insults that had already come from the queue over the past thirty minutes.

'Right, you in there,' he told Hassan, pointing to his left.

Hassan entered without so much as a word of re-assurance to his wife. He had a backpack over his shoulder and he took it with him.

Foxy didn't know what depressed him more – the idea that women were still so repressed in some parts of the world, or the fact that all of the racist taunts he'd witnessed had come from middle-class office workers looking to have their passport pictures or driving-licence-renewal forms stamped. 'Would you like a cup of tea?' he asked the woman.

She shook her head.

A skanger in a Millwall jersey fell through the door, slugging from a can of Amstel, shouting and roaring about the squad cars parked on double yellows, and how it was one set of laws for him and another for the pigs. Foxy buzzed the button under the counter for assistance to help get rid of him.

'Here, you!' the drunk called out to the woman, who visibly shrank a couple of inches.

'Lid on it,' Foxy warned him, coming out from behind the counter.

'Me?' He gestured to the woman. 'What about that thing? She could be a shoe bomber for all we know.'

Foxy was all set to kick him out of the station when he spotted his daughter, Sal, walking through the door. Her face was wet from crying.

He hurried over, relieved to see a couple of uniforms emerge behind him. He pointed out the drunk and they moved in on him, leaving Foxy to concentrate on his daughter.

'I thought you had swimming practice this morning,' he said. 'What happened?'

'Philip asked me if I wanted to go into town instead.'

Philip was one of the special needs kids in Sal's group.

'He said we could go to McDonald's,' Sal went on. 'But someone took my money in the queue, and I couldn't buy anything. Philip didn't have enough for both of us.'

'Where's Philip now?' Foxy asked, worried.

'Gone home,' Sal said. 'I'd no bus fare. I said I'd come and see you instead.'

Foxy gave her a big hug. 'Poor love. That was a long walk. You should have phoned me to come and get you.'

Sal hung her head.

'Got your phone, too, did they?'

She nodded.

'Are you hurt? Any cuts?'

'One question at a time, Dad, I've forgotten the first one already.'

'Bruises. Are you sore anywhere?'

She shook her head.

'OK, I'll tell you what. Let me just get you a nice cup of sugary tea for the shock you've had, and then we'll head off. You can tell me everything, one thing at a time, OK?'

'Can we go to McDonald's on the way home?'

'Course.'

'Can I have two Big Macs?'

Foxy hugged her. Sal was his life. Her mother, Dorothy, had left twelve years ago, the night before Sal had had open-heart surgery. He found it hard to remember what Dorothy even looked like now.

After phoning the group Sal was in to tell them what had happened, and to ask someone to wait for Philip at the other end of the bus ride, Foxy held his daughter's hand and started to lead her to one of the quiet rooms upstairs.

The woman in the burka glanced up, and Foxy sighed and waved at her to follow. He'd been going to take them to the detective unit, where he intended to sit them down at a free desk, but then he heard a couple of cops sniggering. So he carried on into Jo's office, pushing a swivel chair along the way, and closing the door behind him.

'I'll get you both a cup of tea,' he said, introducing Sal to the woman, who said that her name was Neetha.

When Foxy returned two minutes later with mugs in both hands, Sal was nattering away happily, using her feet to spin this way and that on the swivel chair. Neetha was still standing in the exact same spot where he'd left her.

'Please, sit down.' He gestured to Jo's chair behind the desk. 'You can stay here till your husband's finished downstairs. Nobody will bother you.' He handed them their tea.

On his way back across the detective unit, one of the cops asked him, 'What's the story with *Not Without My Daughter*?'

The others cracked up. Foxy ignored them and carried on into the corridor, glancing back and noting with relief that inside Jo's office Neetha had sat down and started sipping from her mug.

He was crossing the public lobby when he spotted Jo clipping up the steps. She'd a bunch of DVDs under her arm. Foxy went to greet her.

'Hassan's here,' he told her. 'But I've got a situation I have to take care of. I can't interview him. You'll have to do it yourself.'

He watched Jo push her hair out of her eyes. It looked different, he noticed. It suited her. Made her look younger, somehow. He sighed. He'd like to have stayed, helped out, but looking after Sal was his priority, and always had been. Jo understood that.

'He's in interview room one,' he said, as he went back upstairs. 'His shadow of a wife's waiting, so you'd best make a start.'

* * *

Jo stared after Foxy for a couple of seconds, then reached under the public counter for a pad of statement forms, tore some pages free and rooted out a pen to bring with her to the interview. She wheeled a TV on a set of shelves with a DVD player underneath out from a control room on the right, and pushed it across the lobby and into the interview room, dislodging the fire extinguisher as she did so.

Inside, Hassan's hands rested on either side of his crotch. From under a bushy set of eyebrows that met in the middle, he watched Jo organize herself at the table.

Strictly speaking, Jo should have had another officer in there with her to witness everything; even a camera wasn't considered watertight protection against a harassment allegation or an assault, but right now she didn't have the time or the patience to go looking.

After cautioning Hassan that he was being recorded, as per regulations, Jo sat opposite and started to quiz him about the previous night.

'I've already told you what I know,' Hassan complained. 'Look, I got tickets to a match in Croker. How long is this likely to go on?'

Jo leaned forward. 'We're talking about a little boy who's missing. You must have seen something. You got kids yourself?'

Hassan didn't answer.

'I've got kids,' Jo said. 'If anyone hurt them and I got my hands on them, I don't know what I'd do.'

'I had a son,' Hassan said solemnly. 'He died of meningitis six years ago. He was three.'

He looked at the floor, his face hard. 'We lived in Iraq at the time. Antibiotics are like gold dust over there because of the sanctions. That's why we came to Ireland. I couldn't face losing another child.'

There were moments in interviews that presented opportunities to exploit a subject's emotions. Sometimes they never returned. Harsh as it might have seemed to an outside observer, this was one of them.

Jo stood up, walked over to the TV and DVD player, and reached for the porno movies she'd taken from his shop.

She pressed the first disc out of the box, and slid it into the drive.

'What are you doing?' Hassan asked.

The sounds from the movie said it all – a woman was crying and wailing in obvious pain, but in-between her pleas a man was making the grunting noises of high arousal. The images were equally despicable – the woman was being raped in a wood, while a line of men waited, laughing and joking. Jo felt ill.

Hassan turned away.

Jo hit 'stop', and 'eject', reached for the next disc from the pile, slotting it in.

'Ah, bestiality,' she said, surveying the cover.

The screen came to life and a naked woman smiled to the camera as she brushed the coat of a German Shepherd.

'Turn it off,' Hassan said.

Jo reached for the next one. 'What age did you say your son was?' she asked, studying the cover. 'Tell you what, why don't we get your wife in to watch with us?'

Hassan held his palms up. 'I'll tell you what you want to know, as long as I don't have to testify in court. I'd be a dead man walking.'

Jo noticed he was sweating.

'The cow who's caused all the trouble, who said her kid was taken, the one who tried to leave without paying for her petrol – you can't believe a word that comes out of her mouth. She's a hooker.'

'Tara Parker Trench?'

'Yes!'

'Why do you say that?'

He didn't answer.

'Is she in one of your movies?' Jo reached for another DVD, all set to put it in the player.

He looked panicked. 'No, one of the customers told me.'

'Name?'

'I only ever knew him as Marcus.'

'What does Marcus drive?' Jo asked, reaching for the pen.

'A HiAce.'

'Colour?'

'Wine.'

'Year?'

'1998, something like that. You'll get it on the CCTV.' Hassan zipped open his backpack and put two more DVDs on the table. 'This one recorded what was going on inside the shop, this one outside.'

'So you're expecting me to believe someone driving a battered van is able to afford the services of a top model.'

Silence, and then he spoke. 'No, he works with her in some hotel.'

'Where?'

'I dunno.'

Jo raised her eyebrows.

Hassan sighed. 'He's got a cleaning firm. Specialist. It only does pools, hot tubs, steam rooms – that kind of stuff.'

'You know a lot about him.'

'I read it on the side of his van.'

'Bit of a coincidence that Tara should have been in at the same time as him, isn't it?'

Hassan shrugged. 'He was paying for petrol when she came in. I said, "Phoar!" or something like that.

He said anyone could have her at this hotel if they'd enough readies.'

'And which one is that, then?'

'I told you, I haven't a clue.'

Jo leaned across the desk, so she was right up close to him. 'Well, you'd better find out, Hassan, and you'd better find out fast, or you and your wife will be on the next plane back to Baghdad. I can guarantee it.'

14

Sexton's stomach rumbled as he was led into Jeff Cox's bank manager's office. He was starving, that was why. He'd had no lunch, and no breakfast, either. Usually he was able to slip out across the road to a little greasy spoon opposite the station for a Danish or an almond croissant to keep him going, but this morning he'd made the mistake of heading in to Jo to see if she needed a hand shifting a television and had been pressed into service ever since. When Jo got her teeth into a case, you couldn't shake her off until she'd solved it. He sighed. He'd been like that once. Before Maura had died. In those days the job had dominated his life, too. Well, he'd learned the hard way where putting work before your home life got a person.

If he'd had his eye on the ball two years ago, his wife and unborn child might still be alive. These days the more he worked, the more guilt he felt. Now, if he cut hours here and there, it was only time he was owed in lieu of all the extra time he had put in over the years. And yet, when he did take afternoons off, he didn't do anything in particular, just kept moving, like the man a few sandwiches short of a picnic he used to pass on the way to work. That bloke had spent the day walking from home to town and back again, just for the sake of it.

The bank manager's office turned out to be a corner of the bank, boxed off by those dodgy blue felt partition-stands that hide nothing from the chest up. The manager had bottle-glass lenses, and examined Sexton's ID an inch from his face, before agreeing to organize a set of the Coxes' accounts. He left Sexton alone to go in search of paper for his bleeping printer.

Sexton rubbed his stomach miserably. He didn't know where his next meal would come from. He didn't keep any food at home any more, as it only went mouldy before he had a chance to eat it. His apartment wasn't really a home in the true sense of the word, anyway, more like just somewhere to put his head down. A home was a place you wanted to go to, and Sexton didn't like being on his own. He hadn't enjoyed getting drunk since Maura had died, either. If he allowed himself to remember the point-lessness of her death – which was all he did when he was on his own or drinking – he got sucked into that way of thinking. He wished someone would explain, in the information leaflets that told depressives to ring the Samaritans or to talk to someone, that actually suicide was the ultimate act of selfisness. It ended the pain for the victim all right, but it devastated the lives of those left behind. What Maura had done had had a domino effect. These days, Sexton spent more time thinking about dying than living.

Daphne had picked up on his state of mind the moment she'd seen him. He'd never been one for counselling, but on her first day in the station she had taken him aside and told him if he needed to talk, she was there. It happened to be the second anniversary of Maura's death, and his head had been all over the place. He'd gone to her boxy little office, not to talk, but so he wouldn't be on his own. He hadn't meantto tell her about the note. It had just come out. She hadn't made him feel like a freak for carrying it around, the way Jo had. Daphne had told him he'd open it when he was ready. And he would. Not to order, as Jo would have it. But when he was ready.

The manager was back with a stack of paper, which he proceeded to insert in the printer, making small talk as he did so. Sexton put his hand in his pocket, and held Maura's note.

'Shite!' The manager cursed.

Sexton looked up. The paper had jammed in the printer again.

'Sorry,' the manager said.

Sorry had to be the most misused word in the English language, Sexton thought. *People used it all the time when they shouldn't, and never when they should*. He wished he'd said it more often to Maura, though. The last time he'd seen her, he'd brought her breakfast in bed. She'd been texting someone, but had stopped when she'd seen him and slipped the phone under the pillow. He remembered how she'd been wearing new lingerie. She hadn't looked right in it. 'What's the occasion?' he'd asked her. But she'd merely smiled. He never had got an answer.

'We have to sign off for every last pencil now, never mind the paper,' the manager said, opening the printer and throwing the screwed-up pages into the waste-paper basket. 'The powers that be are worried we're all about to start a sideline in stationery supplies.'

Do I look like I give a flying shite? Sexton thought. Maura had taken one look at the scrambled eggs he'd made for her that morning, then bolted for the en suite, and knelt in front of the cistern to chuck. Sexton had watched her through the door, as she had held her long, brown hair back with one hand. She'd been pregnant, and it tore him up every day to think that he hadn't known or guessed.

'Has something happened to Imogen or Jeff Cox?' the manager asked. 'Is that what this is about?'

'I'm afraid I'm not allowed to go into the details yet,' Sexton answered.

The manager started clicking his mouse. 'Must be serious, then. You guys never release details of a death until the family's been informed. A robbery would be different. You'd want to get the details out as quickly as possible in that case. I saw the gardaí chopper out there earlier and wondered what was going on. I bet it's something to do with this, right?'

Sexton stood up, impatient. 'I am under time pressure here.'

The manager turned back to the screen. 'Just give me a sec . . . Imogen and Jeff Cox. Here it is.' He coughed self-consciously. 'You know I heard on the news there'd been an incident in Killiney and a woman had been hurt. That's where they live . . .'

Sexton sighed, willing himself to relax. It was nothing personal, just his luck that he'd got the most talkative bank manager in the city. 'Like I said, I can't discuss it.'

'I heard the woman was in her forties, just like Imogen Cox, and that she was taken to hospital with head injuries.'

Maura had been going to get her hair done the day she'd died. She'd never kept the appointment. Why had she bothered to book it at all? She had been a little distant with him, yes, but unhappy? No. She'd got herself a little supermarket job, which had involved dressing up as one of Santa's elves for work each day.

'Well, I don't have to tell you that they were a wealthy couple,' the banker said.

Sexton tightened his fingers around the note. Of all the feelings – guilt, sorrow, anger – the waste was the worst. Having someone top themselves was worse than having them murdered. At least if someone you loved was murdered you could feel angry at whoever had done it. But how could Sexton be angry at Maura? She was the most inoffensive person he'd ever met in his life. The hardest bit with suicide was having to listen to stories every day on the news: about people looking for transplants; people fighting for their lives after random street-attacks while their families held vigils; people left paraplegic after tragedies – all of them grateful for any small extension to their lives.

'The mortgage on the house was paid. The modelling business had been running at a loss for years, was insolvent, in fact, but there were frequent cash deposits, and there's two million euro in their current account.'

'Two million euro? How long had the modelling been losing money?'

The manager typed something into the keyboard, then looked at what the computer threw back. 'For as long as we keep records before moving them on to the archive facility – seven years.'

'So how do you know the cash wasn't connected to the modelling?'

The manager shrugged. 'Their business was always cheque-based.'

'Any unusual activity in the account?'

'It depends on what you call unusual,' the banker said, looking at the spreadsheet the printer had just spewed out.

'Well?' Sexton prompted.

'There's been a cash withdrawal of nine hundred and fifty euro every Monday at the same time – 3.30 p.m. – and from the same ATM machine in Sandymount, for the past six weeks. It's not the only cash withdrawal during that time, but the others are for varying amounts, and taken out at different places. The Sandymount ATM is used consistently every time. Nine hundred and fifty euro is also the maximum amount that can be taken out with their card. If it was a payment it would be more usual for it to go through as a direct debit or a standing order.'

Thanking him, Sexton took the printouts, folded them into his breast pocket with the note, and left the bank as quickly as he could.

In the car park, he reached for his phone to dial Jo and tell her about the new development, but the call went straight to her voicemail. He hung up and glanced at his watch. Today was Monday. It was three p.m. If he went to the ATM now, maybe someone would show up.

He turned his key in the ignition. He wanted to impress Jo, show her he hadn't lost it. He didn't ever want to see her looking like she felt sorry for him again, the way she had at the Coxes' house. The ATM it was. And then he'd call her.

15

He stood in the doorway, all six foot four and two hundred and eighty pounds of him. His body was pure blubber, but every bit as powerful as a stack of hard muscle. He also had a walrus moustache of grey, wiry hair over his top lip, and on the bottom a four-inch metal spike screwed into a piercing. Some of the girls didn't believe it when he said it was to impale the testicles of punters who wouldn't pay up, but Tara had seen exactly what he was capable of when she'd been sent to a casino to escort a gambler who'd bluffed about a big win and then been unable to produce the readies. It wasn't just that Big Johnny hurt people – he liked hurting people.

He advanced another step, his tattooed arms moving as if they weren't connected to his body, his huge shoulders leaving no room for a neck.

'That's far enough,' Tara warned him. She'd let go of Fitz, who was gasping for breath on the massage table, his face purple.

Big Johnny's flip-flops stopped squeaking on the tiles. He held up his arms a little, and she could see how wide the damp circles had spread under the arms of his loose, white T-shirt. He flashed a twisted smile, showing a set of gums that were twice the size of his undersized teeth.

Tara held up the razor blade she'd taken from the ladies' changing room, then moved it to Fitz's throat. He gave a harsh gagging sound as she made her first cut. A tiny trickle of warm blood coiled down the steel on to her fingers.

Big Johnny glared. 'If you think you're going to be able to put this one down to PMT you've got another think coming, my darling.'

'My little boy,' Tara said, her voice loud in the silence. 'I know Imogen's behind this – Imogen and Fitz – and I want you to understand that I will do anything – anything to get him back.'

'Put that fucking thing down before you make me really angry.'

'Just get me my boy.'

'You've got five seconds,' Johnny said.

'I want Presley back.'

'You weren't thinking about your little boy before you started this, were you? I'm counting now. Four.'

Tara looked up sharply. 'What have I started? They didn't tell you what happened in Morocco, did they?'

'Three. Don't play the innocent, sweetheart. You

have something that doesn't belong to you, so it seems only right and fitting that something of yours was taken out as a little insurance policy to make sure you didn't have any more bright ideas. Good thing, too. Now, put that blade down. Nice and easy now . . . two . . .' Johnny held out his hand.

'I never took anything, I swear on my little boy's life . . .'

Fitz thrashed weakly.

'Your car was full of gear,' Big Johnny told her. 'Marcus was supposed to pick the drugs up from the john at the garage. But with all the heat, it was left in your car instead, for safekeeping. And just in case you got any ideas, your boy was taken as well.'

Tara gasped. 'But the police took my car!'

Big Johnny took a step towards her. 'If you'd kept your trap shut, none of this would have happened. You want your boy, you get Fitz's gear back. That's all you have to do. One.'

Tara straightened up and dropped the blade. 'Look, my car's in the station pound. I'll get it back. But you have to let me at least see Presley first. I want my little boy.' She started to sob.

'Good girl,' Big Johnny said. 'Now, come to Daddy.'

16

Jo was not happy. Having let Hassan go, she was standing in her office trying to get through to Tara on the phone. Why the hell wouldn't Tara answer? Banging the phone down, she plugged in the DVD player she'd 'borrowed' from the interview room. Slipping one of the CCTV discs in, she turned the telly on and pressed 'slow fast-forward'. She sat on the edge of her desk, looking between the time on the bottom right-hand corner and the wad of receipts she'd confiscated from Hassan in the station. They were about four inches deep and it took a couple of minutes to sift out any transactions that had occurred between 8.50 p.m. and 9.10 p.m. – fifteen in all, she counted.

Busy night, she thought.

Sitting on a swivel chair that she realized hadn't been there earlier, she ran her finger down each receipt, and, still keeping an eye on the TV, examined the lists of purchases, this time to see if anyone had bought anything unusual. She picked one out: there was no fuel listed. It seemed odd to Jo that the customer hadn't paid for any petrol, but had bought two other items. The first was listed as 'GL' and had cost 22 cents. 'Government Levy' she realized, recognizing the price of a plastic bag. The second was labelled 'Sanitary', and had cost €11.99 – too dear for a bottle of shampoo or a packet of sanitary towels.

She picked up the phone on her desk and rang the service station number cited on the top of each receipt. When the call connected, she identified herself to a man with a Chinese accent, and asked to check the item, calling out the barcode numbers. He told her to hold.

She aimed the remote at the DVD and hit 'pause'.

'It's night pants,' the assistant told her.

'What?'

'Night pants . . . for children at night, that's what the barcode says the product is.'

'Do you mean nappies?'

'Yes, for toilet-training . . . when the toddler goes to bed.'

Jo thanked him, and hung up. She stared at the receipt, perplexed. It could be just a coincidence that someone had bought that particular product on the night Presley had vanished but, as convenience stores went, the garage was pretty uninviting. Maybe the other shops in the area were closed at that hour. Then again, wouldn't most toddlers be in bed by nine at night? She looked at the receipt again, and cursed under her breath when she saw it had been a cash transaction. A visa card number would have led her straight to the purchaser. She'd have to cross-reference the time with the CCTV footage to see if she could ID the person in the shop with the car they'd climbed into; that was presuming they'd driven . . .

She focused on the screen. The time on the bottom right-hand side of the screen read 20.58 p.m., and she could see Tara's car's distinctive striped bonnet in a bay. Ideally, she would have watched the comings and goings building up in the hour before that to see if she could see any suspicious activity, but she was under pressure time-wise and had to be selective. The good news from her point of view was that the garage used a state-of-the-art system to record, so the image wasn't grainy like some of the CCTV systems still in operation around the city. It was like watching TV, but without the sound.

Turning the bunch of statement forms she'd used to interview Hassan upside down so she had some blank sheets of paper – at a premium in the station – she swivelled them to the landscape position and tried to mark up a rough map of approximate distances based on what she was seeing on the screen. Top of the page, in the middle, was the entrance to the store; to the right of that was the door to the public toilet. She drew five lines across the page underneath to represent the six bays, numbering them from left to right. In the fifth she drew a rectangle with an 'x' in it to represent Tara's car.

Using the remote to inch the images forwards, she worked out that the car at the fourth pump, to Tara's left if facing the store attached to the garage, was a white Mitsubishi. Jo drew a box and jotted the registration inside.

In bay three she made out the wine-coloured HiAce whose significance she was beginning to understand, thanks to the interview with Hassan. Again she represented it with a rectangle, making a note of the registration with an arrow between it and the box.

The petrol pump in bay number six – on Tara's right and the one closest to the road – she judged was out of order, having seen two motorists who'd made the mistake of driving in and then tried to reverse and rejoin the queue, causing whatever the equivalent of road rage was when there was no road involved. Jo could imagine the shouts based on the hand gestures and heads being stuck out of windows.

The vehicle in bay number one also got her attention because a camper van was peculiar in this part of the inner city, and at this time of year. The registration was Polish, she noticed. It could just have been someone visiting family the cheapest way possible, she decided, though many of the Poles in Dublin had gone home since the recession.

After a lot of aiming the remote, pausing and playing, she wrote a rough biographical note about the motorists attached to the vehicles, having watched each fill up.

'Teenage male, dressed in baggy jeans with a trucker cap, two male passengers – similar,' she wrote, describing the Mitsubishi occupants.

Jo had to rewind to see Marcus, the HiAce driver, filling up five minutes previously. The sign-writing detailing his business, mentioned by Hassan, must have been on the other side of the van, because the side Jo was looking at was blank. She described Marcus as a 'red-haired male in his forties wearing a navy fleece, jeans and runners'.

The camper van couple in the first bay were 'in their sixties, with bum bags around their waists, and cameras around their necks', she wrote, thinking: *tourists*.

Then it was Tara's turn. Jo watched her patting the air outside her window, and wondered who she was trying to appease. She fast-forwarded through Tara filling up, to try and ID the car behind.

Jo spooled on to see Tara running into the shop.

A motorcyclist on a high-spec bike pulled into the sixth bay, which Jo had presumed wasn't working.

He didn't flick his visor up to read the digital display, or reach for the pump. He just stood there waiting for a few seconds, staring at the garage window. Jo jotted down the registration of his bike. Now he was walking towards Tara's car. Jo sat up. He looked towards the garage again, then stooped to look in the car. The man pulled Presley's door open, pulled a glove off, and seemed to make contact – it was impossible to tell without seeing the child inside. Instead of taking him out, however, he closed the door and went back to the bike before speeding off. Jo exhaled. *What the hell was that about?*

Seconds later, Tara came running out of the station and got into her car, followed by Hassan, who charged out of the shop and banged on the driver's window. The car did a bunny hop, and cut out. Tara shoved her door open, making Hassan flinch as it connected with his body. The HiAce seemed stalled in front of Tara's car. As Marcus got the vehicle going, he sped off, and Tara drove her car out of view. Seconds later she walked back into shot, and entered the garage, Hassan close behind her. The car behind her pulled up, but didn't stop for petrol – it drove straight through and out of shot.

That's odd, too, Jo said to herself, drawing a box on the page behind Tara's car, describing it as a Jag, and noting the registration.

Tara came out of the shop a few minutes later,

disappeared momentarily, and reappeared running and in a panic.

Jo numbered on her page which of the drivers she considered most relevant in order of priority, based on what she'd seen. Number one was the man on the motorbike – why was he so interested in Presley? The biker hadn't taken him, but he'd opened the door as if he'd considered it.

Number two had to be the HiAce driver, Marcus, based on what she had already learned from Hassan.

Three, the Jag owner, because it made no sense to queue for fuel if you didn't want any. Jo hadn't been able to make out who was behind the wheel, but she'd have given a good punt it was a female.

Four, the kids in the Mitsubishi, who were only acting the maggot, in her opinion.

She numbered the camper van five.

She pressed 'eject' and slid the disc out. She needed to run all the registrations listed on the page through the computer to ID who each vehicle was registered to, especially the HiAce, which she hoped would lead her to Marcus. But first, she wanted a quick look at what had happened inside the shop, and who was there.

Jo slid the second disc in and fast-forwarded to the time she'd seen Tara first enter the shop, 21.02 p.m.

The camera was positioned behind the teller this time, so, at 21.02 p.m., she had a clear view of Tara, wearing a short dress, entering and joining the queue. There was a row going on at the top between the teller and a guy with a shaved head. Next in line was a man in a suit and looking agitated. Third, an old man Jo hadn't seen entering while the cars were filling up. Jo wondered how long he'd been there and which of the vehicles was his. Tara joined the back of the queue. A short time later, she was followed by a youth with a face Jo couldn't make out because his hoodie was pulled up.

A couple of seconds later, the camper van man came in.

Jo watched the disturbance kick off just as Tara had described, with the man with the shaved head firing cans of drink up at the counter. She could see Tara pointing her key fob at the window, obviously trying to flick her alarm on. Then the shaved-headed man's dog bolted up and started to maul the guy in the suit – the paedophile Tom Burke, she realized. Jo watched Tara turn and make a break for the exit. A middle-aged woman with long brown hair and sixties-style shades nearly bumped into her at the door.

'Where did you come from?' Jo asked, checking her drawing. 'Were you in the Jag?'

On cue, the brunette reached up to one of the shelves. A set of perfectly French-manicured nails, white at the tips, gripped something.

'Bingo,' Jo said, freezing the frame.

The woman held a square packet with 'DryNite' clearly legible across the side.

It looked to Jo like Tara Parker Trench was telling the truth.

17

Sexton was standing across the road from the ATM he was keeping an eye on in Sandymount – a leafy suburb on the south side – leaning against a bus stop. He was the only one waiting, and he took a step back when a double-decker bus started to pull in, straight for a deep puddle that sprayed up, soaking his trousers and socks. *Bloody chilblains to look forward to on top of everything else*, he thought.

It was three thirty, and he decided to give the stake-out another sixty seconds max. He still hadn't managed to get through to Jo, and his heart just wasn't in it today. So far the only people who'd shown any interest in the cash machine were a bunch of school kids messing on the way home. A harried-looking mum was heading towards it now, pushing a buggy. She looked like she was having about as good a day as he was. The rain-cover protecting her toddler blew off suddenly in the wind, and as she stretched over for it, the buggy nearly upended with the weight of her shopping on the handles.

Sexton pulled his phone out of his pocket to try and ring Jo again, but discovered the damn thing was wet through, too. He gave it a shake, but there was no jizz in it at all. He'd had another one that had slipped out of his pocket and into the bog. It had dried out after a couple of days, so he hoped this one would work again, too, but he could forget about using it today. *Fuck this for a game of soldiers*, he thought. He'd had enough.

He had started to walk towards his own car when a big, flash, brand-new Audi jeep pulled up directly beside the cash machine, blocking the pathway and forcing the mother with the pushchair to step into the bus lane to get round it. This really pissed Sexton off. She looked like she was a good mum, and had been giving the kid's nose a wipe when the jeep veered in. She shouldn't have to put herself and her kid at risk because a selfish prat who liked spoiling himself couldn't be arsed to park where he was supposed to.

Sexton decided to give the driver a ticket. If he was under forty, he was also going to do him for dangerous driving, he decided. If he was under thirty-five, he was taking the car off him.

Sexton rapped on the driver's window. To do that, he had to stand on the road himself, meaning the driver couldn't do a runner without knocking him down. When the window slid down and the driver grinned out at him, Sexton threw his eyes to heaven, walked around to the passenger door, and climbed in.

'Hello, Gav, how's tricks?' Murray Lawlor said, moving his wallet off the passenger seat and placing it on the dash.

Sexton pointed for him to move out of the bus stop and Murray held his hands up. 'I was just leaving.'

Sexton made sure the mum had angled her buggy back on to the path before studying his companion properly. Murray looked more like an investment banker than a former cop who'd packed it all in to be a bouncer. He was thirty-three tops, with Frankie Dettori slicked-back hair and the jockey's lurid taste in shirts. He'd bailed out of the force a few years back because a nixer he had going in security was proving more lucrative. He now ran his own business, and the secret of his success seemed to be his hiring policy. His staff were all ex-guards he'd coaxed away from the force because they knew the law and, as far as Sexton was concerned, how best to evade it. He'd tried to headhunt Sexton, too, around the time Maura had died, but Sexton's head hadn't been in a place that could take any more upheaval, and he'd declined. Based on the size of Murray's cufflinks, this was a mistake – he was clearly creaming it.

'What are you doing here, anyway?' Sexton asked.

Murray didn't bat an eyelid. 'I had to pull over to answer a call on my mobile.'

Sexton glanced from the expensive hands-free set to Murray's wallet sitting on the dash. 'That right?' he said. 'You wouldn't know Imogen and Jeff Cox, by any chance?'

Murray shifted uncomfortably in his seat. 'Nah. Why?'

'Imogen Cox got whacked this morning.'

Murray looked surprised. 'Murdered?'

'You knew her, then?'

Murray rubbed his forehead. 'Yeah, I knew of her, through some of her models. They're always in and out of one of the clubs I cover.'

'Where's that?' Sexton asked.

'Jesus, shouldn't you be reading me my rights?' Murray reacted, half-joking. 'The Blizzard – the nightclub in the Triton. Imogen's girls all have VIP passes. They come in, so do the blokes.' He glanced at his chunky watch. 'Christ – is that the time? I've really got to get going.'

'I thought you worked nights,' Sexton said.

Murray grinned, and changed the subject. 'Bet you regret turning down that job offer on wet days like this. You look like a drowned rat.'

Sexton reached for a tissue for his dripping nose from a box Murray kept between the seats – all nice and plumped and ready to be used. He blew hard in it.

Murray grinned again. 'You know, I'm always

looking for good people. Tell you what, meet me tonight for a jar, and we can discuss it then.'

Sexton was still thinking about the wallet and what it meant. 'Why would I want to do that?'

Murray rubbed his hands together. 'Because I'll be bringing some girls. Between us, we'll see whether we can persuade you to make a decision you'll never regret.'

Sexton sighed. 'OK,' he said slowly. 'Where and when?'

'Say eight o'clock, in the bar of the Triton Hotel? I'm on the club door after.'

'The Blizzard?' Sexton asked.

'That's the one.'

Sexton nodded, and pulled open the passenger handle. 'What's she like to motor, anyway?' he asked as he climbed out.

'Mate, I'm going to spare you,' Murray said, pulling out into the road. 'See you tonight.'

18

The brief's name was George Hannah, and, physically, he was everything the King wasn't: five foot five, and nine stone tops. The King was only five foot ten but he weighed twice what Hannah did. Hannah was wearing a navy suit, white shirt, and white satin tie; the King – jeans, trainers, and a black T-shirt that looked to have been painted on.

Prison was clearly making Hannah uncomfortable. He was carrying a cardboard folder against his chest in that defensive way only barristers do in court, and was trying to avoid eye contact. The King was carrying a Tesco plastic bag with the possessions he needed when away from his cell – a toilet roll and a bottle of water. He was staring at his lawyer.

'Mr Roberts, in the future I can't just drop everything like this to see you,' Hannah said, looking nervously along the row of ten prisoners and their visitors, facing each other along a long bench, and separated by small partitions. King was in the first

142

seat, beside the screw supposedly monitoring contact – who was actually reading the *Sun*, as he knew better than to start sticking his nose into the King's business.

On their right, a lag was wearing the face off a blonde, who was dressed the way a woman should dress: in next to nothing. She'd looked over at the King more than once during the clinch. Clearly she knew who he was, too.

The King slapped his hands down on the table. The letters tattooed on the tops of the fingers of his right hand spelt 'KILL'. The left one said 'PIGS'.

'Let's get this straight,' he said to Hannah. 'I'm paying you.'

Hannah visibly shrank as he opened his folder.

'I don't want tomorrow's murder case to come to court,' the King said, nodding at the folder.

Hannah looked up in surprise. 'There's nothing I can do to stop it.'

The King frowned. 'Not strictly true. Your friend owes me money. You got him off the hook the last time he was in trouble with the law. I want you to do the same for me.'

Hannah pulled a hankie from a pocket and wiped his forehead. 'I don't know what you mean.'

'Your friend was charged when he was caught in that chopper of his with something he bought off me. You made the case against him disappear. I want my case to disappear, too. And I'm holding you personally responsible. Understand?'

'That was different. He had something up his sleeve.'

'Better tell him to pull it out again, so that he gets me out of here. Tell him that way we'll all be quits. Do you understand?'

Hannah was sweating with fear. The King smiled. 'I've got another bone to pick with you: the consignment that went AWOL on Sunday night. That five million is down to you. You don't get it back, you're in serious trouble.'

19

Jo drove through a set of tall wrought-iron gates and past a gate lodge as she headed towards an imposing Renaissance-revival house set back from the road, with one Grecian nude too many along the driveway. The Clontarf address was listed in the system as the home of the registered owner of the Jag, one Rosita Fitzmaurice.

Jo's boots crunched on the gravel as she climbed out of the car and walked up to the double set of doors. Based on the number of cars parked in the driveway and the fact that the gates had been open, it looked to Jo like someone was entertaining, though half past three seemed a funny time for guests. Jo surveyed the mix of cars as she rang the bell. There were roughly ten, and judging by the models and their varying ages, the owners mixed in all kinds of circles.

It was Rosita who answered; Jo recognized her from the set of her neck and shoulders. Her hair looked different from that of the woman Jo had watched buy nappies on the CCTV footage filmed inside the garage. The realization that Rosita had been wearing a wig and shades in the garage only deepened Jo's suspicions.

Rosita was in her early fifties, with a severe blonde bob. Her make-up was a shade too dark for her skin, her lipstick a pearly pink. Her eyelids had a heavy, sedated look, and her perfume had to be very expensive to smell that bad, Jo reckoned. Rosita put a hand to the side of her face as if surprised to find Jo there, which seemed strange considering the amount of people inside. She had a perfect set of French-manicured false nails, Jo noticed, reaching for her ID. Before she got the chance to produce it, Rosita stepped back, holding the door open. 'Come in,' she said.

Jo stepped into an open, wood-panelled room where people from all walks of life – if their dress sense was anything to go by – sat with their backs to her on chairs facing a temporary dais.

A Filipina girl, shabbily dressed with downcast eyes, was standing on the dais. Jo put her at no more than eighteen years old.

A young man with bad skin, dressed in a sharp suit, walked behind Rosita and put his hands on her shoulders. 'I thought I told you to stay upstairs, Mother,' he said sharply.

'I wanted to get some air,' Rosita said.

'Who's this?' he demanded. 'You should have called me.'

'What's going on here?' Jo asked, still watching the young girl.

The man clicked his fingers, the spectators turned to look, and two women sitting in the front row reacted to him, waving the group away by jumping to their feet and hurrying the Filipina out of the room.

'Wait right there,' Jo told the girl, but she kept walking.

Jo made to follow but the man blocked her path. 'Who are you?' he demanded.

Jo held out her ID.

'She doesn't speak English,' he said about the girl. 'We're hiring new staff for the estate.'

Jo watched her go. 'Your name is?'

'Hugo Fitzmaurice. What's this about? Have you got a warrant?'

'Why would I need one?' Jo asked. 'What's going on here?'

'Who is she?' Rosita asked her son, squinting at Jo's ID.

'A member of the gardaí, mother,' Hugo answered. 'She's called Detective Inspector Birmingham.'

Rosita started to fan the air in front of her face with her palm.

'Is it Charles?' Rosita asked, heading for a chaise longue and taking a seat.

Jo's back straightened as she put 'Charles' with 'Fitzmaurice', and realized she was in the home of the multimillionaire who owned the capital's glitziest hotel – the Triton. Jo would bet her life that when Hassan came through with the information about which hotel Marcus worked in, it would be the Triton, too.

'Why don't you go take a little nap, Mother?' Hugo suggested.

'Not before we talk,' Jo said. 'You do, of course, have the right to refuse, in which case I will organize an arrest warrant.'

'On what grounds?' he asked.

'Your mother was in a petrol station last night when a little boy was snatched from a car. I'd like to ask her about it.'

'I didn't see anything,' Rosita said.

Jo shook her head. Rosita's natural reaction, if she had really known nothing, would have been surprise. She would have asked what had happened, and expressed interest in the welfare of the child.

'Fine,' Hugo said. 'You can speak to Mother in Dad's private study. I'll come with you.'

'I want you to go and get that young girl back so I can see her paperwork,' Jo said.

'I'll get Lee to show you she's here legally. But she

won't thank you for it. She can kiss goodbye to her job if she has to leave with you. I need cleaning done. If she has no work visa, she most certainly will be here illegally – and facing the prospect of immediate deportation back to a life of impoverishment and hopelessness, I'm afraid.'

'Bring her so I can talk to her, along with whatever translator you must have had to help her get through the interview,' Jo replied.

Hugo led Jo and Rosita into a study, also wood-panelled and covered with framed photographs. He took his mother's hands in his own and stared at her. 'Mummy, don't answer anything that you'd rather not. Just tell the nice detective if anything makes you uncomfortable, won't you?'

Rosita nodded, and lowered herself stiffly on to one end of a wine-coloured leather couch.

Jo walked over to the wall of photographs. Fitz was in most of them, schmoozing with well-known faces: riding in golf buggies with a former president of the USA; shaking hands with a former African dictator currently on trial in the Hague for war crimes. Jo had her back to Rosita. 'Your hair looks different from the way it did on the camera in the garage.' She glanced over her shoulder.

Rosita touched it absently.

'It was longer and darker. Why were you wearing a wig?'

Rosita looked startled. 'That's personal. You're making me uncomfortable. Hugo said if . . .'

'Tell me what happened in the garage last night.'

'Absolutely nothing that I saw.'

'It's a bit far out for you, isn't it?'

'Not at all. I'd been shopping in town. I had to collect Fitz from the hotel, he'd been drinking, so I stopped off for petrol on the way.'

'But you didn't buy any petrol.'

'What?'

'Petrol,' Jo said.

'Didn't I?'

'No.'

'That's right, the queue was too long. I was afraid I'd miss Fitz. I knew I'd enough petrol to get me there, there's a garage near the hotel.'

'In which case, why did you go into the shop?'

'Did I?'

Jo sighed.

'Oh, that's right,' Rosita said. 'I thought I saw someone I knew inside.'

'Did you?' Jo asked.

'No,' Rosita replied.

'Why did you buy nappies?'

'I had to buy something. I didn't want them thinking I was a complete lunatic.'

'And you weren't worried about being late for Fitz at that point?'

Rosita sat back. 'Are you married, Detective Inspector Birmingham?'

'Yes. I mean no,' Jo answered.

'Was there another woman involved?'

Jo shifted her weight to her other leg.

'I've been married for forty years,' Rosita said. 'In that time the male ego has become a subject of fascination to me. It's so terribly predictable. From time to time it's necessary to make a man wait. It keeps his ego in check.'

'Ever consider divorce?'

'It may come as a shock to you to learn that some people mean it when they say "for better or worse", Inspector . . .'

Hugo arrived back with the young Filipina and an older Chinese woman.

'Well?' he asked his mother.

She gave a dismissive wave.

Jo turned back to the pictures, and stared at one of Charles Fitzmaurice shaking hands with Blaise Stanley. It looked relatively recent. There were other faces in the background, and Jo's eyes locked on a woman over Fitz's shoulder – Imogen Cox. Jo crossed her arms and walked over to the Chinese woman. 'Ask the girl her name, please.'

The Chinese woman said something sharp. The girl answered, starting to sob.

'Lee Cruz,' the Chinese woman said.

'Ask her why she's crying.'

'She doesn't want to have to go home,' the Chinese woman said.

'Ask her,' Jo instructed.

Hugo sighed.

The Chinese woman said something to Lee, then flatly repeated to Jo, 'She doesn't want to go home.'

'Ask her what age she is.' Jo said.

After the translation, the girl's eyes shot up guiltily before she answered.

'Eighteen,' the translator said, handing Jo a photocopy of Lee's birth certificate. The DOB tallied, but it was only a photocopy. A second sheet was an application for asylum, and it had the necessary immigration stamp.

'Satisfied?' Hugo asked.

Jo ignored him. 'Ask Lee if she wants to come with me now. Tell her she can stay in my home, and I'll help her find a job.'

The Chinese woman said something. Lee shook her head panic-stricken.

'I'm afraid I'm going to have to ask you to leave, Inspector,' Hugo said. He handed over a card. 'Here's our lawyer's name and number if you've any further requests.'

Jo threw her eyes up to heaven when she read George Hannah's name on the card, and after hesitating, in order to take one last look at the Filipina, she started to make her way towards the door.

'What did you do with the nappies?' she asked Rosita, turning around.

'I dumped them, of course. I had no use for them.'

'If he's here, if Presley is here, he'll need his medication very soon,' Jo said. 'If he doesn't get it he could die.'

'I don't know what you mean. Who's Presley?' Rosita answered.

20

Jo figured it was no coincidence that the same solicitor who'd arrived at Jeff Cox's home that morning should also represent the Fitzmaurice family. She immediately phoned George Hannah's office, and learned he was in court. After she had emphasized to his secretary how urgently she needed an appointment, Hannah sent word by text that he was willing to meet Jo in the coffee dock of the courts complex just after four. The case he was involved in should have finished by then.

Dublin's Criminal Court had recently moved – from a building with limestone Doric columns blackened by traffic fumes – to a modern, round construction of glass and wood at the entrance to the Phoenix Park.

With twenty minutes to spare, Jo decided to have a quick scope at the proceedings of the rape case she'd been planning to sit in on that morning. Joining the queue at the security check, she emptied her pockets of change and her mobile phone, placing them in a plastic tray, and slipped off her jacket, which had numerous metal zips.

Maurice – the security man, who had a goatee – was arguing with a teenager with a goatee that stab vests could not be worn into the courts, and saying that the teenager could remove his trainers for inspection, too, while he was at it.

Jo walked under the metal detector arch, setting off red lights and bleeps, just as her belongings started to emerge from the conveyor-belt flap. 'It will be my bloody belt, or maybe it's my bangles,' she said.

Maurice looked up, and waved her through. 'I was expecting you this morning,' he said.

'Got bogged down with something else,' she answered. 'What did I miss?'

'Only legal applications for reporting restrictions. The defendant took the stand just before lunch. You should still catch some of it. Court 17.'

The teenager was indignant. 'Here, how come she is setting off every alarm in the building and can get in no problem?'

'She's a hottie,' Maurice answered.

Jo crammed her stuff back into her pockets, then headed across the marble floor towards the two glass lifts with their exposed cables and metal girders.

A barrister a few steps ahead of her, dressed in a full wig and gown, covered his hand with the corner of his cloak as he jabbed the button for the lift.

'You worried about swine flu?' Jo asked.

'No, static shocks,' he replied. 'This building's a health hazard. There are panes of glass shooting straight out from their frames. Oh, and the lift keeps getting stuck – that's when you can get one. The Courts Service says it's all part of the building's "settling-in phase". Can you believe that?'

Jo could believe it all right. She was having her own settling-in problems with the Tara Parker Trench case. On the face of it, the model was an unreliable, self-harming anorexic who could well be suicidal, if, as Jo suspected, she had recently been beaten-up or half-drowned. Not to mention the fact that she was a pathological liar and an attention-seeker to boot. Maybe bloody Oakley had been right all along, and she had Munchausen's by proxy too.

After a minute-long wait, with both lifts permanently working the higher floors, she gave up and took the stairs.

Six flights later, Jo emerged from the stairwell panting, even though she was relatively fit. Every floor in the building consisted of a circular balcony around a central shaft of space that allowed natural light to flood in from the glass ceiling to the ground floors. You could see each of the other floors from the balcony ledge. Jo took in the view, her heart racing like she'd just run a marathon. She wondered if this was what a panic attack felt like, and, for peace of mind, tried to think of the reasons for and against putting Tara Parker Trench's case behind her and concentrating on this one instead.

But before she could come to any conclusions she had reached the door of the court. She pushed through and went inside.

21

Court 17 was a modern take on the old Central Criminal Court. The window behind the judge was a wide rectangle that curved with the building. Quirkily shaped pews had replaced the old colonial-style ones in the central area, and it was all set off by a blood-red carpet. The main difference was electronic. A TV screen could be lowered from the ceiling so protected witnesses could give evidence while cosseted from the accused and the press. Cameras recorded proceedings, which could be screened to the public on the ground floor when the court got too full. The judge even had a computer. Jo watched him check the angle of his wig in the reflection on the screen, and wondered if he had any other use for it.

To the right, the twelve members of the jury were listening avidly to the accused, who sat facing them on the left.

Jo's gaze turned to him. He was in his forties,

short and wiry, with a pale face, crooked facial features, and an ill-fitting suit. The only thing remarkable about his appearance was how ordinary he looked. In a crowd, you'd have thought him the kind of person who cold-called at estate houses, trying to sell stuff nobody needed.

Ignoring the custom of giving a stiff bow to the judge on entry or exit, and instead winking at the court registrar, who she knew of old, Jo moved to a back bench and slid into a seat. She put her phone on silent and crossed her legs. Instantly the top one started to jig.

Jo glanced around for the victim. There was only one woman in the courtroom not looking up. Her sleek black hair was pulled sternly off her face, and her clothes were too baggy for her body. She had olive skin, and was sitting between an older couple.

Jo pulled three files from her bag that she'd put into Manila folders, and after reckoning she had fifteen minutes left before her meeting with Hannah, reminded herself of the victims' details. The first had been raped and murdered in Portlaoise five years earlier. She'd been a nineteen-year-old student teacher out having some post-exam drinks in a pub with friends. The killer had waited in the middle cubicle of the pub's toilets and then climbed over when the student had locked herself into one alongside. He had slit her throat. Nobody had heard a thing. The second victim had been twenty-one and worked in a bar. She had been raped and murdered three years ago in Dublin city centre, after travelling to an open-air concert with a group of friends. She'd got a bus back into town with them, and then left to wait at a taxi rank. Her body had been found in the automatic toilet on O'Connell Bridge – her throat had been slit. The third victim had been an eighteen-year-old still in school. She had been raped and murdered after travelling to Limerick on a school trip. Her throat had been slit and her body found in a toilet in a Supermac's restaurant less than a year ago.

The similarities were impossible to ignore.

The defendant on trial for this separate rape was a taxi driver who'd been nominated as a suspect for the three killings by a highly regarded forensic psychologist reviewing cold cases. He had picked this perp as his best bet, because he was so accomplished at what he did, despite having no criminal convictions. Someone who could kill a woman in a public place would have a similar level of competence, the shrink had suggested.

But on first impressions, Jo did not think he was her man. All of the other victims had been around the twelve-stone mark in weight. The man in the box did not look more than ten, maximum, and he had a serious disability. His right arm ended at the elbow. The victim was thin, too, though Jo suspected she might have lost weight since the attack. But how could this man have climbed over a toilet cubicle quickly with only one arm? And there was another crucial difference between this case and Jo's other three. This victim was alive . . .

It was possible that all the victims were linked by his profession, since he was a taxi driver. Cabbies travelled to where the work was, and all of the women had been some distance from home at the time of their murders. Maybe they'd flagged him down, or been approached by him offering transport.

And his handicap hadn't prevented him from abducting this victim, a Spanish student, from a car park, which was a public place. He must have had plenty of practice to have become that brazen. Maybe he was her man.

Jo watched as the accused's barrister, who had his thumbs tucked into the armpits of his black-buttoned waistcoat, finally asked a question she was interested in hearing the answer to.

'Did you rape her?'

Jo sat up.

'Yes, the first time,' the accused answered. 'But the other times she asked me to make love to her.'

The victim gave little shakes of her head.

Her parents were obviously the people sitting on either side of her. A middle-aged woman with the same black hair held the girl's hand, an older man, in his best suit, had his arm around her shoulders. Their faces were etched with the frustration of not being able to give their side of the story. A translator sat alongside whispering to them what was being said.

It made Jo's blood boil the way victims were treated like second-class citizens in court. She willed the state barrister – a woman with long, black hair and heavy make-up, taking copious notes – to object, but she didn't seem to have registered what the accused had just said.

The judge, meanwhile, looked on the verge of nodding off. If separate legal representation for victims had been implemented – as Justice Minister Blaise Stanley had promised Jo that it would be – a scene like this would not be happening.

'You say there was an element of consent,' the accused's barrister led.

'Yes.'

'And that you felt the victim was originally flirting with you in the bar. Isn't that right?'

'Yes.'

'It's a pack of lies,' a man sitting behind the Spanish family shouted, jumping up. His face was red. He looked very young. He was probably the student's boyfriend, Jo reckoned. 'That animal was stalking her.'

The judge moved his face close to his microphone. 'Get this man out of my courtroom before I hold him in contempt.' He indicated to the registrar sitting in front of him his intention to leave until order was restored.

'All rise,' the registrar declared.

Jo sighed as she stood. It was impossible for victims and their families to leave their emotions at the door of the court, as required by the system. That was the point she'd been trying to make to Blaise Stanley. But if the justice minister was implicated in a crime – as that note Jo had received with the sex tape had suggested – then it wasn't so surprising that her pleas had fallen on deaf ears.

Jo began to move sideways to exit the court. She was glad she'd come, because her intuition told her the man on trial was not responsible for her stack of unsolved cases. Why wouldn't he have killed this victim, if he'd murdered the others? Didn't serial killers usually become more violent, not less? The modus operandi was different, too: a knife hadn't been used. Instead, the accused had attempted to suffocate the student. Jo felt she could now meet George Hannah without being concerned, as Dan, Sexton and Oakley were, that the Tara Parker Trench case was taking her away from a more important investigation.

She was grateful that she'd been reminded what rape did to a woman: how it left her picking up the pieces, sometimes for the rest of her life. If Tara had been brutalized the way the Spanish student had – or even more cruelly – then she was in a very vulnerable place, and desperately in need of professional help.

22

George Hannah was waiting nervously for Jo at the door to the barristers' restaurant. He pushed it and held it open the instant she appeared on the second floor. He checked his watch when Jo stopped momentarily to salute a member of the court staff she hadn't seen in a number of years.

'What couldn't wait, Detective Inspector?' he asked, as Jo ducked under his arm less than a minute later and sat at a table for two. He put down a cardboard folder and lowered himself into the chair.

'Make mine a latte, and I'll explain all,' Jo answered. She didn't want the coffee, but her time was every bit as valuable as his, and she didn't mind letting him know it.

Hannah could barely conceal his irritation as he headed off towards the counter, sifting through the change from his trouser pocket and making great play of the fact that he might not have enough.

As soon as his back was turned, Jo opened his folder. Inside was an application to the High Court for a judicial review. Jo glanced up and saw Hannah trying to work out what buttons to press on a drinks dispenser. She turned the page. The client he was representing was Barry Roberts. Jo scratched her head. Roberts was at the other end of the criminal spectrum from the likes of wealthy business people like the Fitzmaurices and Coxes. Roberts was a drug dealer, nicknamed 'King Krud', who peddled death and misery. He'd been knocking off his adversaries recently, in a feud that had seen some of the worst bloodshed in years.

She turned the page to see what the issue Hannah wanted to thrash out in the High Court on Roberts's behalf was, but was alerted by the sound of a ringing till. She looked up to see Hannah lifting the coffees and turning towards her.

Jo closed the folder, and smiled wanly.

'You were saying . . . ?' Hannah said, looking from the table to Jo suspiciously as he set the coffees down. He turned the folder the right way around.

'How well do Jeff Cox and Rosita Fitzmaurice know each other?' Jo asked.

'This is the first I've heard of any acquaintance,' Hannah answered.

'Jeff Cox was sleeping with the mother of a child taken from a garage last night, and Rosita was in the garage when the child was taken,' Jo said. 'They're both your clients.'

Hannah took a mouthful of coffee. 'So . . . ?'

'That little boy is out there somewhere. You know exactly what people in this city are capable of. I'm appealing to your conscience. Do you know anything that could help me? You must have had a good start in life to end up so highly qualified. You must have had parents who guided you, who wanted the best for you. And to pick law as a profession, you must at some point have believed in the concept of justice.'

Hannah didn't react. 'I don't know anything that can help you, I'm afraid.'

'Then it's too bloody late for you, too,' Jo said.

23

Jo looked up as Dan walked in. He didn't take his hands out of his pockets as he sat down.

'I'm glad you're feeling better,' he said.

It wasn't exactly the apology she wanted, but she knew it was as close as she'd get. She nodded, spotting dark circles under his eyes. 'I would never undermine you, Dan,' she said. In the old days, she'd have added, 'Because I love you.'

He twisted around, giving her office the once-over. 'So how's Rory? I'm sorry I haven't been around much lately.'

'I noticed,' Jo said. It sounded harder than she'd intended. She wished they could stop their constant tit-for-tat sniping. She hated it that she still snapped at him, and that standing anywhere near him still turned her legs to jelly. But she was never going to get over him cheating with his secretary, not now his future was going to be tied to Jeanie's for ever by the birth of their child.

She straightened up. 'And Jeanie. How's she getting along?' It sounded so formal she wanted to tear her hair out.

'Good,' Dan said, putting his hands on his knees. 'Great. Yeah, she's really terrific, thanks.'

This was torture. Jo cut to the chase. 'Why are you here, Dan?'

He scratched the stubble appearing along his jawline. 'I want to know where Foxy and Sexton are. Have you got anywhere with the rape investigation? We should have a case conference if you have. I don't want to be sidelined any more. I want to be kept in the picture.'

Jo glanced at her watch guiltily. It was five o'clock. She'd made several attempts to get through to Sexton's phone, but had gone straight to his voice-mail, and hadn't a clue where he was. Foxy had technically gone AWOL, too. 'We are working on something, but it's not the rape investigation.'

'So what is it?' Dan asked flatly.

'You know exactly what, Dan. It's the same case I've been harping on about all day, the missing tot – Presley Parker Trench.'

He stood up. 'Why am I getting a distinct impression of déjà vu . . . ?'

'I think Imogen Cox, the woman who was murdered in Killiney this morning, was pimping out her models – girls like Presley's mother, Tara. I suspect that's why Imogen's dead. It also means Presley could be in even more trouble than I originally thought.'

'And I know exactly how this one ends,' Dan said, his eyes cold. 'You've just told me you're not undermining me, yet you've already put a team together, ignoring my direct instructions.'

'Can you stop being so bullheaded and contact Dalkey Station? I want to head up the Imogen Cox murder inquiry while I'm at it. We're guaranteed to find Presley if we find who killed Imogen. If she took Presley, whoever killed her may have taken the child, or at least know where he is.'

Dan threw his arms up in the air in frustration. 'You're not listening to a word I'm saying—'

Jo cut him off. 'When I interviewed Tara this morning her lips were blue. At first, I thought she was cold, but the heat in the station's stifling. So, then I thought maybe she was in shock. But even after I got some breakfast into her, her lips were still as blue as the first second I saw her. The thing is, I've only ever seen lips that colour on people lying on a slab in the morgue, who've drowned.'

Dan stared in disbelief, his mouth partly open.

'I also noticed she had all these little pinprick blood spots under her eyes. The last time I saw anything like that, Professor Hawthorne was examining a drowning victim during an autopsy. He said that little burst blood vessels scattered about under the eyes meant the person had fought for their life. Tara's nose was running as well, also consistent with asphyxiation caused by drowning. Plus, there were bruises on her torso, suggesting she'd been manhandled. My hunch is that whoever left those marks on her either saved her from drowning or had tried to drown her. And since anyone who knows me knows the only rule of policing I've ever really adhered to is that there's no such thing as coincidence, I'd say the chance that two such recent catastrophic events in her life – being attacked, and losing her child – are unconnected is virtually nil.'

Dan sighed heavily. 'Blue lips, blood spots, a runny nose, and a bruised belly. Why don't I ring the commissioner right now? Better yet, why don't you do it? Let's face it, you've more chance of getting through to him than I have. Or, how about this – come back to me when you have some real hard evidence and not just supposition?'

Jo felt a surge of anger. 'Tara's kid goes missing, Dan. A short time later her boss is murdered. And now I can't get in touch with Tara. You have got to put me in charge of this investigation before anyone else gets killed or disappears. I have the hard evidence you want right here. I have a DVD showing that Imogen Cox was involved in the sex industry.'

Dan took a breath and sat back down. 'Show it to me.'

Jo pulled open the desk drawer. It was empty and so was the one under it. She slapped her hand off the top, sides and bottom of both to be sure, then did the same with the two on the other side. There was something stuck to the roof of one of the drawers, but no Jiffy bag, and no DVD. The video of Imogen Cox, and the note that had come with it, had been taken.

'Well?' Dan asked.

Jo walked to the door and called to the detectives working in the office outside, 'Anyone been in here this morning when I was out?'

Detective Sergeant Roger Merrigan's arm shot up like a schoolboy's, much to the other detectives' amusement. He was the office clown, and Jo knew that when he'd worked with her on the Bible case he'd reported her every movement back to Dan. She gave him a stiff nod to enter, and waited with her hand on the door until he was inside before closing it.

Dan's eyes followed her.

'Who's been in here while I was out?' she demanded.

'Here?' Merrigan asked, looking at Dan with raised eyebrows.

Jo put her hands on her hips.

'Can't say I noticed anyone. I thought you were

172

calling the register, that's why I put my hand up.'

'You must have seen if someone came in? There's a new bloody chair in here. Wheel itself in, did it?'

'Oh, yeah, Foxy's daughter was in all right,' he answered. 'The one who's got that—'

'Sal?' Jo asked. 'Her name is Sal.'

'Yeah, the mongoloid one—'

Jo put her hands on his shoulders and turned him back towards the door. 'On your way,' she said.

'I have to go,' Dan said, also heading for the door. 'Jeanie's expecting me. Don't you have to pick up the boys?'

Jo glanced at her watch, reached for her jacket, and remembered something. Turning back to her desk, she picked free the slip of cardboard stuck to the roof of the drawer. It was an antenatal appointment card for Holles Street Hospital with Jeanie's name on it, citing the date of an appointment some months back for a rhesus positive injection.

Sighing heavily, Jo tossed it on to her desk and locked her office door on the way out.

24

The kid was yapping away, it wasn't normal. Not that she knew much about little kids, but weren't they supposed to button it around strangers? He was doing her head in, talking about this, that and the other.

Her room was pokey at the best of times, but the kid hadn't nodded off on the couch till near midnight, and he'd been up again at six, his motor mouth going non-stop. She was sick to the teeth of listening to him rabbiting on. Even now, he was plonked in front of the TV talking right through the cartoons, which she had on at practically full volume to try and drown him out. She couldn't hear herself think. She hadn't had a wink of sleep last night worrying about the trouble she could get in if she was found with him.

Marching between him and the box, she put her hands over her ears, shut her eyes and yelled, 'Quiet!'

His chin wobbled. 'I want my dad.'

Taking him by the hand, she pulled him off the

couch. Having him here was turning into a real pain. She couldn't even open the curtains in case someone saw him.

The kid started to wail.

'Shut up,' she said, shaking him roughly. 'Shut the fuck up!'

But snot and tears were rolling down his face and he was hollering louder. She put her hand over his mouth. 'OK, you want me to ring your dad? I'll do it,' she lied. 'That's it, good boy, keep it nice and quiet and I'll have him here in no time.'

She held him, feeling the little shudders travelling through his ribcage, hearing the tight wheezing sound he made as he gasped for breath. Cursing some more, she put him down, and picked up her mobile, pretending to dial.

'Hello, it's me. Little Presley wants his daddy. Can you come and get him?'

It worked. The kid was calming down.

'You're on the way? That's fantastic.'

'I want to talk to him,' the kid said. 'He's getting me a present on his holidays.'

She put the phone down quickly. 'Sorry, too late. But don't you worry, he's coming right over. Here, if you're a good boy we can get you chips and sausages. Would you like that?'

The kid nodded.

'Your dad asked if I would wash your hair for you

to make you nice and smart, so you've got to be a good boy and come into the bathroom with me, OK?' She held out her hand. 'Otherwise he won't give you your present.'

Looking startled, the kid took a step back, opened his mouth and started to cough.

25

Tara sat on a high stool at the bar in the Triton, downing a third glass of Cristal. She needed it after what had happened in the massage room. The emergency wrap of cocaine she'd stashed with her change of clothes was helping to numb the pain of the kicking Fitz had given her for threatening and cutting him. Still, right now she was buzzing as she waited for Big Johnny to bring Presley back like he'd promised. Then she was going to take Presley in a cab to the police station, and she wasn't going to leave until someone gave her back the keys to her car.

She twisted around to look at the bunch of yummy mummies in the corner of the bar. They were sitting at a table, wearing the kind of condescending expressions women only ever got after they had landed on their feet in a single-income household in a nice part of the city, with two big cars parked outside. Tara had gone to a private school, too. She'd been accepted at university, could play piano, and hold her own in conversation with anyone. She wanted what they had, too, one day – a big house, an SUV, and a nanny. *I'm just taking the scenic route*, she told herself, taking another mouthful of bubbly.

'Have some more,' the man who had bought her the drink said, pulling the magnum from the ice and refilling her glass. She didn't know him from Adam. He was fifty-something, with high-waisted trousers and a black polo neck so tight that the loose skin on his neck dangled over it.

Nico, the barman – an Italian chef who had switched to bar work because of the size of the tips ladies like the yummy mummies gave – headed over and put his fingers to his lips. 'Not too much more, bellissima,' he told her. 'Fitz is around tonight.'

'Yeah, don't I know it,' Tara answered, holding the glass up in a toast, then knocking it back, too. She banged the empty glass back down on the counter, and sniffed.

The man put one arm around her, and rubbed a clammy hand up and down her skin from shoulder to wrist. It was six o'clock, and the cocktail of drink and drugs was starting to wear off. Her mood was becoming maudlin. *Where the hell were Big Johnny and Presley?*

'You're so sexy,' the man told her.

Tara held out her feet in their glossy red, strappy Manolo Blahniks and twisted her ankles around admiringly. The sight of her expensive shoes always made her feel good, no matter what else was going on. Men who moaned at the prices didn't understand that it wasn't about value for money. Shoes like this, designer bags and dresses, they were a status symbol. They reminded her how far she'd come, how much she'd achieved. Even when she got Presley back, she was never going to return to the bad old days when she hadn't had enough to pay the rent. It was all very well Jeff telling her she needed to get herself straight, but how was she supposed to pay for it?

Tara reached for the bottle and poured herself another glass, toasting Nico – he really was gorgeous, but too broke to be an option. *Been there, done that, worn Mick's T-shirt*, she thought. She stood up, almost upending the stool in the process. Flicking her hair, she tottered on to an imaginary dance floor, put her hands above her head and started to pump the air. Tomorrow she was going to wake up with the same problems, but tonight she was determined to be a superstar. She was going to get her boy back.

26

They were home. Rory pushed the passenger door of
Jo's car open, grabbing his schoolbag from the
footwell before Jo had finished parking in the driveway. He'd been giving her the silent treatment ever
since she'd picked him up from school. She hadn't
noticed at first, because she'd been too busy talking
to Foxy on the hands-free set when Rory had climbed
in at the school gates. Normally she'd have put the
call off till after she'd chatted to her son about how
his day had been, but she needed to make sure Sal
hadn't taken the sex tape from the office, as the
thought of what Sal might see filled her with dread.

In the course of the conversation, Foxy had picked
up on Jo's stress levels and offered to work tonight if
Jo could provide a babysitter. She'd told him to bring
Sal over to hers, that Rory would do it. Foxy could
then head to the airport, as Jo had established from
an earlier call in the car that Tara's ex was due to fly
back from his holiday tonight. If problems cropped

up Jo would have to go to the station, too, to be in on any interview between Foxy and Mick Devlin. She also wanted to spend part of the evening running checks on the registrations she'd lifted from the CCTV in the garage. She had another try at getting Sexton, but his phone went to voicemail again.

Jo unstrapped Harry from his car seat, and as she set him down took his chunky little hand in hers. Harry held a velvet blanket he used as a comforter against his cheek as they followed Rory inside. It made Jo's heart lurch to think how independent her baby had become since Dan had left. She, on the other hand, felt as if she was regressing as the months turned to years and passed without him. It was hard to come home after a day's work, and not be able to sit down over dinner and thrash out the day with him. It was harder still to sit on a couch when the boys were asleep and stare at the TV on her own. She couldn't have a nightcap alone without feeling like an alcoholic – and without a nightcap, or an adult conversation, or a pair of arms wrapped around her, there was nothing to take the edge off the day. She didn't even want to think about how she was ever going to fare when she was ready to meet someone new. She was still relatively young at thirty-six, but how was she going to find the time to get out and about again? Where did you go when you were single and looking for a date these days? And who was going to want to go out with her, anyway, when she had a family ready-made?

Rory was pulling a towel out of the hot press by the time Jo had turned the alarm off, brought in Harry's crèche bag and closed the door behind her.

'Let's get you fed, darling,' she told Harry, kissing his little cheeks as she scooped him up.

In the kitchen, she put a set of blocks on the red and green chequered floor for him to play with while she got his tea ready. He'd be nodding off in under an hour. She hated seeing so little of him during the week, but whatever options she might have had if Dan had still been around, in terms of going part-time, were gone now she was a single mum and paying her own way.

Something struck her suddenly. Running down the hall, she banged on the bathroom door. 'Let me in, I need to ask you something.'

'What is it?' Rory answered, sounding bored.

'You only ever have a shower when you come in if you're planning on going out again. Tell me you're not planning on going out tonight.'

He pulled open an inch of the pine door. 'I'm going to the Mezz with Becky.'

'No you're not. It's a school night.'

'It's her birthday.'

'I need you here. I've got to go out again. And Foxy needs someone to mind Sal.'

'So I gathered in the car. You should have asked me. I'd made plans.'

'Yes, I should have, I'm sorry. But please, ask Becky to come up if you like, or take her out at the weekend instead. I'm working on a case that I can't clock out of. There's a little boy who's missing.'

'I've booked the tickets, Mother.'

'Look, this missing boy, he's only a year older than Harry. He's got asthma, and he has to be found before he needs his inhalers.' She glanced at her watch.

'Seriously, Mum, this is not my problem. You've worked your shift. Let someone else worry about it.'

'You're getting more and more like your father every day, do you know that?' Jo snapped.

He opened his mouth to answer, as she quickly held her hands up. She had, she realized, managed to upset almost everyone she cared about today. 'You're right. I'm sorry. I've been putting work first. You take the car, meet Becky. I'll work something out.'

'What about the little boy?' Rory asked.

'Not your problem,' Jo said, walking away. 'Go out, enjoy yourself. Just get home at a reasonable hour, will you? I don't want your principal on my case again.'

Rory tugged her sleeve. 'Becky will understand if I postpone—'

Jo threw her arms around him and started kissing him on the cheek.

He screwed up his face as he pushed her back. 'And in return I want your Visa card to pay for a meal for two, and a full tank of petrol in your banger of a car.'

'Deal,' Jo said, smiling.

After Foxy had dropped off Sal and agreed to head to the airport, and Jo had settled Harry down for the night, she stuck her head around the sitting-room door to check on Rory and Sal, whom she'd treated to a pizza. They were watching a repeat of *Britain's Got Talent* – Rory looking through spread fingers at a skimpily dressed very old lady singing her heart out.

'I don't think she's out of tune, Rory,' Sal said.

'It's not the tune, it's the dress,' Rory explained, winking at Jo, who gave him a thumbs up. He'd such a good heart, she could forgive him anything.

'What's wrong with the dress?' Sal asked. 'I love red.'

Jo went into the kitchen, switched on her laptop, and began scouring holiday destinations in Morocco on the internet until she found a hotel with an onion-shaped roof like the one she'd seen in the background of the sex tape. It was called the Atlantis, in Marrakesh.

Next, she logged into her remote access to Pulse, the garda computer system, in order to check the registrations she'd noted on the diagram she'd drawn up in her office. The first number she ran belonged to the HiAce. It threw up Marcus's surname and his address in Sandymount, making Jo look upwards and whisper, *thank you*, quickly. With his name and address she was able to get his social security number from another database on Pulse. Tomorrow she would contact the Revenue to find out the names of his clients, which would hopefully include the Triton Hotel. She curled her lip in surprise when she realized he lived in such a nice suburb, unaffected by the slump in property prices. Especially considering he was driving a van that looked like it was about to collapse.

'Mum, Sal is falling asleep in there,' Rory said, arriving in.

Jo stood up and walked into the sitting room. 'Would you like to go to bed now, darling?' she said.

Sal looked up sleepily. She was only twelve, and it had been a very hard day on her. Jo felt guilty about taking Foxy up on his offer to work that night.

'Yes, please, Jo.'

Jo walked Sal down to the spare bedroom.

'Dad packed my night clothes just in case,' Sal said, taking a Miley Cyrus rucksack off her shoulder.

'Good thing, too,' Jo said, plumping her pillows.

'Good night, Jo,' Sal said, putting her arms out for a hug.

'Night,' Jo answered, kissing her forehead.

'Jo?' Sal asked, as she was closing the door.

'Yes, love?'

'What age were you when you had to start wearing a bra?'

Jo scratched her neck. 'Let me think, must have been about your age, I'd say.'

'Right,' Sal said. 'Thanks.'

'Tell you what,' Jo said. 'We can go shopping for one, if you like, at the weekend?'

'That's OK, thanks,' Sal said. 'I just wondered. Don't say I said so to my dad, OK, Jo?'

'Course I won't,' Jo promised. 'That's girl stuff.'

Jo's mobile was ringing as she re-entered the kitchen. It was Reg, the superintendent in Dalkey, who'd treated her shabbily earlier in Howth.

'We've arrested Jeff Cox for the murder of his wife,' he said.

'End to a perfect day . . .' Jo answered, adding, '. . . not,' quickly. 'Has he admitted anything?'

'The only thing he's saying is that he wants to speak to you,' Reg replied. 'Can you get over? We've already extended his detention once, so it's urgent.'

27

In the bar of the Triton Hotel, Sexton looked around at the blinged-up women with tangerine skin, and the men in chinos and deck shoes, their car keys lined up along the bar like a dick-measuring contest. He'd been so hungry he'd bought a takeaway curry after meeting Murray Lawlor at the Sandymount cash machine. He'd eaten it in the car, and fallen asleep, only waking up just in time to rush here. He still hadn't had a chance to ring Jo.

He was sorry he'd come. He felt shabby still dressed in his work clothes – a grey suit, white shirt, skinny pink tie, and a pair of Dr Martens soles. There was a familiar-looking woman dancing at the far end of the room in that stupid way only the very drunk do. It was a scene he'd have expected to see in the early noughties, before the country went belly up. In the current climate it reeked of bad taste. He felt a bad bout of indigestion coming on, and was all set to turn around and leave when he spotted Murray to the back right, in a blue shirt with a white collar opened one button too low, waving him over. Murray's chest had been shaved and oiled, and if he'd squeezed his pecs together you could have used them to open your beer. There was a motorbike helmet with a black-tinted visor on the table in front of him.

Sexton spotted a couple of well-known faces at the bar and a rugby international heading for the john as he walked over. He felt himself breaking out in a sweat. He liked to disappear in a pub, yet everyone in this place wanted to be seen, as far as he could make out. They were all facing the door, looking up to see who'd arrived, with identical bored expressions on their faces. He got the impression that if Angelina Jolie walked through the door, their faces would stay the same.

Murray had his arms around two babes, who seemed to be hanging on his every word. Sexton stared at them. On second thoughts, maybe he should start looking after himself more, join a gym perhaps, get himself a pair of pecs that could take your eye out, like Murray.

Murray stood and put out his hand to make a meal of his arrival. *Well, with birds like that, he's entitled*, Sexton thought. But what tickled him more was the way the girls stood, too. Like bloody geishas they were, like they didn't have minds of their own.

One of the women was a ringer for the Charlie's

Angel he'd a crush on as a kid, Sexton realized. She'd the same long black hair and killer black eyes as Jaclyn Smith. The blonde beside her was more of a Farrah Fawcett than a Cheryl Ladd, too much make-up, but a Kelly Brook body built for sin. *And doesn't she know it?* Sexton thought. Her short, sequinned dress was cut so low you could see the rim of her bra, satin red.

'Ladies, this is Gavin, a very good friend of mine,' Murray said. 'Better watch what you say, he's a policeman.'

'What happened to your face?' Farrah giggled. She'd spoken in broken English and sounded Eastern European.

Sexton touched the scab on the bridge of his nose; he'd completely forgotten about it. 'I headbutted a dirtbag a couple of weeks back.'

She reached for her drink. The ice cubes tinkled as she drew it to her mouth. Looked like a G & T with a splash of lime. He used to work with a cop who said you could tell all you needed to know about what made a woman tick by the drink she wanted. Her choice told you the kind of hit she was chasing, and, from that, you could generally work out why. A girl into shots wanted to forget, therefore she would need lots of fun to keep her mind off the past. A girl into lager wanted a laugh and generally a commit-ment, in which case – steer clear. But a girl on G & T was perfect – gin made a woman emotional and needy; in other words, anxious to please.

Jaclyn's eyes widened. 'What did he do to deserve that?' she cooed. She sounded like an Essex girl, and judging by the strawberry on the rim of her glass, Sexton reckoned she was drinking champagne, meaning she was high maintenance.

'Gav, give me a hand at the bar, will you? I've got to keep the ladies here feeling refreshed,' Murray said. He was wearing jeans with pleats ironed down the centre and those tan, square-toed poofter shoes Sexton hated. 'Same again, girls?'

Farrah Fawcett shook her head, grinning. 'A Bacardi Breezer for me this time,' she piped up.

'And me,' Jaclyn rowed in.

Sexton felt depressed. Drinks like that were for kids. Kids shouldn't drink.

'Still got the silver tongue, I see,' Murray said when they were out of earshot. 'What are you talking about nutting someone for?'

'She asked me a question.'

'Yeah. Well, let's keep it nice and light from here on in, shall we? Everything's on a need-to-know basis, understood? Now, which of them do you want?'

'Yeah, like I'm in with a chance.'

Murray rubbed his thumb off his first two fingers. 'Everyone's in with a chance when it's a level playing field.'

'You are joking,' Sexton said. 'They're hookers?'

Murray put his hand on Sexton's back and turned him away from the girls. 'Can you keep it down? Discretion is the key here.'

Sexton looked over his shoulder, and lowered his voice. 'I just don't get it. The women on the street I meet in the job all have baggage – they were abused as kids or have drug problems. These girls have everything, their whole lives ahead of them. How did they—?'

'Questions, questions,' Murray answered, zipping his lips. 'Are you up for it or not?'

'Nah, paying is the last gasp, mate,' Sexton said.

Murray put his weight on Sexton's shoulder, and leaned in close. 'Just so you get it straight, you're not paying them for sex. Any man can get sex any time, anywhere, as long as he's prepared to lower his expectations to fit the situation. You're paying them to fuck off afterwards, to disappear, to forget it ever happened, to be discreet – in other words everything your ordinary woman won't do after sex.

'These girls are really special for another reason. They don't lie in bed expecting you to do the work. They come to bed to spoil you, treat you like a man. And don't start worrying that you can't afford it. Tonight's on me. Consider it a gesture. You come to work for me, this is the kind of life you'll be leading. These girls are one of the perks. Course if you want them both together, you can forget about a month's notice. I want you on the job tomorrow.'

Sexton felt his heart rate step up a pace, not because of what he was being offered – the thought of paying for sex made him feel sick – but because now he knew he had a lead, something Jo would be interested in. It was possible Murray was taking payments from Jeff Cox for supplying him with prostitutes. Jo had suspected Tara of being on the game, and, having seen Murray waiting at the ATM in Sandymount, Sexton was pretty sure that he'd been meeting up with Cox there on a weekly basis. This also meant they now had evidence of a motive for Cox to murder his wife, despite Jo's first thoughts on the subject.

He exhaled as he mulled this over. 'I thought you were driving,' he said, nodding at the motorbike helmet.

'I'm allowed one,' Murray said.

'Why the switch to a motorbike? You were in a car earlier.'

'Questions, questions. I always take it on a job, if you must know. Best way to follow someone in case of traffic.' He nudged Sexton's shoulder with his own. 'Get these in, will you? I'm going for a slash.'

The change Sexton got back from a fifty euro note for the round was only worth sticking into the collection box on the side of the counter. He stared at the handful of copper coins. He didn't want to insult the street kids of Calcutta by dropping it in.

He watched as Murray emerged from the Gents, earlier than he should have, rubbing his nose with his finger once too often, the spring in his step too springy, grinding his jaw.

Sexton was handing out the drinks when his arm stopped mid-air.

Another drop-dead gorgeous female had just come over – the same one Sexton had seen dancing when he'd been on the way in. She threw her arms around Murray's neck.

'Look what the cat dragged in,' Murray said, extricating himself.

Sexton stared in disbelief. The woman was Tara Parker Trench. And her pupils were fully dilated. She was completely out of it.

28

Foxy stood in the arrivals hall of Dublin airport feeling guilty as hell that he was still working. He rarely worked overtime, as Sal always came first, and he didn't like disrupting her routine. But he'd never known Jo to be wrong when she got this worked up during a case. He wouldn't forgive himself if anything happened to an innocent little boy because he hadn't backed her up, especially after he'd had to bail out of work for a chunk of the afternoon.

He scanned the display board over his head, which claimed the flight back from Fuerteventura had arrived twenty minutes earlier. He knew from bitter experience that luggage collection and passport clearance were notoriously slow. He and Sal went to EuroDisney every Christmas and getting out of Dublin airport regularly took longer than the flight.

He held a sheet of paper against his chest with Tara Parker Trench's ex's name written in bold caps on it. If he'd had a bit more notice, he might have been able to organize a picture of Mick Devlin through Facebook, the greatest asset to police forces around the world because it provided lists of associates as well as photographs. Foxy had done a course in how to use it, but he still couldn't grasp why anyone would want to show complete strangers their treasured family albums. *Must be getting old*, he thought.

He watched couples embrace as they caught sight of each other, and grandparents with arms outstretched as they spotted returning grandchildren. Everybody needed someone to pick them up at the airport, as far as he was concerned.

Ordinarily, he'd have gone through customs and waited for Devlin as he disembarked from the plane, but Jo had specified their inquiries be kept low key, as there'd be hell to pay if Dan found out what they were up to.

He noticed that some of the passengers starting to stream into the arrivals hall were wearing shorts and T-shirts, and he started to study the men coming through the automatic frosted-glass doors behind trollies stacked with luggage. His focus shifted from a black-haired man in a denim shirt to a pot-bellied guy with shades who was much the same age, early twenties. They were heading in different directions, and neither had seen his note. Foxy chose to follow the guy in the denim shirt for two reasons. Firstly, he had model good looks, so would probably have had plenty of experience pulling gorgeous women, and not have been intimidated by Tara Parker Trench. Secondly, he was on his own – no sign of any mates – while pot belly had a bird hanging out of his arm. Foxy thought it more likely Mick Devlin would have given up on women. And last, but by no means least, denim shirt had a remote control car in a box under his arm, which seemed the perfect present for a three-year-old boy.

'Mick,' he called. 'Are you Mick Devlin?'

The guy stopped and turned. He looked from Foxy's face to the sign, and the colour drained from his face.

'What's going on?'

'I need to have a word.'

'Not me mam or dad?' Devlin glanced beyond Foxy, like he half-expected to see the surviving half in the background.

'Let me buy you a coffee.'

'Oh Jesus, it's not Presley, is it? Tell me that cow hasn't done something stupid. Tell me my boy's all right.' He reached into his back jeans pocket and pulled out a mobile phone.

Foxy spoke quickly. 'We haven't been able to contact Tara, and Presley's missing.'

Mick bent double as though he'd been punched, and with his hands on his knees took a few deep breaths. 'What happened?'

'We don't know. I need you to tell me anything you think might be relevant to his disappearance.'

'Like what?'

'Anything irregular about what was going on in Tara's life that might lead us to her and your son?'

Mick straightened, and glared at Foxy. 'You wouldn't be asking me a question as specific as that without knowing the answer.'

'Please, don't hold back on me. It's too important. Why did you two split?'

'I thought she might be on the game.' He checked Foxy's reaction. 'I can tell it doesn't come as a surprise to you. Is she?'

'Why don't you tell me why you came to that conclusion?'

'The hours, the money, the way she was getting dolled up. The fact that there were never any pictures she could show me for all the supposed jobs she was going to. And she stopped . . .' his voice trailed off.

'Stopped what?'

'Liking sex.'

'But you never had any proof of what she was doing?'

'I never caught her with anyone in our bed, no.'

Foxy chose his words carefully. 'Do you know anything about the men Tara might be involved with?'

'Only that they're rich.'

'Any names?'

'I told you, she denied it—'

'If you suspected something, it must have been with good reason. Did you notice any admirers?'

'Yeah, I suspected someone. That old fart who sent his Bentley around to bring her to the airport, because a taxi was never good enough.'

'And who was that?'

'She called him Fitz. He owns some swanky hotel in Dublin, fancies himself as Richard Branson with his helicopter out back. He's a dodgy bastard. He used to send her flowers as well, give her jewellery. I mean, what would you think?'

'Do you mean Charles Fitzmaurice?' Foxy asked.

'Yeah, that's the one.' Mick stepped closer, his eyes wide with tension. 'Now, tell me. What's happened to my son?'

'Hello, love, what a nice surprise,' a woman said, tapping Foxy's shoulder. 'You always did have a thing about being there to collect someone after a flight.'

It took a couple of seconds for Foxy to place her. The last time he had seen her had been the night before Sal went in for open-heart surgery. And yet here she was, larger than life, and acting as if nothing had happened. Dorothy. His wife. The woman he hadn't seen for twelve years, or managed to divorce.

29

Dalkey Garda Station operated out of a converted Edwardian house with sea views, at the end of a quiet cul-de-sac populated in the main by writers and artists. The joke was that if you got stationed here, you needed amphetamines to unwind. It was gone ten in the evening by the time Jo arrived, and as she walked into one of the draughty holding rooms she wondered how its faded grandeur was making Jeff Cox feel. It made her edgy and out of sorts, because of what it said about the justice department's attitude to policing.

Jeff's eyes were bloodshot, the slick look of the morning gone. 'I d-d-didn't do it,' he said. 'I didn't kill Imogen.'

'Yeah, yeah,' Jo answered. She made a talking hand to illustrate. 'I'm innocent. I loved my wife. I wasn't there.' She glanced at the uniformed male sitting at the door. 'Any chance of a cuppa?'

The uniform stood up slowly.

'Tiny drop of milk, ta. You want one?' she asked Jeff.

He shook his head.

Jo looked at the camera lens and winked at Reg, the Dalkey superintendent, now watching intently from the other side.

She examined her nails. Not one of them was worth filing into anything, but if Jeff Cox wanted her attention, she was going to make him work for it. She suspected he was used to paying for sex, and she knew he was vain, both of which suggested an ego-centric and self-serving attitude. He'd be full of remorse, for himself . . .

'I-I- thought you – of all people – believed me. You said so at my house, in front of my solicitor. That you d-d-didn't think I d-d-did it.'

'Not exactly. And, besides, that was this morning, when I thought you were a kept man and incapable of bludgeoning your wife's head in with a rock. That was before I found out you'd a girlfriend on the side, who – from what I hear – was putting it about to anyone who'd pay.' Jo looked around. 'Where is your esteemed brief, by the way? Let me guess – he had to go to watch some cricket match being played live in India. Personally, I'd have gone for a brief based in or around the Bridewell, the sort more likely to be cheer-ing Eric Bristow along, if you know what I mean. They're particularly good at finding ways not to let a mere "bludgeoning someone's head in with a rock" charge stick. Plenty of practice, you see. Your lawyer's strengths are alimony and personal injury suits against plastic surgeons.'

'I d-d-didn't kill Imogen.'

Jo frowned. 'Your wife was older. You hated her. And to add insult to injury, she was your boss – and not just at home, but at work, too. Did she put you down in front of all the beautiful women she managed? It must have been degrading being paid by her. But the lifestyle made it all worthwhile. You couldn't just walk away. And you needed it if you were going to keep a certain young model in your life who was willing to have sex with you. The fact that it was for money was a by the by to you. Tara gave you back your mojo, made you feel like a real man. Not like your wife. You needed to find a way of getting Imogen out of your life, and Tara in.'

His eyes widened. 'I d-d-didn't d-d-do it.'

Jo held up the bank statement she'd taken from his room.

'What happened? Did Imogen decide you were spending too much of her money? Did you have a blazing row? Did you decide to teach her a lesson? Show her what a real man you were?'

A bead of sweat ran down Jeff's face. 'I d-d-didn't kill Imogen.'

'So you keep saying. But if you didn't, who did?'

The uniform came back with the tea.

'Perfect,' Jo told him, walking over. 'Just what I needed. Raining out, is it?' She could see Jeff fidgeting out of the corner of her eye, and she kept the conversation going with the uniform. 'The things men want in bed never cease to amaze me. Do you know what "rimming" is?'

The uniform shrugged.

'It's licking out someone else's . . . well . . . you know,' Jo pointed to her behind. 'The girls have to wear dams on their teeth to avoid catching hepatitis. What about "roasting"? Have you heard of that?'

The uniform shook his head.

'It's a girl who services two men at the same time. Think of a pig, skewered both ends and turning on a spit.' Jo took another sip and spoke over her shoulder to Jeff. 'Course, I'm sure Tara only ever imagines your face when she's working.'

The uniform sniggered.

Jeff stood up, his face tight with anger. 'Tara's not like that,' he shouted, his stammer gone.

Jo turned to face him.

'She was t-t-trying to get out, put all that behind her,' he said, more quietly.

'Job satisfaction missing, was it? Not getting the same kick out of it any more?'

He banged the table with both fists. 'She was

gang-raped. You happy now?' After a pause, he sat back heavily in his chair.

Jo walked over to her chair and sat opposite him. 'In Morocco?'

Jeff nodded.

Jo thought of the DVD she'd started to watch that morning. The girl she'd seen in the pool could have been Tara, now she came to think about it. Tara had certainly had enough bruises, by the look of her. 'By whom?'

He put his head in his hands. 'By animals. They could have killed her.'

'Were they businessmen? Or film stars? The kind of men kids want to be like, that they look up to, that women dream of dating? Who were they?'

'Footballers.'

Jo raised her eyebrows. 'What were their names?'

'I don't know.'

'Bullshit. Imogen was there, too, wasn't she? Who were they, and why didn't your wife do anything to stop it?'

'The b-b-business was d-d-disappearing. All the Irish girls were dropping out. The b-b-big money was gone. She needed to keep the clients happy until she sourced new girls.'

'Where's Presley?'

'I don't know. I thought Imogen must have taken him, to keep Tara quiet, and Tara thought so, too, but my wife swore she hadn't. Imogen couldn't have children herself: she got chlamydia when she was young, and that was the end of it. It made her even more of a b-b-bitter, twisted b-b-bitch, if that was possible. She sucked the life out of everyone she met. A vampire, that's all she was – no b-b-better.'

Jo sighed and rubbed her eyes. She believed him about not knowing where Presley was. The Dalkey gardaí had searched the house after he'd been arrested, but found absolutely nothing to suggest the little boy had been brought there.

'Well, the bad news, from your point of view,' she told him, '. . . is that failing to summon emergency services immediately to help your wife is a very serious crime. Your only hope now of leniency from the courts is to cooperate fully with our investigation. If your expensive solicitor was here, he'd tell you the same thing. Do you have the film of Tara being raped?'

'No.'

'Why not?'

'We were burgled. It was one of the things taken.'

'I want the names of the footballers involved in the assault.'

Jeff looked panicked.

'I told you, I don't know their names. It was a club outing. They were all Melwood Athletic, that's all I know. I swear to you—'

'So what was the last row with your wife over, anyway?'

'T-t-the same thing it was always about – me spending our money.'

'On Tara?' Jo asked. She didn't wait for his answer. There wasn't time.

Reg was waiting for her on the other side of the door.

'Well done.'

But Jo was really worried. 'How the hell am I going to get an APB on all the ports and airports at this hour of the night?'

'I don't follow,' Reg said.

'If Imogen Cox was running out of girls, she might have started sourcing them from abroad. If this case leads to a human trafficking ring, Presley could be absolutely anywhere in the world by now.'

30

Fitz was in his dressing gown, having waved away his private nurse, who was fussing over a blood pressure monitor and the bandage on his neck. He didn't want any distractions while he watched Tara on one of the screens in the control room of the hotel, which was rigged up like the *Big Brother* house.

Tara, he was starting to believe, knew a lot more about what had been going on in the garage than she'd maintained. Well, once he had his drugs back, he'd teach her a thing or two. He wasn't going to take any more chances.

She was cocking her ass at him as she leaned in to take another glass of champagne from Nico. Fitz's champagne. Now she owed him for that, on top of the five million euro which the haul in the back of her car was worth.

'Is she on something?' he asked Big Johnny, who was standing behind him.

'Nothing, boss. She asked, but I refused.'

'She's on something,' Fitz grumbled. 'If she fucks this up, I'm holding you personally responsible.'

'Yes, Fitz,' Big Johnny said.

'Where's the kid?'

'Upstairs. Yolanda's watching him. He's safe, I guarantee it.'

Tara had moved over to the tables. Fitz watched the way she let her tits brush against Murray, how her leg touched another man's thigh while she pretended to be completely absorbed in what he had to say.

She was air-kissing the new guy now, working her magic, running her fingertips along the back of his neck. She threw a worried glance in the camera's direction like she knew he was watching. Good. He wanted her scared. It was part of the turn on.

She sashayed over to some of the other girls in the bar, heels clicking along the tiles, the new guy's hard-earned cash ching-chinging as he paid for a round of drinks. Oh, she really fancied herself, all right; really thought she was something very special. Not for long, though. He was going to take her down a peg or two. No better man. Not here, not yet. But when she found out what he had in store for her, she'd end up begging him for more. He felt his groin spring to life in a way that hadn't happened for twenty-odd years. He smiled at the screen. He was going to give Tara Parker Trench the seeing-to of her life. It would be her last.

He sat up suddenly. 'Who's that guy with Murray?' He jabbed a finger at the screen.

Big Johnny looked surprised. 'I don't know, boss.'

'Well you'd better find out. And you'd better find out quick. Because we have plans for tonight, and we don't want him getting in our way.'

31

In the flesh, Sexton thought Tara Parker Trench even more stunning than in photographs – with her silky, shoulder-length sandy hair, olive skin, and jade-green eyes. She wore a skimpy silver dress and red shoes that were so high she had to keep one hand permanently on the bar for balance. She was movie-star beautiful, but that wasn't why Sexton was staring. He couldn't believe she could be out partying when her kid was missing. Or was she? Perhaps Presley had been found. Sexton cursed his sodding mobile for the umpteenth time today. Given Jo's lecture about his heart not being in the job, there'd be hell to pay tomorrow, especially if she had been trying to contact him. But still, if Tara's boy had been found, how could she be on the lash the first night her kid was home safe?

'Got anything for me?' she was asking Murray. She had a gravelly voice that was sexy as hell. Sexton did not like where his instincts were going.

'He didn't show up,' Murray answered.

Tara looked put out.

Murray wasn't giving her the time of day, Sexton observed. He wasn't even looking at her, just standing there straight as a beanpole. Sexton didn't know if he'd be able to stay that aloof if she started fawning over him.

'That's not good enough,' she told Murray. 'Jeff owes me. I need the money.' She whispered something directly into Murray's ear.

'Not now,' he said in a clipped tone, nodding in Sexton's direction sternly.

Tara pursed her lips like she was sulking, then began talking to Sexton. 'Have we met? You look familiar.' She air-kissed him, running her fingers along his neck.

'I was just going to ask you the exact same thing,' he replied.

'A comedian,' she said, pulling a bored face.

'Actually, Gavin's a copper,' Murray said, emphasizing the last word.

The smile fell from Tara's face, and after a drawn-out second, she turned back to the bar and reached for her glass.

Murray stepped into the gap. 'A word of advice,' he told Sexton, lowering his voice. 'Steer clear of that one. It'll only lead to trouble.'

'You two were talking about Jeff Cox, weren't

you?' Sexton asked. 'That's who you were meeting today, right? What exactly is your new job description, Murray? What did Jeff owe Tara money for?'

Murray looked around nervously. 'Button it, I'm warning you.'

Sexton was getting sick of his attitude 'Or what? What do you know about Imogen Cox's murder?'

Murray held his hands up and gave a big, false smile, his eyes hard. 'Look, all I'm saying is, Tara's trouble.'

Sexton glanced around for the nearest payphone. He needed to speak to Jo urgently. He thought there might be one in the lobby.

But before he could make a move, a group of men streamed through into the bar, joking and jostling. In tracksuits and carrying holdalls, they managed to bring the place to a standstill. Sexton had been wrong about this bunch – virtually everyone in the bar was now holding their drink mid-mast, and had cut off their conversations to stare at the newcomers. Even Sexton took a step back in surprise. No wonder they had a captive audience. The men were internationally famous footballers.

One of them pointed over at Tara. 'Here, look who it is!'

The guy speaking was called Kevin Mooney. He was probably the greatest living player in the world, in Sexton's opinion. He'd watched every match Mooney had played for the last five years.

Sexton took a deep breath, but before he could say anything, Tara had thrown her arms around him and started kissing him passionately.

'Get a room,' one of the footballers called, amid a sea of whistles.

'We have to leave,' Tara whispered in Sexton's ear. 'We have to leave now.'

32

Foxy stuck the kettle on as Dorothy pottered between the kitchen and the spare bedroom, unpacking her things and getting her bearings. He was counting his lucky stars now that Sal was staying overnight with Jo, and the house was empty. He'd arranged for Devlin to call into the station tomorrow morning to finish up the interview.

Dorothy reappeared and waved a hand down her front. 'What do you think?'

He realized she'd changed into a pink summer dress that was too young for her. It showed a lot of flesh. Her henna-red hair hung loose about her shoulders, and she wasn't wearing any shoes. Her toenails were painted a bright red and she'd a silver ring on the second toe of the right one.

'How have the years treated me?'

He coughed and turned back to the kettle. 'I'd better put the heating on . . . How long did you say you were over for?'

'Hmm? Oh, just a couple of days.' She sat at the

table with a heavy sigh. 'God, my plates of meat are killing me.'

'Sorry?'

She pointed down. 'Plates of meat, you know? Feet. Sorry, I've been away too long.' She peered out the window. 'You should plant a creeper to hide that back wall.'

'No. Sal likes to bounce a ball against it.'

A couple of minutes later, he carried two of his best china cups and saucers through to the living room and placed them on the glass table. There were jam rings on the saucers – Sal's favourites.

'I don't drink tea with milk any more,' Dorothy said. 'I have to watch my figure these days.'

'Oh.' He turned and carried one of the cups back to the kitchen, refilling the kettle at the sink before returning. 'So who were you planning to visit?'

She took a biscuit. 'You, of course.'

'Were you going to ring first?' he asked, alarmed, wondering what he'd have told Sal if she'd opened the door to her mother.

'Yes. I am nervous, no point lying to you. Especially after everything.'

Foxy frowned. It felt like a betrayal of his daughter now to remember how their lives had fallen apart when they had first found out about her condition. It was the shock of going from expecting everything to be OK, to watching the doctors and nurses whispering around the observation table after Sal had been delivered. Foxy remembered how they were told her ears were set a bit low, and this might indicate the chromosomal disorder Trisomy 21: Down's syndrome.

Dorothy had been distraught. 'Everything will be all right,' he'd promised her. 'She's beautiful. She's our lovely daughter.' But he had known, because Dorothy had taken the news so hard, that it wouldn't be all right for her.

'Tell me how you've been.' She put a hand on his knee.

He stared at it. 'Fine. Busy.'

'Any women I should know about?'

Foxy stood up. 'Do you know, you haven't asked me one thing about Sal since you arrived.'

'Well, you'd have told me if anything was wrong with her – anything else, I mean.'

'There's nothing wrong with her. Sal is Sal. She's still beautiful. Still special. Yet you haven't asked me what her favourite thing to do on a Saturday is, or what she likes and hates to eat, or what TV programmes she enjoys . . . anything.'

'I didn't think she . . .'

'What? You didn't think she could feel or think?'

Dorothy shook her head fiercely. 'You know I don't mean that. I love Sal, I always have. I regret what I did every single day. I want to see her again, that's all. And I wanted to see you. We were happy together once.'

Foxy felt a rush of anger. 'Let's get one thing very clear: I don't want you back, not like that.'

Dorothy threw her hands up in the air. 'For your information, I wasn't offering. I have a partner, thank you very much.'

'So why didn't Frank come with you? Give you a bit of support when you meet the daughter you left for dead?'

Dorothy's eyes welled up. She sniffed.

'I'm sorry,' Foxy said with a sigh. 'I'm not judging you. Really I'm not. I just know you, Dot, and I don't think you've changed a bit.' He paused, and looked at her. 'He's left you, hasn't he? That's why you've come back. You never could bear being on your own.'

Dorothy pulled a tissue from her sleeve as the tears started to flow. 'Frank didn't leave me – he died, poor bugger.'

Foxy walked over and put his arm around her. 'I'm sorry.' He gave her shoulders a squeeze. 'I only ever spoke to him on the phone but he seemed ... reliable.'

She blew her nose. 'I want to come home, John. It wouldn't have to be like old times. I messed that up, I know. But I could be a companion – cook and clean for you and Sal, make all of our lives a bit easier. Don't answer me straight away. Just give me a couple of days to prove to you and Sal that home life is better with me in it.'

'Look, I can't have you swan in to her life as her mother, then take off again if it doesn't work out. You'd break Sal's heart.'

Dorothy clutched his hand. 'She's the only reason you're saying no, though, isn't she? I can see it in your eyes. If it was down to you, you'd have me back. Right?' She tried to touch his face.

He leaned away. 'You can stay tonight, but to-morrow you have to go. I need time to think this through.'

Dorothy sighed. 'Can I see her tomorrow?'

'No. You should go back to Brighton. That's where you live now, isn't it? If we do arrange a reunion, I need to prepare Sal gently for what's coming.'

Dorothy closed her eyes and gave a resigned nod. She reached into a pocket, pulled out a tiny plastic band, and handed it to him. It was Sal's hospital wrist ID, less than an inch in diameter, he reckoned.

'You might as well have this, too. Maybe you can show it to her when you're telling her about me?'

He took it, read Sal's name on it.

'I kept it to remind me how tiny she used to be. That's the way I like to remember her, everyone still treating her like she was normal because they couldn't tell. My doctor said I had post-natal depression, did you know? He said that was why I found it so difficult to cope.'

Foxy felt a pang of guilt. 'Look, you'll have to leave early tomorrow morning. I'm sorry, but I have to think about what's best for Sal.'

33

In the hotel suite they had adjourned to, Sexton was standing in the shower, tilting his face into a jet of steaming water, and soaping under his arms, keeping one eye on the crack in the door, which he'd left ajar. It was just coming up to eleven at night, and he'd only given into Tara's insistence that he wash because she was frantic, completely convinced that they were being watched. She'd said Presley's life would be in danger if they didn't keep up the pretence that they were about to have sex. She'd agreed to tell Sexton everything if he first went through the motions, as a client would have done.

He'd decided to cooperate to calm her down. There was no point arguing with someone on drugs; and she was definitely on something – completely paranoid, and jabbering away. But some of the things she'd told him on the way up in the elevator about the footballers in the bar had convinced him she was about to come clean. If he played his cards right, he believed he could have this case solved for Jo by the morning. Tara had even slipped her dress and shoes off and handed them to him to convince him she wasn't going to do a legger as soon as his back was turned.

He snapped the head off one of those miniature shower-gel bottles and soaped it through his hair, rinsing the suds out quickly, and stepped out of the shower. He smelt of strawberries, and he shook the water off his hair as he dried himself. There was a dressing gown on the back of the door and he pulled it on. It was too small, and he felt like a plonker, but if all this got Tara to talk to him, it'd be worth it.

He swiped the condensation off the mirror so he could see himself, and spiked his hair to seem younger, or at least trendier. He wasn't bad looking, he supposed. He'd never had any problems pulling before he got married. After Maura died, he just couldn't be bothered trying any more. Even so, a woman like Tara would never have given him a second glance.

He went back into the dark bedroom. She was lying on her back diagonally across the four-poster bed, wearing only suspenders and a pair of stockings. Her breasts were a little too big for his taste. But, overall, she was perfection.

'OK, I kept my side of the deal,' he said, using the

towel around his neck to scrub the back of his hair.

But Tara didn't answer, or react.

Sexton stepped in closer, trying, in the dim light, to make out what was wrong. Then he saw it. A trickle of vomit was running from the corner of her mouth. He put two fingers to her neck, and held his breath as he waited. The pulse was faint, but it was still there. Tara Parker Trench wasn't just out cold, she was in a really bad way.

34

It was nearing midnight as Jo swung her car across the East Link Toll Bridge, towards the city centre. Stays tinkled against the masts of yachts in the marina to her right. The other side was the city's preferred spot for suicide jumps.

Steering past the rundown harbour warehouses dotted along North Wall Quay, she mulled over what Jeff had just told her. If Tara had been gang-raped, and the whole thing filmed, that sex tape in the wrong hands could bring down a lot of important people. The amount football clubs paid for top players was probably worth more than the GNP of the bloody country these days, after the interest on the IMF debts had been paid. Those players who had hurt Tara would have to face criminal charges. If they were prosecuted, and went to prison, the knock-on effect on their club's fortunes would be incalculable. Worst-case scenario: relegation, terrible press, even bankruptcy. The sex tape would be the linchpin of any prosecution. No wonder it had been taken from her office. But by whom?

The streets were empty. Even the homeless had bedded down for the night, Jo realized, scanning the quay. The car's heater was broken again, and her breath fogged in the night air. She'd kept the radio on to help her stay alert, though it was one of those chat shows where callers ring in to abuse each other and the DJ takes the high moral ground to stir them all up. *Who had sent her the tape?* she asked herself. Tara could have done so, but why give Jo only half the story when she was so desperate to find Presley? Jo felt sure Tara had been trying to hide that part of her life when they'd met.

Her phone beeped with an incoming text and Jo angled it at the top of the steering wheel, clicking the message open. She glanced between it and the road ahead, greasy under the streetlights after a recent shower.

It was from Rory, typed in that phonetic way kids had of spelling that was indecipherable unless it was read aloud. He was letting her know Harry and Sal were sleeping soundly and he was off to bed. He ended the text with one of those sleeping head emoticons. Jo smiled to herself. He was a good kid, and she'd make it up to him at the weekend. She always felt she was failing to maintain the work and home balance.

Pulling up on the kerb outside the Ever Oil service station where Presley had been taken, she shifted the gearstick into neutral, turned the radio off, killed the engine, dimmed the lights, and stared in. She needed to see the place at night in order to imagine what it had looked like to whoever had stolen him. It was well-lit, the vivid red and orange brand logo even more garish illuminated in the dark. The forecourt was empty; metal shutters had been pulled behind the doors. A pay hatch with a slot for cash was manned – she could see a shadow moving inside.

Something about this garage had vexed her ever since this morning, when she'd first entered it with Tara; it had niggled at the back of her mind all day. The place itself was so dingy, and in desperate need of basic upkeep, let alone major renovation work. The staff this morning had been foreigners, sometimes a sign of people who were being paid under the counter with lower amounts than the minimum wage.

Personally, she would only have stopped here for fuel out of desperation. All over the country, well-maintained garages were shutting down. It was becoming really difficult to get from A to B without running out of petrol. But this one was right in the heart of the city and, with the right investment, should have been a money-spinner. No matter which way she looked at it, the location just didn't gel with the set-up.

Jo watched a drunk wobble from the street in the general direction of the pay hatch. His smashed-up face gave him a down-and-out look, and made it impossible to estimate his age. His runners curled up at the toes, several sizes too big. She watched him shout through the speaker set in the Perspex, could see his frustration as he banged his fist against it to try and get some attention from the shadowy figure inside.

Her gaze shifted to the state-of-the-art CCTV camera over the door. She thought about the footage she'd watched today from inside and out, how clear the images had been.

That's bloody well it, she said to herself, as she worked it out at last. If all the signs were that the owner didn't give a toss about his staff, and was paying them next to nothing, and if he didn't want to invest in the place, why did he have such an expensive security system? A much cheaper one would have done the same job. Something else was going on in this garage, and Jo suspected it was so lucrative it dwarfed the revenue from fuel.

'That's why Tara was here,' Jo said to herself. 'And that's how whoever took Presley knew she'd be here, too.'

Jo kicked her shoes off as soon as she got in the door of her house. She stood and listened to the 2.30 a.m.

silence, then carried on into the kitchen. There she pulled open the washing-machine door, fetched a laundry basket, and scooped out a wash she'd put on before heading out that morning. Taking a clothes horse from the hot press, she arranged the wet clothes on it near the embers of the sitting-room fire. No point in putting them out tonight, rain was forecast.

Then she went to the dishwasher and removed the ware, putting it away quietly into the presses, and stacking the contents of the sink into the emptied trays. She wiped down the surfaces with a cloth and anti-bacterial spray, and swept the floor. It needed a mop, and the sitting room needed a hoover, but both would have to wait. It was only day one of the case, and already the domestic chores were backing up.

Rubbing the back of her neck, Jo padded down the hall, sticking her head into Sal's room to listen, before carrying down to the next room – Rory's – where she did the same.

Then she went into her own bedroom, where the sound of Harry snoozing in his cot lifted her heart. Unzipping her skirt, she let it slip to the floor, un-buttoned her blouse, and unhooked her bra. Moving to the wardrobe, she pulled out one of Dan's old shirts, and after burying her face in its homey, safe, manly smell, she pulled it on over her head, and climbed into bed and oblivion. It had been a long, hard day.

Tuesday

35

Jo was back behind her desk by 8.45 a.m., stifling a yawn as she pored over a bunch of witness statements taken at the garage the night Presley had been snatched.

She'd had to get up at six to do the housework -- make beds, hoover, sort laundry and clean out the fire - before dropping Sal off at her day centre, Harry to his crèche, and Rory to school on time.

Somehow, she'd found an extra ten minutes to spend on her appearance, and was now wearing her best tailored suit - a matching black skirt and jacket with a pair of killer heels. If she was going to have to persuade Dan that she couldn't continue running around like a blue-arsed fly and find Presley on her own without any back-up, she wanted to feel feminine while doing so.

The skinhead in the service station who'd caused the trouble by throwing cans of drink had been charged with criminal damage and resisting arrest, Jo noted. His name was Henly Roberts, and he'd an address in Portmarnock, a plush suburb on the north side. His DOB was 1969. Jo sat back in her chair and chewed the top of her biro. It wasn't every day you got a skinhead in his forties named Henly from a nice part of town. Maybe he'd gone into the service station with the deliberate intention of causing a disturbance, to distract everyone from what was going on outside. Jo glanced at the detective unit outside her office. Once Sexton arrived, she was going to send him to Portmarnock to find out. She made a note to remind Sexton that the dog Henly had had with him needed a licence. She was going to ask Foxy to doorstep Marcus Rankin, the registered owner of the HiAce in the garage, who Hassan had mentioned in his interview. Hassan would need to be brought back in for further questioning, too, about what was really going on in the garage he ran, she decided.

She pushed the swivel chair a couple of steps sideways to the computer, and pinged it on. Once it booted up, she was planning to run a check on whether Henly had any previous convictions.

She continued thumbing through the witness statements while she waited. The computer stopped whirring and Jo double-clicked on the Pulse icon on the screen. Sliding her finger across the mouse pad, she entered her ID number. Yesterday, she'd traced and interviewed the Jag's owner, Rosita Fitzmaurice. Now she realized that someone else in the queue at the garage had the same surname. She read the relevant statement more carefully. According to his DOB, Hugo Fitzmaurice was twenty. Jo guessed he must be the young guy she'd seen on the tape, his face partially hidden by a hoodie. Hugo had exactly the same address as Rosita Fitzmaurice, and Jo realized, with a start, that she'd met him: the young man with bad skin and a sharp suit who'd been ordering Rosita around and calling her 'Mother' in Clontarf. But there was absolutely no mention in either of their statements that they'd been at the garage together, which was highly suspicious.

The Fitzmaurices owned the Triton Hotel, and Jo suspected that the owner of the HiAce van, Marcus Rankin, worked there with Tara, too. If Tara, Marcus Rankin, Rosita and Hugo Fitzmaurice were all linked to the Triton, and if they were all in the same garage on the night that Presley disappeared, then that in itself was an incredible new lead.

She picked up the phone, and ran Marcus Rankin's social security number through the Revenue to check on his employers. She was just getting the details she needed when she stopped short at the sound of a rap on the door. Dan was entering, with a grave expression on his face. Jo cut the call short and put the receiver down.

'OK, you've got your murder and missing boy inquiry,' he said, sinking into the chair opposite. 'Who and what do you need?'

Jo clapped her hands together, then studied him more closely. 'Why the sudden change of heart?'

Dan exhaled. 'Because Tara Parker Trench turned up in intensive care with a suspected drugs overdose last night.'

Jo gasped.

He leaned forward and picked something off her desk. 'Why've you got Jeanie's hospital card here?' he asked, standing up.

'It was in the drawer of her desk,' Jo said. 'Give it back.' She tried to take it from him.

He stretched his hand up out of reach.

'It's old,' Jo said. 'I was about to dump it.'

'So why didn't you?'

'Look around. I haven't made it to IKEA yet. I don't have a wastepaper basket. Can you just tell me what's happening with Tara?'

Dan ripped the card in two, and slipped both pieces in his trouser pocket. 'Tara was found unconscious in a hotel room in the Triton,' he said.

'The Triton,' Jo said, clicking her fingers. She stopped as she realized Dan was glowering. 'What?'

'Sexton was with Tara when she OD'd,' Dan said.

'You're joking. Where is he now?'

'Donnybrook Station. He was arrested at the scene.'

36

Charles Fitzmaurice stepped into his Bentley and put the radio on, hearing the pips go for 9.30 a.m. It was only a short walk from his Clontarf home to his garage, but, given his weight, he was panting like a sprinter after a race. He was also hung over from the ten-odd units of twelve-year-old Jameson Gold Reserve whiskey he'd consumed the previous night. His fondness for fine cigars meant his sinuses were at him, and on top of that he was hacking his lungs up, as he did most mornings. To cap it all, he was groggy as hell, having tossed and turned all night after yesterday's events. The only thing that could improve his mood now would be the news that the socialite and model Tara Parker Trench had died. That was why the radio was on.

Sixty-two-year-old Fitz was hoping against hope that things would work out. It wasn't just rock and roll stars on massive blowouts vacuuming charlie up with a deviated septum who dropped dead from overdoses. Middle-class, well-bred beauties like Tara, using cocaine as a recreational way of prolonging the party, were going overboard all the time. At least if she died, it would be the end of the problem. Otherwise, it might come back to him, and he could lose everything. Someone's head was going to have to roll, and as far as he was concerned that someone was Murray Lawlor, for getting too big for his boots . . .

He adjusted the tuning and tweaked the volume as he drove along the coast road. He was a bag of nerves. It wasn't so long ago that he'd had to bribe a reporter who'd been commissioned by a newspaper to dig the dirt on him. The dogs in the street were barking about his extra-curricular activities, apparently. His wife, Rosita, had even taken to following Tara, after finding out about what she believed was an affair. That's how Rosita had ended up in the garage the night everything had gone belly up. If she asked for a divorce, the banks were going to start making demands he couldn't meet.

By the time he reached the lock-up in North Wall, Fitz was in a lather of perspiration. His doctor had done a stress test on him some years back, using a pulse monitor and sweat detectors on his palm. This morning, the doc could have multiplied those levels by ten.

At the warehouse, Fitz sank into his black

presidential chair, and picked up the phone to phone his lawyer, aware he was going to have to take some drastic measures.

When Big Johnny appeared ten minutes later, Fitz's heated discussion with George Hannah was winding up. The brief was demanding the Morocco sex tape be couriered over for safe storage in his office. When Fitz informed him he didn't have it, that it had been burgled from Imogen Cox's, the lawyer told him he was going to have to come up with five million quid to keep the drug-dealing scumbag, Barry 'King Krud' Roberts, from killing them all. To top it all, Fitz had just learned he'd lost money on a dog at Shelbourne Park the previous night. A lot of money. Money he didn't have.

'The little boy needs a doctor,' Big Johnny announced, as Fitz slammed down the phone.

'Better call an ambulance,' Fitz said, before stretching over and slapping the mobile out of Big Johnny's hand. He jabbed his temple. 'Have you lost the small ounce of sense you've got?'

Big Johnny looked at the pieces of his phone scattered around his feet.

'You should have gone to that room before lover boy called the emergency services last night. What am I paying you for? Not to think, that's for sure.'

Big Johnny spread his arms wide. 'But Murray said he was a pig. If I'd gone in there . . .'

Fitz smoothed his hair sideways over his scalp. 'If he went to a hotel room with a hooker, he had a price. I knew she was on something.'

'I swear to God, Fitz, I gave her nothing.'

'Murray must have, then. I watched him last night. He's getting too big for his boots. They are my girls. I say who rewards them with what. He needs reminding exactly where he comes in the food chain.'

Big Johnny didn't answer.

'What's the matter with the kid?' Fitz asked.

'Yolanda says he can't catch his breath. She went to a pharmacy last night but they wouldn't give her anything without a prescription. They said he needed a nebulizer, steroids, and regular doses of an inhaler. They told her to bring him straight to a hospital before he needed oxygen as well.'

Fitz's eyebrows soared. 'Tell me she didn't do something as stupid as that.'

'No. But she's getting jittery. She's afraid he'll pass out on her.'

Fitz sighed hard through his nostrils. 'He's no use to us any more, now his dozy cow of a mother is in a coma. You make sure she doesn't come out of it. And get rid of him. I'm not risking him getting sick all over the chopper again. You got any idea how much it costs to get one valeted?'

37

Jo felt a chill running down her spine. 'What do you mean, they've arrested Sexton?' she asked.

Dan leaned back in his chair. 'A bunch of guests in the Triton witnessed Sexton snogging Tara in the bar. They then booked a room together. Apparently, Tara was fine, the life and soul of the party, before she went off with him. About half an hour later, Sexton dialled 999 from the room, claiming he thought she'd OD'd. They were both virtually naked when the paramedics arrived.'

'That's ridiculous,' Jo said. 'Sexton wouldn't sleep with a call girl. That's the bloody problem with him.'

Dan looked surprised, opened his mouth to say something, then closed it again quickly. 'You said you couldn't get in touch with Tara yesterday,' he said finally. 'Did you know Sexton was with her?'

'No,' Jo said reluctantly, remembering how she'd tried to contact Sexton in vain the previous day, too. 'But I trust him completely.'

Dan folded his arms. 'But he has been acting differently lately, you have to admit that. He's never around, for starters, and when he is, it isn't long before he disappears again. If he's got a drug habit, it would explain a lot.'

'Of course he hasn't got a drug problem. It's Sexton, for Christ's sake. He lives the job.'

'He's been under a lot of stress,' Dan said.

Jo rolled her eyes. 'Who hasn't?'

'You seem to know a lot about his love life. Maybe there's another reason you can't keep an open mind . . .'

Jo threw her hands in the air. 'Here we go again. I'm supposed to be bloody shagging Sexton now, as well as the justice minister, is that it? God, I've been having a rare old time since you left. '

Dan stood up slowly, then walked over to the door and closed it. Their raised voices had ensured a captive audience outside. His eyes were stony when he turned back to her. 'What I mean is, it's possible you've been working too close to him to see what's staring you in the face.'

Jo shook her head. 'Don't try and turn this around. I know what you meant. If you want to know if I'm sleeping with someone, why don't you just come out with it straight, and ask me like a real man?'

Dan stepped close enough to slip his hands around her waist. 'Are you sleeping with anyone?'

'Mind your own bloody business,' she said, turning away and pulling her jacket from the back of the chair. She caught a glimpse of Tara's Mini, still impounded in the yard outside, as she moved.

'Listen to me, Jo. You still answer to me on this inquiry, and I'm telling you to call a case conference asap.'

'I'll do it as soon as I've spoken to Sexton.'

'Forget it, you can't see him. He's in custody.'

'We'll see about that,' Jo said, pushing past him to open the door.

In the car park, Jo headed towards Tara's car and unlocked the door she'd watched the motorcyclist in the garage open the night Presley had disappeared. If the investigation had run its proper course, the car would have been impounded for forensic examination. Given the haste to put the case to bed, Jo suspected it hadn't even been searched. She climbed in and saw the floors and seats were clear. She ran her hand between the joins and the backs of the seats – anywhere something could have been wedged. There was only some loose change and a child's toy car there. She got back out and went around to the boot, pulling out two doors which opened in the middle. She lifted a buggy from the back, and ran her palms along the carpet, finding only a car jack.

She was about to put the pushchair back in when

it occurred to her that the jack should have had a compartment of its own. She fiddled with a couple of plastic knobs, lifted the carpet up and out, and stared in disbelief. What looked like clear, plastic-wrapped bricks of fresh snow were wedged in tightly there. She reckoned there were enough to keep south Dublin partying up to Christmas and through the New Year.

Walking purposefully back around to the door she'd just climbed out of, she got in again, and this time scoured the ceiling, the lining, and finally the padding covering Presley's car seat, which she freed from the rear. That's when she found something she'd only ever seen in intelligence bulletins. It was the size of a kid's marble, but no mother would ever risk leaving it where a child might put it in its mouth. It was a tracking device.

38

With one phone call made on the steps of the station, Jo arranged to meet Blaise Stanley for lunch, and asked him to cut through the red tape so she could pay Sexton an unorthodox visit in Donnybrook Station. Tara's car was towed to the forensic lab where it belonged. The tracking device was sealed in an evidence bag and given to Dan, who was put in the picture. And less than an hour later, Jo walked into Sexton's interview room.

'Thank God you're here,' Sexton said. His whole body slackened as he pushed his chair out from the table in the windowless room.

'Interview suspended at ten a.m. to allow subject to speak to Detective Inspector Jo Birmingham, Store Street,' the interviewing officer announced. His sing-song voice told Jo he wasn't happy that strings had been pulled. Jo wouldn't have been either, but her faith in Sexton was non-negotiable.

Clicking his tongue in annoyance, the officer tucked

his notepad under his arm, and banged the door on his way out.

Jo leaned on the table with her two hands and lowered her voice as she glanced around for the camera. 'What have you done with the sex tape that was in my desk?'

Sexton looked taken aback. 'I don't have it. I didn't even know you'd lost it.'

'You knew where it was. And when you disappeared yesterday afternoon, it did, too.'

'Jo, I swear to God—'

'So where've you been? I tried to call you all afternoon. What the hell have you been doing?'

'I've been working. I know you don't believe me, but I went to the bank like you asked, and then, based on what the manager told me, I went to an ATM machine in Sandymount to see if I could find out why the Coxes were withdrawing a large amount of cash there every Monday afternoon.'

'So why didn't you ring me to keep me in the picture?'

'I tried, honestly I did, Jo, but my phone was . . . well, it got wet. Look, I know it sounds like one of my pathetic excuses, but, Jo, I wouldn't . . . I mean, I didn't . . . I was working. I swear on . . . on Maura's memory.'

Jo sat down on the side of the desk and crossed her arms. He was telling the truth. 'So what did you establish?'

Sexton told her about his encounter with Murray Lawlor at the ATM – reminding her who Murray was – and went on to say that Tara had been terrified by the sight of a group of international footballers at the Triton Hotel. He told Jo how he and Tara had headed upstairs, and how Tara had then explained what the footballers had done to her in Marrakesh a couple of nights earlier.

'Do you know who they were?' Jo asked tentatively.

'Of course,' Sexton said. 'If Tara hadn't jumped me, I'd have been asking for their autographs. They're all Melwood Athletic.'

Jo gave a little victory clench of the fist, then made him detail exactly what had happened when he'd met Murray in the bar the previous evening. 'Hold it,' she interrupted. 'Did you just say Murray was on a motorbike?'

'Yes. I thought it was weird, Jo, because, like I said, he was in the big flash Audi jeep earlier in the day. But he made a point of saying he always took the bike when he was working.'

'There was a motorbike in the garage the night Presley was taken,' she said as she pulled out her phone and started to dial. 'I haven't had a chance to run the registration yet. But I'll bet you any money when I do it'll come back to Murray Lawlor.' She winked at him as she waited for the call to connect.

'Well, it seems I owe you an apology. In spite of all this' – she indicated the room they were in – 'yours was an afternoon and evening very well spent yesterday. As a matter of fact, what you've discovered might just have given us a major new lead.' She tousled his hair. 'Nice one, my son.'

He grinned, and she saw a flash of the boyish old Sexton back. Jo asked the duty sergeant who answered the call to enter the registration of the motorbike, which she read out from her garage diagram.

She waited, and nodded when the duty sergeant confirmed that Murray Lawlor's name was listed on the system as the registered owner of the bike. Jo thanked the officer and hung up.

'We'll need to pay Murray Lawlor a little visit,' she told Sexton. 'He's in this up to his eyes.'

'Fill me in on what's happened,' Sexton said.

'I found drugs and a tracking device in Tara's car. The drugs should be enough to get you off the hook for now, or at least buy you enough time to have some tests carried out,' Jo said. 'I'll bet you when they're profiled they'll crossmatch in content and purity with whatever Tara took last night. It looks as though Murray Lawlor was making sure he knew exactly where Tara was at all times. Not just for Jeff Cox, either. Jeff was only small fry. Murray must have been concerned about what was in the back of her car. We need to find out who he was working for. Now, hurry up and extricate yourself from this situation you've got yourself into, because I'm calling a case conference in the station this afternoon and I want you on my team.' She straightened her suit. 'But first, I've got a few questions for Blaise Stanley.'

39

Blaise Stanley was tucking into a bread roll when Jo arrived at Patrick Guilbaud's restaurant, having followed a maître d' down some stairs and into a dining area where some of the country's most notable artists were on display on the walls. She'd refused to hand over her jacket. She didn't plan on getting comfortable.

Stanley pulled his napkin free of his shirt collar and, after dabbing the corners of his mouth with it, deposited it on the table. He stood and air-kissed Jo on both cheeks. The first one made her uneasy, the second made her feel she had sold out.

'How's your friend holding up?'

Jo sat down and gave her table napkin a quick flick before smoothing it over her lap. 'He'll be fine. He's innocent.'

'To what do I owe this pleasure?'

'I just thought it time we had a little tête-à-tête. There was no mention in the budget yesterday of funds being allocated to fund the separate legal representation proposals you've backed to make life easier for victims of crime in court.'

Jo had negotiated lawyers for victims in court with Stanley during the Bible killer case, but the policy had yet to materialize.

Stanley plucked a leather-bound wine list from the table and studied it, his gold dice cufflinks flashing against a pair of starched white cuffs. 'Patience, Birmingham, I always look after my friends. The country is banjaxed, in case you hadn't noticed, meaning certain projects have to be long fingered. Bond holders, IMF, you must have heard . . .'

'We had a deal,' Jo argued, really annoyed.

'As I said, I always look after my friends. Do you like your new office?'

'Meaning?'

'Meaning that I'm doing my best for you, that I have your best interests at heart.'

Jo sat back. 'Tell me what's going on.'

'At ease, Birmingham. I know I don't have to remind you that if I lose my office, and my enemies do manage to bring me down, your campaign to advance the rights of victims goes with me.'

'You make it sound like a threat.'

'Do I? You've got other issues, haven't you?'

'Yes.'

'Well, tell me about one. I'll get my advisers to prepare a paper.'

'You need to end the system that allows prisoners on murder or rape charges out on bail,' Jo said. 'The numbers reoffending while waiting to go to trial are startling. Then there's the fact that even after being sentenced, prisoners earn an automatic entitlement to remission for good behaviour. These things add insult to injury for the victims.'

'You have a point,' Stanley said. 'Now, do you have a wine preference? I've developed quite a taste for the New World lately.'

'I'll pass,' Jo said, putting a hand over her glass.

'Spoilsport.' He chuckled and reached for a bottle of water, then checked the label. 'Still or sparkling?' he asked.

'Either will do fine,' Jo said flatly.

He poured her a glass, and set the bottle back down.

'How well did you know Imogen Cox?' Jo asked.

'Who?'

'The former model-turned-model-agent. She was murdered yesterday. You must have heard of her. I'll bet your office has been fielding calls all day looking for quotes from you on the country's crime levels.'

'The name means nothing to me.' He lifted the menu. 'Can I recommend the monkfish? It's sensational.'

Jo studied him closely. 'How come nobody ever

raves about the chicken? It's always the sole, the cod, the plaice. It's always the fish.'

'What's your point?'

'That people are sheep. They pretend somewhere like this makes them comfortable, when really they'd be much happier in their local. They say the fish is divine, when actually they'd much rather be getting stuck into a plate of chips. It's all appearances, and you – more than anyone else – know how important those are.'

'Have you something on your mind?'

Jo leaned forwards. 'Were you in Morocco on Sunday night?'

'No.'

'What about Tara Parker Trench? Do you know her?'

'The model? No, again. Why?'

'I'm going to ask you one more time, and I'm going to ask you to really consider what I'm asking before you answer. Did you know Imogen Cox?'

Stanley waved to a waiter over the heads of the other diners, then spoke very quietly. 'Let me reiterate, I categorically did not.'

The sommelier arrived and began the ritualistic uncorking process.

'Pity you won't join me in a toast,' Stanley said, rolling the liquid around the bottom of his glass, sniffing, tasting and then clicking his tongue on the roof of his mouth.

He signalled he was happy for the wine to be poured, the sommelier duly obliged, and Stanley raised his glass. 'I'm going to promote you. Hence the office. How does chief superintendent sound?'

Jo's mind raced. The potential pay rise would be a lifeline – she was struggling to manage the cost of running the house now she was on her own. She might even be able to afford some help. But there was only one chief superintendent per division, meaning she'd have to be transferred.

Jo took a mouthful of her water. 'Where do you have in mind?'

'I want you to replace Dan,' Stanley said coolly.

'Why? Are you promoting him, too?'

'No.'

Jo tried to process what he was saying. 'Hang on. I was the one who wanted a transfer. You can't move Dan.'

'I'm not going to. An internal investigation has found he was completely compromised during the serial killer investigation you solved. Here are their findings.' He reached sideways into a briefcase on the floor beside him and pulled out a spiral-bound set of sheets, which he tossed in front of her.

Stamped 'Private and Confidential', the title read 'Inquiry into Policing Conduct and Standards during the Walter Kaiser Investigation, Store Street'.

Much as Jo wanted to read every page, she wasn't

about to give Stanley the satisfaction. There was no question in her mind that Dan's decision to tell no one that Anto Crawley – the country's biggest drug dealer and one of the serial killer's victims – had been one of his informants, had held up her investigation. But the punishment was heavy handed in the extreme.

'He'll think I've had something to do with it,' she said quietly.

'Does it matter? I thought you'd separated.' Stanley reached for another bread roll and sliced it in half.

'He knows already, doesn't he?' Jo said, suddenly understanding Dan's pent-up anger that morning. 'He thinks I'm behind it, that I've been manoeuvring behind his back.' She stood up so quickly the napkin fell on the floor and her glass of water overturned. 'No, I'm sorry, I can't accept on these terms.'

Stanley reached for some more bread, spread a corner with butter, and spoke out of the side of his mouth as he chewed. 'Suit yourself. But if this report gets out – and there's a very real chance it will – somebody's head is going to have to roll, and it's not going to be mine. You solved the case, it seems only right and fair that you should be rewarded. My spin doctors tell me that if you're promoted, we will minimize the negative ripple effect.'

'Dan is a good cop. He made an error of judgement. We all do it. No harm came of it. We got the killer.'

Stanley leaned back and smiled up at her. 'If you don't want the job, I'm sure one of your colleagues will be more than happy to step up to the mark. All I'm doing is giving you first right of refusal.'

40

The prison officers were wearing white Tyvek over-alls, and plastic masks over their noses and mouths, so they wouldn't catch anything from contact with the King. He was sitting in the back of the van bring-ing him to court, smears of excrement caked to his face. The screws had tossed a coin to decide who should sit in the back with him; the smell was that bad. There should have been three officers alongside him, but they had reasoned it down to one – a butty kid sitting opposite, whose eyes watered over his mask. The other two officers were up front with the driver, only a reinforced Perspex window separating them. The King's ankles had been cuffed and chained to his handcuffs as an extra precaution. There was no garda escort because the resources for organized crime had taken a hammering in the budget. The cops were planning to meet them at the courthouse instead.

Every time the King looked at the screw opposite,

he doubled up laughing like he'd just heard a really funny joke.

'What's so funny?' the officer asked eventually, his voice muffled through the mask and his face shiny with perspiration. He'd a stab vest on underneath, and the van was reinforced with bulletproof metal. It was like sitting in an oven.

The King was holding on to a handle grip so tightly his knuckles had turned white. 'You look like one of those Tellytubbies my kid used to like to watch,' he answered, cracking up again.

Then, with a sudden, deafening jolt, the van jack-knifed at such speed it overturned and did a double spin. The King's grip ensured he did not bounce off the roof. Holding himself steady, he aimed his feet at the young screw's head, building up momentum with the motion, and connected. The screw's face spurted blood, and his eyes rolled up and closed as he passed out.

The van stopped moving, and the King threw himself on the floor, face down.

He listened hard as, up front, the sounds of breaking glass, metal crumpling, and cars piling up drowned out the high-pitched yells of terror.

Then came the staccato thud-thud-thud of a machine gun, as the King's men finished off the screws in the driver's compartment.

When the shooting stopped, the King grabbed the

young screw's set of keys he needed to open his restraints, grinning as he did so. He'd taken out an insurance policy in case his brief let him down in court today, and it looked like it'd paid off.

The champion of the world was a contender again.

41

Jo was back in the office by two thirty, holding her door open with her back as the three detectives she'd requested for the first conference filed past, wheeling chairs in front of them. First was Detective Sergeant Aishling McConigle, a plump, rosy-cheeked new graduate in her mid-twenties, who'd already been promoted for her bravery after an undercover vice operation on prostitution. She'd suffered a kick to the torso after a pimp got territorial, and lost her spleen, but against all expectation had returned to the job. Jo had picked her for her mettle and her knowledge of the sex industry.

Behind her, Detective Sergeant Neil D'Arcy looked more like a computer nerd than any cop Jo had worked with. That was exactly why she wanted him. He'd done several courses in mobile phone analysis, and given that the escort business relied so heavily on mobile communication, he could bring invaluable expertise to the table. The fact that he had a reputation as being a closet anorak when it came to football could prove equally useful.

Third in the line-up was Detective Inspector Al Lovett, a hardworking detective in his forties who'd just concluded a secondment to the cold case unit reviewing old missing persons cases, and identifying the flaws in previous investigations. It hadn't made him popular, but that was a character reference in its own right in Jo's book.

Last, but not least, was Dan, who closed the door behind them as he settled into his seat, stretching his legs out in the pokey space and crossing them at the ankle. He didn't need to be there – ordinarily Jo would have briefed him afterwards. But he was making a point, and since meeting the minister, Jo understood why.

Foxy, Jo had learned from a phone conversation minutes earlier, was on his way. He'd been mysterious about where he was, but had promised he'd be back shortly, and had made no apology for not being on time.

Jo had another twenty lower-ranking officers at her disposal for the dogsbody duties that would need to be carried out. Dan had promised to double that number again within twenty-four hours if Presley was still missing. Once the three in front of her had had their instructions, they could draw on those resources – to help complete the jobs Jo set them.

She rolled up her sleeves as the group arranged themselves, Dan behind them and nearest to the door. Sitting
on the edge of her desk, a marker in hand, Jo glanced
outside to where Oakley and Merrigan clearly had the
hump on the other side of the office wall. They were
locked in conversation, and taking regular over-the-
shoulder glances in her direction. Jo had been quite
prepared to let bygones be bygones and invite Oakley
to join them, but he'd kicked up when she'd asked him
for the photograph of Presley which Tara had given
him, and had tried to refuse to hand it over. He hadn't
had a leg to stand on, and after Jo had reminded him of
as much, she'd had the picture blown up, laminated,
and fixed with a coloured magnet to a wipe board
'borrowed' from the detective unit outside. But she had
also washed her hands of Oakley. Presley was the only
one who would suffer from Oakley's attempt to turn
this into a contest.

The image of a cherubic-looking little boy with blue
eyes and a mop of blond curls stared innocently over
Jo's shoulder, giving everyone there solemnity and
focus.

Not wanting to waste any more time, Jo gave the
briefest synopsis of the case, sticking to the facts. Some
links in the chain of events, such as the allegation
that Tara Parker Trench had been raped, needed
corroboration, she explained. Some – such as Presley's
abduction and the murder of Imogen Cox – were fact.

She censored nothing, and gave them the full details, including the allegations against the justice minister, though this raised a worried look from Dan. A team was a team, as far as Jo was concerned. The fact that the station's local pub was shared by four news-papers, operating out of a city-centre office block nearby, was not something she was going to let divide them. There were stiff penalties for breaching the Official Secrets Act, but cross-pollination was inevitable, especially on Friday nights. Anyway, if what Dan was dreading panned out, the story was leaked to the press, and they started to dig the dirt, they'd be doing her a service. Ultimately, they might help her save Dan's job. Jo concluded the summation by telling the team that their goal in sorting the wheat from the chaff was to establish how the various crimes were linked. Only then would they find Presley.

Then she slid a DVD into the player. It was the CCTV footage taken from the security camera outside Store Street Station. She'd asked the officer who'd copied it for her to edit it down to less than a minute, in which a figure could be seen dropping a Jiffy bag into the station's letterbox.

Unlike the quality of the footage filmed in the garage, the graininess made it almost impossible to make out the figure at all. Everything was also in a muddy colour somewhere between dark grey and navy.

'This is the person who delivered the sex tape to the station,' Jo explained.

The time on the lower right-hand corner of the screen said it was 5.10 a.m.

It was hard to tell if they were even looking at a male or a female. The individual was wearing a three-quarter-length coat, the colour of which was impossible to identify, though it had white ridges, which made a large square pattern. A trucker cap pulled low on the forehead made it impossible to see the face, or length of hair.

'And that's all we've got,' Jo said, pressing 'eject' and sliding the disc out.

'Right,' she said, winding it up. 'Aishling, I want you to concentrate on the Atlantis Hotel in Marrakesh this afternoon. We need the hotel's client list and the names of any guests who checked in and out on Saturday and Sunday night. I also want the names of all the passengers aboard Tara's flight to Marrakesh. Oh, and the guest list from the Triton Hotel on Sunday night, too, OK?'

Aishling nodded as she made a note.

'D'Arcy, I know this can't happen overnight, but I'm going to need you to illustrate on a map of the city what masts Tara's mobile was bouncing off, to try and approximate her movements. OK?'

He gave a thumbs up.

'And Lovett, can you organize a press briefing for

early evening? We'll need more photos of Presley, as up to date as you can manage.'

'Won't that bring undue pressure to bear on us?' he replied. 'We don't want the press to start dictating what leads should be followed up, and skewing the direction of the investigation, do we?'

'It's a risk we have to take,' Jo told him decisively. She hoped he wasn't going to question every instruction she gave, as this would be time-consuming and annoying. 'Presley's nan lives nearby, but I expect she'll be keeping a vigil at her daughter's bedside. Which reminds me, we need to keep Tara Parker Trench under protection in intensive care ASAP.'

She took a deep breath. 'Right, Aishling, if I'm bringing in foreign girls to work on the game here, where do I source them?'

Lovett cut in. 'All the newspapers run those classifieds for private masseuses where you get to pick all sorts from Chinese exotic beauties to Caucasians,' he said.

'But that's for punters,' Jo pointed out. 'I'm talking about sourcing girls for work in the first place.'

'We could get on to the ad managers in the papers who are indirectly profiteering.'

'We'd have to prove it, and we don't have time. Aishling . . . ?'

'The internet,' she replied.

Jo stood and wrote it on the board, with an arrow

pointing sideways from it to the word 'computers'. 'Now we're getting somewhere.' She turned to Dan. 'We'll need to seize the Triton's computers.' He took the cue and headed for the door. They'd need search warrants, signed by a judge.

Lovett looked deflated, but Jo didn't have time for egos. Drawing a line to the right from the top of the board to the bottom, she created a second column. 'So I'm a pimp with a bevy of exotic beauties that I've sourced from the internet, and plan to fly in. How do I get my girls into the country without work visas?'

'You don't,' Aishling said. 'You set up a front – you know, a company that looks legit.'

'Go on,' Jo encouraged.

'Remember that model in the nineties, Samantha Blanford Hutton?' Aishling said.

'She had a brother who was a jockey?'

'Yeah, that's the one. Well, she was a model-turned-high-class-hooker who set up a cleaning company, registered it, the lot. She sourced all these girls from Brazil by placing ads in newspapers over there, and got the employment visas she needed rubber-stamped. She brought them over, and withheld their passports to force them on to the game. One of the girls went missing, and some of the others broke their silence – that was the only reason it all came to light.'

Jo thought about the young Filipina girl she'd seen at the Fitzmaurices', and remembered how Hassan had said that the HiAce driver, who was in the garage the night Presley vanished, had a specialist cleaning firm. She wrote his name at the top of the second column with a question mark. 'According to the Revenue, Marcus Rankin works at the Triton. Let's find out the name of his cleaning firm, and if he's got anyone working for him. If he has, let's determine their gender, age, and nationality.' She turned to Aishling. 'How do you know so much about cleaning agencies, anyway?' she asked. 'I thought your speciality was street workers.'

'Samantha used to babysit for me. I grew up a few doors down. I could write a thesis about what went on in that house.'

Jo grinned. 'Only in Ireland ... Right, we also need to establish if the Triton has been recruiting foreign staff for menial labour – waitressing for instance – through a registered firm,' Jo said, drawing a fresh line on the board to create another column. At the top of it she wrote 'Charles Fitzmaurice, owner of the Triton'.

'I want every spit and cough on this man,' she said. 'I want to know if he's got any previous, and if not, why not. If he's ever rung us to so much as ask for directions, I want the details. After the press conference, I'll be heading on to the Triton. Anything you can get for me for that interview could make the vital difference.'

She listed the names of the footballers in a fourth column on the board. 'I also want you to contact

Interpol, Europol and Scotland Yard, and find out if there's anything that's ever rung alarm bells about any of these men, proven or not.'

Out of the side of her eye she saw Foxy hurrying towards the office.

'And last, but not least, can you get someone to bring Hassan and his missus, and Marcus Rankin back in here? For the moment we're only requesting their co-operation. I don't want detention warrants running out on us before I've had a chance to speak to them.'

Foxy had reached the door, and once inside he put his hands on his knees and leaned over trying to catch his breath.

'You'll give yourself a coronary if you keep that up,' Jo said.

Foxy straightened up, then reached into the pocket of his donkey jacket and pulled out a disc, which he handed over to Jo. Oakley, outside, was straining to look over his shoulder and get a view of what the object was.

'What's this?' Jo asked.

'Your sex tape from this morning,' he said. 'Hassan's wife took it when she was waiting up here for him.'

'Up here?' Jo said, glancing out angrily at Merrigan.

Foxy nodded. 'It's a long story. I just paid her a visit.'

'Right,' Jo said. 'We'd better watch it, then.'

42

Jo moved to the side of the TV as the DVD started to play. She pointed to the woman on the screen standing with her back to the camera, between the man's legs.

'I haven't watched this through yet, but if our information is correct, that is Tara Parker Trench. If anyone recognizes the man she's with, please pipe up. Again, hopefully we'll get a better view of him shortly. If we're on the right track, he's a Melwood Athletic player.'

'Christ,' Dan said, leaning forwards.

With a burst of shouts from the screen, the group of men in shorts – who Jo had first seen the previous day – started jumping into the pool. 'Again, from our inquiries, we believe these men could also be MA players,' she explained. 'Sexton got two possible names off Tara last night, before she passed out. Let's pray we get a view of their faces at some stage.'

Aishling tucked a strand of hair behind her ear. 'Jo,

the man being, um, pleasured, looks like Kevin Mooney . . .'

'You can't see his face at that angle,' Lovett objected.

'No, I know, but the tattoo on his ankle . . .' Aishling leaned closer to point.

Jo jabbed 'pause' on the remote, and they all studied what was not much more than a speck on the screen.

'She's right,' D'Arcy said. 'Mooney's got a football boot tattooed on his right ankle, exactly the same as that one.' He turned to Aishling. 'I didn't know you were a footie fan.'

Aishling grinned.

'Can we save the chat for later?' Jo asked. 'But that was well spotted, Aishling. And Kevin Mooney is one of the names Sexton got, too.'

Jo pressed 'play' again, pointing to the couple sipping cocktails about twenty feet beyond the pool. 'Meet Imogen Cox, now deceased. Presley was taken the same night she flew back to Dublin from this hotel with Tara.' Jo's finger moved across the screen, 'This man may be Blaise Stanley . . .'

The detectives glanced at each other.

Dan put his hands together at his mouth like he was praying.

Jo spoke directly to him. 'We need to establish where Stanley was on the night in question, if we're going to substantiate the claim.'

'Let's fly someone out to Marrakesh as soon as possible,' Dan said. 'See if we can't find that hidden camera and whoever knew about it.'

'Why do you think it's hidden?' Jo asked.

'There's no way a politician as long in the tooth as Stanley would be naïve enough to allow himself to be filmed with that going on,' Foxy answered. 'If it's Stanley, it's a hidden camera all right.'

The conversation stopped as, on the telly, the men in the pool started to shout crude words of encouragement at the man getting the blow job.

'There's a Yorkshire accent in there,' D'Arcy remarked. 'Greg Duncan is from Barnsley, is black, and plays for Melwood Athletic.'

Jo's eyes moved to the only black man in the pool, to the far right of the group of four who had made a semicircle around the woman. She moved to get a better view of the screen. She hadn't seen much more of the rest herself.

The men were closing in on the woman. One of them started mauling her breasts from behind. As she reached back to push him off, Kevin Mooney grabbed her by the hair and forced her head into his lap again.

The woman shot up, and turned around to give the man feeling her up a shove, her face finally coming into view as her hands landed on the man's chest. It was Tara all right. Jo sighed with relief. It was another piece of the puzzle. She checked on Foxy, who was standing at the door, gazing out with a pained expression on his face. When he spotted Jo looking at him, he tipped his head in the direction of the unit outside. Jo nodded to show it was OK for him to go. Relief spread across his face.

On the screen, the man who had been sitting on the edge of the pool slid in and stood in the water, clearly put out. Nobody said a word, but more than one of the detectives frowned. Everyone recognized Kevin Mooney now – his face was practically iconic. He was never off the telly, given all the brands he endorsed. Standing beside Tara, he looked short but broad, with dense brown hair and light-blue eyes.

The atmosphere changed once he was in the pool, Jo noticed. For a start the laddish feel to what had been happening disappeared, and there were no more high-spirited shouts. Instead the other men stopped messing and began closing in like a pack. The black man moved behind Tara and, gripping her neck in the crook of his arm, dipped her head sideways into the water.

'That's definitely Greg Duncan,' D'Arcy said.

'Good,' Jo said. 'Which means we've only two left to identify, if the second name Sexton got is correct.' She withheld telling them what that was, as it would make the verification process better.

The tape was getting harder to watch. Tara was obviously in acute distress. Two of the men moved to her legs, which they pulled from under her and gripped.

Dan grimaced, and looked away.

By now Tara was fully prostrate in the water, which was washing over her face. Mooney moved between her legs and Tara's head was once again dunked back as she attempted to thrash her arms. A couple of long seconds later she re-emerged and gulped a mouthful of air, too winded to shout or scream. The man holding Tara's right leg put a hand over Mooney's shoulder and glanced over at his companion, holding Tara's left leg, who looked back at him. Their profiles were in clear view.

'Watchman and Mansell,' Dan said, with a sigh.

'Yep,' D'Arcy said.

'Melwood Athletic?' Jo asked.

Aishling nodded.

What followed next made Aishling cover her mouth with her hand, Lovett watch through spread fingers and D'Arcy blink rapidly. Dan stood up, knitting his hands behind his head.

Each of the men took turns to follow Mooney's lead. The positions varied, but the result was the same. At one point, screaming and flailing, Tara managed to break free, and made a desperate attempt to escape. She hauled herself up on to the edge of the pool and crawled forwards, water streaming from her hair, before being caught, dragged violently back into the water and raped again. Afterwards her face, half-submerged, said it all. It was completely blank. She had clearly given up.

Jo focused on Imogen Cox in the background. She stood to kiss the man she was with on both cheeks before he headed back to the hotel. The tape ended abruptly, with Imogen walking over to the pool as the last of the footballers hoisted themselves up and out. Behind them, in the shallow end, Tara lay still.

'Was that Stanley?' Jo asked, referring to the man Imogen was with.

'I can't be sure,' Dan answered, slowly.

'I feel sick,' Aishling said.

Jo could tell from the men's faces that they weren't far off, either.

'Sexton saw some MA players in the Triton last night,' Jo said. 'I say we bring them all in right now, while we can.'

Dan nodded.

'Evening paper's in,' Foxy said, arriving back and tossing it on to Jo's desk. The headline got everyone's attention. Jo lifted it up, the team gathering on either side to read over her shoulders. It read, 'Top Model's Tragic Last Interview.' The strapline stated, 'Kevin Mooney's Steamy Desert Hat-trick. How My Affair With Striker Left Me Gagging For More.' Jo scanned the article quickly:

Tara Parker Trench, socialite and model, made secret phone calls from Marrakesh to our paper's showbiz reporter, and he was waiting for her in Dublin Airport with a photographer, where he managed to secure more details. An arrangement was made with Tara, where she agreed to sell her full story, in return for a substantial payment . . . The contracts had been drawn up, but were unsigned . . . On discovering from a tip-off about Tara's condition, which we are attributing to an overdose, the editor has taken the decision to publish . . .

'And be damned,' Dan cut in.

'Surely it isn't all bad to have it out in the open?' Aishling suggested. 'It could bring more girls out of the woodwork.'

'Bollocks,' Jo said. 'They've already started to spin it. All they need now is for Tara to die on them, and those players will get off scot free.' She clicked her fingers. 'Hang on, Foxy mentioned that Tara's ex was going on about that hotelier, Charles Fitzmaurice, paying her too much attention, right? . . . He's got a bloody helicopter pad down there at the hotel. Aishling, can you get on to air traffic control straight away, see if he's booked any flights in or out for today?'

Oakley rapped on the door and poked his head

around it. 'Have they got the Barry Roberts story yet?' he asked, pointing to the paper.

Jo continued to scan the article for details but her ears pricked up. Roberts was one of the city's biggest drug dealers, and although her concern right now was Tara, Roberts's name had come up when she'd sneaked a peek in the file belonging to the dodgy solicitor, George Hannah.

'Why, what's happened?' Dan asked. 'The King's up in court today, isn't he? Tell me he didn't get off on a technicality?'

'He never got to court,' Oakley answered. 'He was sprung from the prison van, and that's not the worst of it. There's three prison officers dead at the scene, and a fourth in Beaumont with serious head injuries.'

43

Sexton pressed the intercom and leaned in close to be heard over the city-centre traffic – honking motorists mostly, outraged that they were going nowhere in the pre-rush-hour build-up. He'd been released at three thirty, with the warning that his file was being sent to the DPP to decide whether there was enough evidence to make a charge. He knew that if there'd been any hard proof there wouldn't have been any need to seek legal advice. He wasn't worried about the results of the blood samples he'd given biting him in the ass, either. He had a horror of drugs, and wouldn't have touched them with a bargepole.

But he also knew that in the policing game, mud always stuck. It was as simple as that. His name had been linked to a hooker, and to drugs, and he was never going to live it down. The fallout would be implicit: in all the jobs he would be assigned from now on, ones guaranteed to turn cold because there were no leads; in the promotion lists, where he'd be passed over time and again; and worst of all, from his point of view, in the way other cops would stop talking whenever he entered a room. If that happened, the job wouldn't be worth doing. He'd seen it with better men than him over the years. They'd ended up like zombies, clocking in and out, just passing time to get their pension. All things considered, he'd decided enough was enough. It was time to make sure Jo cracked this one. He wasn't going to go back to the station until he had something to give her, to reward her faith in him. She was right about Maura's note, too: once this case was solved he was going to read it. He needed to start getting on with his life. The crick in his neck he'd woken up with after nodding off in the car earlier had gotten worse after his arrest. He rubbed his neck painfully.

'Pizza,' he said into the buzzing speaker.

'I didn't order a pizza,' came the response. It was followed by, 'Oh, it's you. Come in, then, but it will have to be brief. I've got to wash my hair. Top floor.'

A set of glass doors slid open.

Murray Lawlor's office was located in a converted mill on Camden Street. There was no reception, just a rack of bike stands attached to the exposed stone wall, facing a line of lockers. Sexton took the wrought-iron stairs instead of the lift. He wanted to see what businesses occupied the other six floors. Solicitors, chartered accountants, and an architect, he realized. Murray was a pimp hiding among professionals. He had chosen well.

At the top a set of doors faced him, made of reinforced steel, with a couple of CCTV cameras angled down over them. The place was bright, but the arched window on one wall was disconcertingly low. He'd have had to kneel and stoop to see out. There was another intercom on the wall, which Sexton was stepping towards when Murray pulled open the door of his office. He was wearing another loud shirt, red this time, with a thin white pinstripe running through it, and he had one of those little metal pins joining the two sides of his stiff white collar under a big, fat, red tie. Gold. His hair was greased back so heavily Sexton thought about asking him how he felt about threatening local marine life.

But Murray got in there first. 'I did warn you to stay away from Tara,' he said.

Sexton drew back his fist, and slammed it into Murray's stomach, shaking his hand as the impact of connecting with sheer muscle reverberated up to his armpit.

Murray barely winced, but as he clenched his right fist in response, Sexton jolted a knee up into his groin, causing him to bend over and yelp.

'Glad we got that out of the way,' Sexton said, flicking his foot to the back of Murray's knee to trigger the reflex, and then hooking his ankle around

Murray's to finish the job and bring him down.

Once he had Murray pinned to the ground, his knee pressed into the small of his back, Sexton let out a hard sigh. 'Now, if that job's still on offer, I'm free for an interview, mate.'

Five minutes later, Sexton had Murray handcuffed to the spindles on the back of his captain's chair in his big fancy office, and had started to riffle through the drawers of a stack of filing cabinets.

'Where did it all go wrong?' he asked. 'Eh? Hotshot. It's not an easy life being in the force, I'll give you that. The money's crap, the public hate you, and relationships, well, I'm living proof of what can happen there . . .' He was walking his fingers through the names on the tags as he scanned, and he stopped when he spotted the word 'Cox'. He whipped the file out and had a quick flick through. It contained photos of Tara in the company of various men: at a candlelit dinner; emerging from a car; smooching. Sexton transferred it to the top of the shiny black desk, and went back to the drawers.

'You're going to regret this,' Murray said through a puffed-up face and a bloody nose. His top lip was also swollen. 'You've no idea who you're messing with. You're a dead man walking.'

'Is that a threat?' Sexton asked.

'It's a fact.'

'But at least before you started sneaking around and paying women to tell you what a big man you were, you could hold your head up. Did you know scientists reckon cops have got a community gene? They want to help make things better?'

Murray cleared his throat and spat at him.

Sexton pulled another file. 'What have we here?' he asked. The label read 'Charles Fitzmaurice'. Sexton pulled out a white sheet with grey type on it, and realized he was holding a summons for Charles Fitzmaurice, dated earlier that month and charging him with possession of class A drugs, with intent to sell or supply. According to the document the drugs had been found at an aerodrome in the north of the city.

The last page in the dossier was a court sheet showing the charges had been struck out.

'Jo is going to love this,' Sexton said with a smile, pulling the contents of the two files out, folding them together and tucking them into his inside pocket. He nodded towards Murray. 'Don't go anywhere. We'll be back soon to pick you up.'

44

Big Johnny pulled in on North Great George's Street, and turned to Yolanda, who was sitting in the passenger seat.

'Right, let's get on with it,' he said.

Yolanda took a quick look at the small boy in the back, who was too tiny to even see out of the windows. Pulling the handle, she hurried around to the back passenger door, which she opened so she could pull Presley out. His lungs were whistling between breaths now. His breathlessness had put her heart crossways during the night. Big Johnny had promised her that if anything happened, Fitz would take care of it, but Big Johnny had also assured her he'd tell housekeeping she couldn't work her cleaning shifts while she was minding the boy, and he hadn't. The boss lady had come banging on the door, gunning for her. Then, when Presley took ill, she had started to panic that he might die in the apartment. What if they blamed her for not summoning help?

The last thing she wanted was a police investigation. Supposing they asked her about her tax payments?

Yolanda needed her cleaning job. She'd dabbled in the escort work, but it was irregular and unreliable. She was in her early forties, but looked a lot older. She could see the disappointment in men's faces when she showed up. That was why she liked working in the hotel. She liked having her own place, the uniform, and she needed to save every penny she could to send back home to her mother in Buenos Aires, who was taking care of her twin daughters, who would be in their teens soon. Having Presley around had just reminded her of how the months she'd been away from her own children were stretching into years. But she didn't want to go back yet. There was no work at home. The Irish thought they were in a recession, but they didn't know what poverty was. Yolanda could make in a week here what she did in a year at home, had even got herself some nice clothes for the first time in her life.

'That's my nana's house down there,' Presley said, wheezing.

Yolanda squeezed his hand. 'Do you remember what I said would happen if you talked about where you were?'

Presley nodded.

'What did I say?' she pressed.

He looked anxious. 'You'll come back and take me again,' he said, trying to catch his breath.

Big Johnny got out of the car and walked up to the front door. 'Chop, chop,' he said, ringing the doorbell.

Yolanda gave Presley a little push and told him to hurry.

The front door opened an inch, and from behind a safety chain a worried-looking woman's gaze travelled slowly from Big Johnny to Yolanda, and followed her arm down to Presley. Then the woman jolted the door shut, unlocked it, and flung it open, dropping to her knees and putting her arms out. She was younger than Yolanda had expected.

The kid tried to run in. Yolanda gave Presley's arm a rough tug. 'Not yet,' she warned.

Big Johnny pushed the door open. 'Hello, Gabriella,' he said, like he hadn't a care in the world. 'Stick the kettle on, there's a good girl. You and I need to have a little chat about your daughter. How's Tara doing, anyway? Come round yet, has she? Talking, is she? To tell you the truth, she's caused us quite a spot of bother.'

45

The press conference was held in a hotel on Beresford Place, just around the corner from the station. Two mules were standing on either side of the door demanding mobile phones in return for entry. The room was warm and stuffy, with a long table at the top facing eight rows of seats, ten across, with a centre aisle. Two TV cameras on tripods were blocking the access there, cables trailing after them. The front and second rows had been taken by photographers who were sitting tight, clearly afraid of losing their seats. Jo had regularly seen snappers come to blows while jostling for position outside court, actually knocking each other off their stepladders to get the shot. The journalists were different. It wasn't about one perfect shot for them. They could get more from talking to each other than from hanging around waiting for a single moment.

Jo sat in the centre seat of the big table with the members of her crack team – Lovett and D'Arcy on her left, and Foxy and Darragh Boyle, a press officer attached to the garda press office, on her right. All bar Jo had changed into their uniforms before heading over, civvies transferred to lockers in the station. Nameplates sat in front of each of them, along with microphones propped on stands – though Jo's was the only one switched on.

Jo had requested Darragh Boyle's presence, because she was convinced the journalist behind Tara's interview was going to show. The byline on the story attributed it to a Frank Maguire. Sure enough, when a short, wiry man in a puffa jacket and CAT boots appeared in the corridor while they were waiting outside, Boyle gave her the nod.

Jo watched him walk into the room and place his digital recorder, the size of a cigarette lighter, on the table in front of her, where it joined a cluster of others that had been left there, red lights flashing in anticipation. He headed to the seats to sidle into the third row. The mules outside had been instructed to snaffle his mobile and make copies of his call log and contacts book. Whatever information they gleaned wasn't evidence they were ever going to be able to admit in a court of law, but it would give them a basic steer into whether the Tara Parker Trench story was authentic.

A poster featuring Presley's face had been attached to the front of the desk with the word 'Missing' typed in large print at the top, and giving details of the little boy's height, size and weight. What he was wearing and where he was last seen were detailed in a smaller typeface at the bottom.

Jo and the others had been at their seats for around five minutes when she leaned to her right to tell the press officer she was not prepared to wait any longer, although the room was only a quarter full. Boyle got up to close the door, causing a last trickle of stragglers to appear, cold coffee cups in hand.

'Thanks for coming,' Jo began. 'I'll give you the details first, and then I'll take questions, but for operational reasons I won't be able to answer many. I'm Detective Inspector Jo Birmingham of Store Street Station, and I'm appealing to the public for their help to find this little boy.'

The cameras began to click incessantly, and the flashes made Jo blink more rapidly. Two men, with earphones on and control packs strapped over their shoulders, angled long sound muffs over her head.

'Presley is three years old,' Jo went on, looking intently down the lens of the TV camera. 'He disappeared from the back of his mother's car in the Ever Oil garage on Eden Quay at around 9 p.m. on Sunday night. At this point in time we'd like to withhold the little boy's surname. If you saw anything in the vicinity that night that you thought was unusual, please contact us. Or if anyone knows what happened, and for whatever reason has kept quiet to date about who has taken Presley, please get in touch.'

She leaned forwards. 'But if you are the person holding Presley, please, please talk to us. It's not too late to undo the damage. This little boy needs medication, and we know he must be really missing his mum and dad.'

Jo reached for an enlarged photograph of a pair of miniature running boots from a stack in front of her, and she held it aloft. 'When taken, Presley was wearing a pair of Nike runners just like these . . .' She held up a second photograph. 'A denim jacket with a Tommy Hilfiger label on the inside collar, and a NY Yankees trucker cap, which was white with black lettering.

'We're in the process of contacting everyone in the garage that night. However, we would urge anyone there in the half hour before the snatch, who noticed any unusual behaviour, to get in touch. Did anyone drive by this garage shortly after 9 p.m. and see a car leaving in a hurry or in a haphazard way? Please get in touch.

'We're particularly anxious to connect with employees working at toll bridges, or at ports, stations, or airports. Again, please, look hard at this boy's little face. We need to get him home. Did you see him on Sunday night or since?

'And that is all the information we can give you at this point. You can contact the confidential garda number on 18000 666 111. Thank you.'

Several voices started to shout at once, but Boyle waved them quiet. 'Hands up, and we'll try to get to all of you.'

Most of the hands shot up. But a couple of reporters began to tiptoe out into the corridor to file, Jo presumed.

'Maria,' Boyle said, pointing to a woman in her late thirties whose hair was cut in a bob and who was wearing a wax jacket.

'Are you following any specific lines of inquiry?' she asked.

It was such a soft question that Jo suspected Maria must have done a deal with Boyle to get leads on the story further down the line in return. She could see the agitation in the other reporters' faces. They wanted to know the child's surname, his condition, why his disappearance was only now being made public – and those were just for starters.

'Several,' Jo answered. 'That's why I would once again appeal to anyone involved in this crime to come to us before we come to you.'

Maguire jumped to his feet. Boyle tried to wave him down, but he wasn't having any of it.

'No, I'm sorry, this is not on,' he shouted. 'If you

want us to inform the public, you can start by giving us some real information.'

Boyle tried to point to someone on the other side of the room, but Maguire wouldn't give up. 'I've got a deadline in half an hour. Who was driving the car the child was snatched from, for starters? What was its make, model and registration? And does this case, coupled with the escape of Barry Roberts earlier today, mean that we have now effectively lost the battle for law and order in the city?'

Jo suspected he was trying to confirm that the car belonged to Tara, and that her child was the one missing. But the way he'd connected the Roberts case to what was happening with Tara had sounded an alarm bell in her head, though not in the way the reporter had suggested. Could the drugs she'd found in Tara's car have something to do with Barry Roberts?

'At this point, all I can tell you about the car is that it was a dark-coloured Mini . . .'

A heavy-set female was waving her arm in an agitated manner. 'Where are the parents? We can't write this as human interest without quotes from them.'

Jo opened her mouth to answer, but she was cut off by the sudden opening of the door from the corridor and the appearance of Merrigan, who walked straight up to the podium and hissed something into Boyle's ear.

'What the hell is going on?' Jo whispered to Foxy.

Boyle stood up. 'Good news,' he announced. 'One of the officers attached to the station, Detective Sergeant Fred Oakley, has found the little boy. Thank you all for your patience. It's rare to be able to wind things up this quickly, but extremely welcome, as I know you'll appreciate.'

46

They were in the station ten minutes later. Conscious that the press pack gathering on the steps outside was increasing by the minute, and not knowing why – given that there was no missing child any more – Jo took a couple of officers in the incident room aside, and asked them what had happened. Foxy, Lovett and D'Arcy came with her, all ears.

'Your appeal went out live on one of the afternoon shows. Presley's granny apparently heard it. She rang in immediately to say the boy had been with her all along,' one of the officers – a tall, skinny man – explained.

'Rang in?' Jo said. 'So why was the call put through to Oakley and not to the incident room?'

Lovett shot her a dismissive look that told her exactly why – because of men's blind loyalty to other men when confronted by a female who outranked them.

'It was,' the skinny garda said. 'Oakley was in

here, back at his desk the minute you were gone!'

'Oakley doesn't have a bloody desk in this incident room,' Jo retorted. 'He's not part of the team.'

Dan came into the room, looking stressed and uncomfortable.

'The main thing is Presley has been found,' Foxy said, putting a hand on Jo's shoulder.

Jo was furious. 'He can't be. Presley's grandmother must be lying.'

'That's a bit harsh,' Foxy said.

She rummaged through her pockets. 'I've got a number for her somewhere. Tara gave it to me. I'm going to ring her right now.'

'Is this the first time you've made contact?' Dan asked, frowning.

'It's the first bloody chance I've had,' Jo snapped. 'But I'll make it my priority now.'

'I wouldn't bother,' Dan said. 'Oakley's with her now.'

'Well, he'd better make way for me,' Jo answered.

Dan sighed, his eyes dark and troubled. 'What are you planning, Jo? To create a scene in the middle of what may be the only good-news story of the day? Because if that's the case, I guarantee you the press will pick up on it.'

Jo sat down heavily. 'What I can't understand is: why are so many journalists still hanging around now Presley's been found?'

'Maybe it's because they've cottoned on to who he is,' Dan replied.

Jo felt another jolt of fury. 'And who told them that?' she demanded, looking around to see whether Merrigan was still hanging around.

'I have no idea,' Dan said firmly. 'But let's hope they don't look too hard at this case, or we're all going to end up in the doghouse.'

'I don't know what game Oakley's playing,' Jo said. 'He told me he'd checked Presley wasn't with his nan.'

'That's not the way he tells it,' Dan said.

'So what is his story?' Jo said angrily.

'Standard police checks were not done. He was overruled by you.'

'And you believe him?'

Foxy cut in. 'Let it go,' he said. 'Sort it out later.'

Standing up, she walked into her office, closing the door behind her.

Five minutes later, the sound of a cheer from the street outside caused her to step up to the window and peer out. Oakley was out there, beaming from ear to ear, with a little boy on his shoulders, and a handsome middle-aged woman beside him – who looked startled by the photographers bobbing around her.

Jo watched, arms folded.

Merrigan was there too, tousling Presley's hair, slapping Oakley on the back and smiling for the shots.

Presley seemed well enough, Jo observed, feeling the first wave of relief since she'd taken on the case. He was pale, but clean and well dressed, if slightly wary at finding himself in the middle of a bunch of excited strangers. He had one of those rice biscuits in his little hand, which he was half-hiding behind and half-eating. Jo didn't know what she found harder to believe – the idea that Oakley had found him so easily, or that he had gone to the trouble of thinking of Presley's teeth by giving him the least sugary treat he could find.

Her gaze moved back to Presley's grandmother. *What was it about her that didn't quite fit?* she wondered. She had to have been watching telly at home if she'd got to the station this quickly, which meant she hadn't been in hospital, in the intensive care unit, watching over her critically ill daughter. Jo wasn't going to judge her for leaving Tara's bedside, especially as there were no facilities in the hospital for family members. No, it was the sheepskin coat that was bothering her, she realized. It looked expensive, something you'd expect to see on a woman from one of the more affluent suburbs.

'Somebody got to her,' Jo said, thinking aloud.

'The main thing is that Presley's safe,' Foxy said,

coming into her office. He waited for her to answer, and when she didn't, said quietly, 'Sometimes the bigger thing to do is admit you're wrong.'

'I'm not bloody well wrong,' Jo said, turning on him. 'You, of all people, should know that. You said it yourself when you saw Tara yesterday morning. She was heartbroken.'

Foxy nodded, then glanced at his watch. 'I'm sorry about this, but I'm going to have to head off.'

'You can't. Not now.'

'I've put in my eight hours, Jo. Now I have to get back to Sal.' He swallowed, and Jo noticed how strained he looked. 'Dorothy's back.'

Shocked, Jo covered her mouth, then went over and put her arm around his shoulders. 'You'd better hurry, then. Let me know how you get on.'

Merrigan appeared in the doorway. 'A couple of reporters want to interview Fred Oakley. Your office is the best place to do it in.'

'I bet it is,' Jo said, bitterly.

'What's the matter, Birmingham?' Merrigan said. 'Aren't you going to give Fred his due?'

There was an uncomfortable silence as Jo absorbed the tone.

'It's the only quiet spot,' Merrigan went on. 'Can they have it?'

Jo was about to answer with an 'over my dead body', when there was a commotion outside, and

Oakley, Presley and Presley's grandmother walked into the incident room outside her office. She didn't even know Tara's mother's name, Jo realized. Maybe she was losing her touch . . .

'Getting more like a bloody crèche every day,' a detective called out, triggering a burst of laughter.

Oakley picked the little boy up and swung him up in the air. 'You're a great lad, aren't you, Presley.'

The child wriggled his way back down to the floor.

'Little scamp,' Oakley remarked as Presley took off across the room. 'Here, he'll make an Olympic champion, at this rate.'

Jo made a beeline for Tara's mother, making sure Presley was out of earshot. 'Do you really mean to say that Presley was never in the service station, and that your daughter lied about everything?'

The woman looked scared. But before she had a chance to answer, Oakley put his arm around her and walked her into Jo's office, tipping his head in the direction of a couple of reporters who had just appeared on the floor.

'All's well that ends well, eh?' he warned, keeping up the big man routine, and making Jo's skin crawl. 'Cute little fella, isn't he?'

He signalled for one of the reporters to follow, then closed the door behind him.

Jo walked over to Presley and knelt down beside him. 'You OK, Presley?' she asked, taking his wrist.

The child looked away.

'Where've you been, little man, eh?'

He twisted out of her grip, and started to run around the room.

'You trying to grill a three-year-old now?' Merrigan said, only half-joking.

Jo looked round. The other side of the glass, Dan was zipping up his sailing jacket, looking as though he was getting ready to leave. She stepped outside, and went over to him. 'You can't go. What about Morocco, the footballers, Imogen Cox?'

'Without a missing boy, we've no claim on any one of them,' he answered, looking drained. 'Besides, you said in your briefing Tara was studying to be an actress. For all we know, she was acting for the cameras on that tape. A defence barrister would have a field day. She hasn't even made a complaint. Quite the opposite, in fact. She's sold her story to the media.'

He started to walk towards the door.

'Where are you going?' she asked, keeping up.

'For a drink,' he said, his shoulders hunched and defensive. 'And if you've any sense you'll join me and let it go, too. This case has been a bloody nightmare from start to finish.'

47

Jo sat at a free desk, keeping an eye on how things were panning out in her office. A camera had been set up, and a big floodlight sat on the ground angled upwards. A circle of silver material had been placed on a stand on the other side of the room to bounce the light back. Presley was sitting on Oakley's knee in Jo's chair. His grandmother seemed to have declined to talk, as she was standing behind the camera.

Jo had rung one of the mums with a child in Harry's crèche and called in a favour, asking her to collect Harry and take him home with her, so she could stop watching the clock. She'd also contacted Rory's school to let him know he should stay on for the study hour. Then, she took out the list of the last twenty mobile phone calls Maguire, the reporter who knew so much about Tara Parker Trench, had made and received. As far as she could see, he'd made several to Tara, but she had returned none, at least not from her mobile. Jo would be able to confirm with the phone provider how long the calls to Tara had lasted, which would straight away tell her whether Tara had spoken to him at any length, or cut him off. There were also several contacts to and from an English number that interested her. She dialled it from the phone on the desk, expecting to get through to Melwood Athletic, only to discover it was the office number of a high-profile publicist who handled celebrities when catastrophes struck. The firm had a reputation for damage limitation.

Jo's mobile rang. She answered it and discovered Aishling McConigle was on the other end. 'For the record,' McConigle said, 'Charles Fitzmaurice did book airspace at lunchtime.'

Jo nodded to herself, and thanked her. She turned back to the tape recorder, hoping to become privy to the conversations the reporter had had with the PR man, when something struck her. Standing up, she walked up to her office, and opened the door without knocking, much to the annoyance of the cameraman and the young female reporter in there, who'd been winding up their interviews. Going over to her desk, she picked up the disc she'd watched with the team earlier, showing the CCTV footage taken from the station on Sunday night.

Back outside, she located a CD player, and put the disc in, looking from the image of the shadowy figure on the screen to Presley's grandmother now in her office. Jo checked the screen again, and confirmed what she'd suspected minutes earlier. There was no doubt about it. The squares on the coat worn by the person who'd dropped off the sex tape at the station were the wool ridges you got at the joins on a sheep-skin coat.

48

It was five on the dot when Foxy got home, and ten past by the time he'd washed his hands and stuck Sal's dinner on – coddle, her favourite. He hoped the sausage and bacon dish would cheer her up. She hadn't been herself when he'd collected her, though she wouldn't tell him why. When he called to say the food was ready, she wouldn't come to the table, asking to eat it in front of the telly instead. Foxy felt a twinge of concern. It just wasn't like her to mope about like this. He wondered if the incident in McDonald's with Philip might be playing on her mind, and decided to take a few days' leave in the hope that she'd open up when she was ready.

When the doorbell rang, he waited for the sound of her footsteps – Sal loved answering the door – but when they didn't come, he hurried down the hall himself. He could tell as soon as he saw the shade of red through the frosted glass pane that it was Dorothy.

He closed the living-room door to his right, and grabbed his set of keys from the hall table to let himself out.

'What the hell are you doing calling here?' he asked, opening the door and stepping outside, glancing over his shoulder.

Dorothy had two shopping bags in either hand. 'I just called around, hoping we could have a cup of tea. You wouldn't have to tell Sal who I am. Just say I'm a friend. I've brought cake and biscuits.' She swallowed, and took a breath. 'I didn't want to leave without meeting her.'

'Well, you'll have to. If you meet, it'll be on Sal's terms and not yours. I'm not going to ask her to—'

He'd caught sight of a movement behind him in the hall. Grabbing hold of Dorothy's arm, he walked her down the short driveway that would be lined with the primroses he and Sal had planted when spring came, and opened the gate.

'All right, all right, I'm going,' Dorothy said, her voice shaking. 'Take the chocolate cake for Sal, though. She wouldn't be her mother's daughter without a sweet tooth.'

The front door opened and they both looked round. Dorothy dropped the bags and froze.

'Hello,' Sal said.

'Hello, my darling,' Dorothy said.

'Sal, this is Dorothy,' Foxy explained. 'A lady I used to know when I was a lot younger.'

Looking puzzled, Sal walked slowly down the path towards her mother. Wordless, Dorothy put out her arms, tears streaming down her face.

Foxy stepped forward to try and intercept his daughter, but it was too late – she and Dorothy were holding on to each other like the world was about to end.

A minute passed, then Sal stepped back. Her glasses were off-centre. The lenses had steamed up.

Foxy put his arm around her. 'Let's go back inside, Sal. It was nice to see you again, Dorothy.'

Sal shrugged him off. 'She's my mum, isn't she?' She turned to Dorothy. 'You sound just like the woman who rang me in the day centre today.'

Foxy's heart skipped a beat. 'How could you?' he asked Dorothy. 'How could you do this to me? And to Sal?'

Dorothy sniffed. 'I have a right.'

Foxy's breath quickened, and he took a step towards her.

'Dad?' Sal said, tugging on his jacket. 'Dad? Is there a cake in that bag? Can we eat it now?'

Foxy looked down at her. She seemed calm and her face was back to normal. 'OK,' he said reluctantly. 'Just the one slice, mind.'

'Would you like some tea?' Sal asked, taking her mother's hand.

Together, they walked towards the front door, leaving Foxy at the gate on his own.

49

Jo opened her office door. 'I'm afraid you'll have to wrap it up now, I need to get back to work in here.'

The cameraman had already started to disassemble his equipment, and didn't seem bothered, but the female reporter who'd been left waiting outside her office was seriously put out. 'I haven't had a chance to interview anyone yet. Can we relocate somewhere?'

'I'm sure Fred would be more than happy to oblige,' Jo said. 'I need Presley and his nan to stay here for the time being, though.'

'We'll have finished up in ten minutes,' Oakley protested.

'I don't have ten minutes,' Jo answered.

The reporter took Oakley's tone as a green light to get bolshie. 'I've told my editor the interview with Gabriella Parker Trench is in the bag. He's marked it in for page one. I'm up against the clock now. I'm only a freelance.'

'If your editor gives you any grief, tell him to ring me,' Jo said. 'And give me your card. I'll have a much better story in a few days, I guarantee it.'

The reporter handed over her card, and they left. Jo closed the door behind the lot of them, and gestured to Tara's mother to take a seat. It was clear where Tara had got her good looks.

'I'm so sorry to hear that Tara is in intensive care. You must be worried sick about her. Have they told you any more?'

Gabriella studied her hands. 'She's . . . she's in a coma,' she said shakily. 'On life support. I don't know what to do—'

Jo leaned forwards. 'I'm so sorry.'

Gabriella still didn't look up. 'My beautiful girl brought sunshine from the moment she came into the world. I can't have her remembered as someone who sold herself for drugs. That's not who she was.'

Jo looked over at Presley, who had curled up on one of her chairs, and appeared to be dozing.

'She never wanted for anything,' Gabriella continued. 'She had brains to burn . . . could play the piano . . . She wanted to be an actress.'

'Yes,' Jo said. 'She told me.'

'You know, I was a single mum, too, but I wanted the best of everything for Tara. I scrimped and saved so I could send her to the best school. She saw what the other girls had, heard about their foreign holidays, got invited to their big houses – and she wanted all that, too. It's natural, isn't it? She was so generous. She'd have given you the clothes off her back if you admired them. That was my Tara. She just wanted everything now. And because she had so much attention from men, she always got what she wanted in the end. Mick was the only man who really loved her.

'I was at the end of my tether when he told me what was going on – the other men, the drugs. So I did the tough-love thing. I thought, *This will bring her back to me. She'll hit rock bottom and come back.* She and I – we had this bond. We were like sisters. I was only a teen myself when I had her. That's why I was so dead set against her having, well . . .' She glanced at Presley.

'Like her, isn't he? Got her bad chest, too. The doctors said her system could have handled the cocaine, or could have handled the drink, but the combination of both was too much, and brought on the heart attack.'

A tear ran down her face. 'I'm so frightened that she's not going to make it.'

Jo took Gabriella's hands in hers. 'I want to bring the people involved to justice,' she said. 'But I need your help. Who took Presley? What really happened?'

'Like I said, he was with me,' Gabriella answered, picking up her bag and searching for a tissue.

'Has someone threatened you?'

Gabriella looked up, startled. 'No.'

'Presley, then?'

'I don't know what you mean.'

Jo sat back, and pushed her hair away from her face. 'It was you who dropped in that DVD to the station yesterday morning, wasn't it? You've spent the last few days trying to protect your daughter, and Tara knew it.' She handed Gabriella the slip of paper Tara had written on. 'She wanted me to come to you if anything happened to her or Presley.'

Gabriella was staring at Jo, her face white with shock.

'I'm going to find the people who did this to Tara, with or without you,' Jo went on. 'I want you to have the satisfaction of seeing them in court.'

But a look of terror had crossed Gabriella's face. 'If you have children, for the love of God, never say those words again to anyone,' she whispered. 'Walk away while you still can.'

50

It was almost six o'clock when Jo met Aishling outside Collins Barracks, near Heuston Station, a well-known haunt for hookers cashing in on the passing trade along the quays. The army barracks had been decommissioned years earlier, and the building was now part of the National Museum.

Aishling climbed into Jo's car and rubbed her hands together, blowing into them to warm them up. She'd just spent the last hour or so asking the girls on the street what they knew about any drug dealing going on in the Ever Oil garage further up the Liffey. Jo was really impressed by her initiative. It was lashing rain, and without the windscreen wipers on their fastest setting, impossible to see out.

Jo had bought them both coffee on the way over. Unplugging one of the polystyrene cups from its holder, Jo handed it over. 'Thanks for sticking with the case,' she told the young detective, as Aishling pulled the hood of her waterproof jacket down.

Technically, now Presley had been found, Jo had no right to request anyone to do anything.

'That's all right,' Aishling answered, blowing under the cup's lid, and closing the car door. 'I told you, I like keeping an eye on them.'

She nodded in the direction of a woman standing on the steps of the hotel opposite, sheltering under the entrance canopy, and looking up and down the street at the passing traffic. She was wearing a pair of long, shiny black boots that came up over her knees, a short, tartan skirt that flashed a considerable chunk of white thigh, and a red leather jacket. Her black hair was in a ponytail; it had the static, flyaway look of a wig.

'That's Daisy,' Aishling said, swiping the rain from her face. 'She's got three kids and a mortgage on a very nice place in Tyrellstown. She was a hairdresser until the recession, got laid off a few years ago. Doesn't look forty-five, does she?'

Jo shook her head. 'How'd she get this spot if she's only new?'

'She's two daughters working round the corner,' Aishling answered. 'There's strength in numbers.'

'You take sugar?' Jo asked, offering a sachet.

Aishling shook her head.

Jo watched as Daisy held her handbag up over her head, and ran towards a Fiat Punto that had pulled up in front of her.

'It's only her pimp, Tom,' Aishling said. 'He's an

evil bastard. He'll be asking her what I wanted. Better head off. I don't want to make things any more difficult for her.'

Jo drove around the corner.

'There's Arlene, her eldest,' Aishling said, as Jo parked up. The girl with one hand on her hip, twenty-odd feet in front of them, was dressed in skin-tight red PVC, despite being morbidly obese. She was holding an umbrella that only managed to cover her head and shoulders.

'Crikey,' Jo reacted.

'You'd be amazed by the trade she does,' Aishling said. 'She's busier than the whole lot of them put together.'

'What's her excuse, then?' Jo asked.

'She makes more hooking than she would as a secretary, gets to decide her own hours, and, believe it or not, enjoys it. Now, don't turn around for a look, but behind us is her other sister, Melissa. She's a junkie, and nothing but trouble.'

Jo glanced in her rear-view mirror at the stick insect in denims and a bomber jacket. 'Did any of them have information worth giving?'

'Yeah, but I'm out of pocket fifty euro,' Aishling said, looking worried.

'That's fine,' Jo said, reaching into her own wallet and riffling out a couple of twenties and a ten. 'There you go.'

Aishling nodded gratefully as she folded the notes and tucked them into her jeans pocket. 'Apparently the row in the garage was over protection money which Hassan refused to pay. That's what the trouble was about on the night Presley vanished.'

Jo looked surprised as she sipped at her drink. 'Did you get a name?'

'Daisy mentioned some skinhead named Henry going in there and causing a fuss. Henry is an enforcer for the gang members who broke away from that Barry Roberts's group, after he murdered Joey Lambert in McDonald's earlier this year.'

'Henry,' Jo reiterated, nearly choking on a mouthful of coffee. 'Trust Oakley to get the spelling wrong! He entered his name in as Henly on the system. I thought he must be a toff connected to Charles Fitzmaurice.'

She and Aishling shared a giggle.

'Has Roberts got some connection to the garage?' Jo asked.

'Funny you should mention that,' Aishling said.

'Go on,' Jo encouraged.

'OK, you know the way all the trucks were supposed to bypass the city centre after the Port Tunnel opened?'

Jo crinkled her nose, trying to figure out where this was going. 'Yeah?'

'Well, some trucker who owes Daisy money keeps

filling up in there. She went in screaming like a dervish telling Hassan she was going to report him, and Hassan warned her that the place was protected by Barry Roberts, and to stay away.'

'No wonder the security system's state-of-the-art,' Jo said.

'And here's the best bit,' Aishling continued. 'You remember those three junkies who died on the street last year, after someone mixed rat poison with their gear?'

Jo nodded.

'It wasn't accidental,' Aishling continued. 'The King poisoned the gear because they owed him money. The girls hate him. It could have been any of them. The junkies only owed him two hundred euro between them, and the youngest was barely fifteen. The girls are all willing to testify in court against Barry Roberts. If we can find him, that is.'

51

Dan was sitting on a stool at the bar in Molloy's, with one foot on the brass rail that ran around it, and the other on a free stool in front of him. After dropping Aishling back at the station, Jo had gone looking for him to brief him about the latest developments. She hoped the Barry Roberts link to the investigation would stop him from shutting it down.

He was watching a football match on TV but, judging by the expression on his face, the running commentary from the resident pub expert behind him was doing his head in.

'Come here often?' Jo asked, taking the free stool alongside.

He glanced at her in surprise, and reached for his glass.

Whiskey, Jo realized. Neat. The way she liked it, too, but she couldn't remember the last time she'd seen Dan go to the pub straight after work.

'What are you having?' he asked.

'Just a water for me,' Jo said. 'I'm driving. What's your excuse?'

'I'm staying in a hotel tonight,' he answered. He paused, and looked deep into her eyes.

Jo turned to study the TV. After a few moments she said, 'I never wanted your job, Dan. I'm not saying I don't want to be promoted. I do. Just not at your expense.'

As he knocked back the contents of his glass in a couple of gulps she noticed he needed a shave.

'I wouldn't hold it against you if you did. You've worked hard, made a lot of sacrifices for the job. You should be rewarded. It's only right. You don't owe me anything any more.'

Jo didn't like the way he said it. 'What sacrifices have I made, Dan?'

'Forget it, I wasn't having a go.'

She drew a breath and twisted back around, leaning towards him. 'Dan, we broke up because I wanted another baby, and you didn't. Whatever chance we had of working things out ended when you started seeing Jeanie. For the record, that's our story.'

'That's not how I remember it,' he said, indicating to the barman, who was twisting open a bottle of still water for Jo, that he wanted a top-up.

Jo pounced like a hawk. 'Go on . . .'

'I don't want to fight,' Dan said, as the barman plucked his empty glass off the counter and moved off.

Jo stood up. If she stayed, a row was inevitable; her blood pressure was rising by the second, not to mention her sense of frustration that this bloody man could still affect her like this after everything. She bit the inside of her cheek to hold back. Each time she gave him an inch and tried to reach out to him, in however small a way, he did this – twisted things around. Well, she was sorry she'd even bothered attempting to mend bridges tonight. She couldn't do it any more.

'I just didn't think you were a natural mother,' he said.

She froze, her back still to him, jaw hanging open. Even by the standards their rows had sunk to in the past, the throwaway comment marked a new low.

'All the energy you put into work, you were always so knackered by the time you got in, you'd nothing left to give me and Rory,' he continued. 'I didn't think it was fair to bring another child into it.'

Jo spun around. 'I hope, for your sake, that tomorrow you can put this conversation down to alcohol, because, personally, I couldn't be prouder of the young man I have reared my son to be. Sorry if I wasn't fit to pole dance by the time we got to the bedroom after a day's work. Here's hoping the new mother in your life manages it.'

Dan pinched between his eyes with one hand, and reached out to grab her arm with the other. 'I'm sorry,

I've been under a lot of pressure,' he blurted out.

Jo pulled her arm free. He stood and took a step closer to her. 'Jeanie and I, we've called it a day,' he said, urgently. 'I've just taken it out on you. I didn't mean it to sound like it did, so bitter. You were a great mother – are, I mean. I'm feeling sorry for myself, lashing out. I've lost someone I loved. Have a drink with me? For old times' sake . . . please . . . Jo. Please.'

She sat down slowly, against her better judgement. She didn't want to think about how she'd react if it turned out he was talking about Jeanie when he said he'd lost someone he loved. She was kicking herself for giving him the benefit of the doubt again, presuming he was talking about their relationship. But much as she wanted to go home before he could burst that bubble, she never could be clinical when it came to Dan.

'I've got to leave to pick up the boys in ten minutes,' she said, swallowing. 'I'm sure you and Jeanie will work things out.'

He was lifting the fresh whiskey to his mouth, but he banged it back down. 'Under no circumstances. She's taken me for a right fool. I'm not going back.'

Jo moved her glass of water around in front of her, unable to take a mouthful; her stomach was churning.

'I don't want to end up one of those saddos in a

B & B,' he said. 'Can I come home, just until I find my feet?'

The know-all behind Dan tapped him on the shoulder before Jo could answer, the tips of his fingers stained from nicotine.

'Any sign of Barry Roberts?' he asked. 'He grew up just around the corner from here, you know.'

Dan ignored him. He slid his arm round the back of Jo's stool and lowered his voice. 'I forgot to tell you. I'm going to resign at the end of the week.'

Jo felt like ordering a double herself at that point. 'What?' She held her finger and thumb an inch apart. 'We're this close to proving it's Blaise Stanley in Marrakesh,' she said.

'The case is closed,' Dan said. 'Don't you get it? The rape happened in another jurisdiction.' His eyes slid towards the punter behind him. 'The only investigation anyone will care about from here on in is the one finding Barry Roberts. If it's any consolation, I'm going to put you over that one before I go.'

Jo was all set to fill him in, but the busybody interrupted again. 'Between you and me, it's all over some drugs deal that went sour,' he said. 'Some big businessman on the south side owes the King money. The drugs disappeared in the garage just around the corner from here the other night.' He put a wavering finger to a set of pursed lips and winked.

Jo stared at him. 'Who told you that?' she asked.

'My lips are sealed,' he slurred, adding, 'half his gang live in the flats around the corner.'

Dan reached for Jo's hand, and examined it closely. 'I'll tell you the real story of us,' he said. 'I didn't want to have to share you with another kid. I thought we had the perfect family set-up: just you, me and Rory. I wanted you all to myself.'

The sound of his voice close up like that had the same effect on her it always did. Jo closed her eyes and tried to remind herself that a couple of minutes ago she'd been spitting nails. She finally took a sip of water from her glass.

'How many of those have you had?' she asked him.

'That's my fourth,' he said about the untouched drink on the bar.

'Let's go home, Dan.'

His face softened.

'I only want to make one stop off on the way,' she said, pulling a tape recorder out of her pocket. 'Don't look at me like that. If I don't speak to Kevin Mooney before drawing a line under this case for once and for all, it's going to get between me and my sleep. Afterwards, I'm all yours.'

52

The King ran out of the pub, across the road, and towards a motorbike being gunned by a man in black leathers. He was moving in steady, even paces, his right arm stiff at his side, to keep the Glock semi-automatic he was holding concealed against his dark leather trouser leg.

He was wearing a black motorcycle helmet, and he flicked the visor up so that he could see the small screen his getaway driver held in one hand.

'The signal moved, literally seconds after you left,' the driver said. 'I tried to ring you but you couldn't have heard . . . It's heading south side. It'll take us less than five minutes to catch it.'

'No, one of the customers recognized me,' the King said. 'It'll have to wait. We'll pay Fitz a visit now, instead.'

53

They got to the Triton just after seven. Dan flicked on the central locking, then put his arm casually over Jo's shoulders as they headed for the entrance. She was not going to let herself think about the idea that he might want her back. Jo had had two years of being logical and careful, and in all that time she'd never found another man as attractive as her ex.

In the lobby, she watched Dan hold up his ID for the receptionist and tell her that they wanted a word with Kevin Mooney.

The girl was young, and pretty, but plastered in make-up she didn't need, with her hair pulled back in a severe bun. She jabbed at a keyboard officiously before announcing that there were no guests of that name staying in the hotel.

Dan wasn't having any of it. 'Don't waste my time. It's more likely you've seen him on MTV's Cribs than running about on a pitch on *Sky Sports*, but I know you know who Kevin Mooney is, nonetheless.'

A door set in-between rows of pigeonholes for room keys opened, and a huge man with a walrus moustache filled its doorframe. 'Problem, Fern?' he asked, eyeballing Dan.

'The gardaí are here to talk to Kevin Mooney, Johnny,' she replied.

'Haven't you told them he's checked out?' Johnny answered, flatly.

'He's checked out,' the receptionist said, turning back to face them.

Dan put his two hands on the marble counter and vaulted it. He grabbed the man by the scruff of the neck and banged him against the pigeonholes.

'Who the fuck do you think you're talking to, boy?' Dan demanded. 'Unless you want a raid on this establishment within the next twenty minutes, you can tell me which room he's in.'

'614,' the receptionist blurted out.

Dan moved to the pigeonholes, took the card key he needed and walked out from behind the counter.

In the elevator, Jo stared at him in disbelief.

'What?' he asked.

'Nothing,' she answered, slipping her hands around his waist and leaning in for a smooch. She thought he was sexy as hell.

'I reckon we've got about four minutes before

320

security gets reinforcements up here,' he said, as they exited on to the sixth floor and walked down the corridor looking at the door numbers.

At 614, Jo pressed her ear against the door, and nodded to Dan, who gave it a hard knock. When there was no answer, she stood back and let Dan use the key.

It was a suite, reputed to cost a couple of grand a night, and Jo noted that though it was bigger than your average hotel room it was otherwise pretty bland.

They walked down the hall and found Mooney lying on his bed in flip-flops and tracksuit bottoms, talking on his iPhone and watching TV. His bare chest was hair-free.

'What the hell is this?' he asked aggressively, holding his phone away from his ear. He was handsome in a Liam Gallagher way, with similar levels of just-beneath-the-surface anger.

'Gardaí,' Jo said. 'We'd like to talk to you about what happened in the Atlantis Hotel at the weekend.'

'Are you having a laugh?' Mooney asked.

'Rape is not a laughing matter, Mr Mooney,' Jo said.

Dan took the phone from his hand and powered it off.

Mooney looked annoyed, and got up off the bed.

'It wasn't rape. We paid her,' he said indignantly.

'You paid Tara Parker Trench for what, Mr Mooney?' Jo asked.

'To party,' he answered, in a way that made Jo's skin crawl.

'Arrest him,' Dan said.

'For what?' Mooney reacted. 'I've got a taxi ordered to take me to the airport. I'm training tomorrow.'

'You can forget about that,' Jo said, pulling the tape recorder out of her pocket. 'I've got you recorded saying you paid for sex, and I've also got a video of what you consider consensual.'

Mooney went pale. 'Give me that mobile,' he said to Dan. 'I need to call my lawyer.'

'Look, you've got the Champions League coming up. How about you do us a deal, and in return we forget about this conversation?'

Mooney sat down heavily on the bed. 'What do you want to know?' he asked, earnestly.

54

After checking up and down the corridor, Jo pressed her ear to the door of the suite next door, and then glanced over her shoulder at Mooney, who nodded. Swiping the key pad in the lock, she opened the door to find two girls in two double beds, both pulling sheets up to cover their nakedness.

One of the women – a blonde – stepped out of her bed, which was very ruffled. 'Who are you?' she demanded, her accent Russian.

'Police,' Jo said. 'And we want you to produce your passports and paperwork sharpish, please. And then you can tell us all about who paid your airfare, and brought you here.'

The blonde shot a dagger look at Mooney, who tried to back out of the room but was blocked by Dan's arm.

'Is this a joke?' the blonde demanded. She was wearing only panties, and she covered her breasts with her arms as she moved towards the bathroom door.

'Not so fast,' Jo said, pushing past her and swinging the door open.

Standing in the bath, hiding behind the shower curtain, were two naked men. Jo recognized one of them as being Greg Duncan, the black man on the sex tape. They held their hands over their privates.

'Put some clothes on,' Dan told them, reaching for a phone to dial the station.

The brunette in the second bed started to cry. She had the features of a Romanian national – dark eyes and hair, olive skin. 'I can't believe this is happening,' she sobbed.

'Right,' Jo said. 'We're arranging squad cars to bring you back to the station, and we'll be needing statements. You'll be asked about any other bookings for tonight, who you're working for, and whether you've been here before. Let's try and get this over with as quickly as possible.'

Jo walked over to a dresser and looked at the little heap of charlie sitting on the counter. She clicked her tongue. 'We might be able to do a deal on the drugs charges if you all come clean on the prostitution racket.'

'I would have done it for free just to say I'd been with any of them,' the brunette said, weeping loudly.

The blonde walked over and put her arms around

324

her. 'We could have sold our stories to a newspaper and made a fortune. We'll know next time.'

'We're models,' the brunette told Jo.

'Course you are,' Dan said.

'Which reminds me,' Jo said, sliding her hands over the surfaces of the walls, and stepping up on a bed to reach the higher spots.

'You see a camera anywhere?' she asked Dan.

The brunette pointed to the light over a picture on the wall.

Jo high-fived Dan as she walked over and spoke directly into it. 'Who's a pretty boy then, Fitz?' she said. 'We'll be after you, next, so don't get too comfortable.'

55

The King was in the Triton, his revolver pressed so hard against Fitz's forehead that the metal had made a red, round ring imprint in the skin. Grunting, he moved the gun to Fitz's lips and pushed it into his mouth. Fitz's eyes bulged out further as he looked over at Big Johnny, who was lying spreadeagled on his front on the hotel bedroom floor, hot blood oozing from a bullet hole in the back of his head.

'This is the last time I'm going to ask you,' the King said. 'And I want you to think very carefully before you answer. 'What are you going to give me back first – the money you owe me, or my drugs?'

Fitz gagged on the gun as he tried to speak, then pointed a trembling hand at the wall. The King lowered the gun, and pulled an ornately framed painting down, tossing it to one side to reveal a small safe.

Slowly he raised his arm and cocked the weapon,

then looked over his shoulder and saw the look of hope in Fitz's eyes.

'You should have told me it was bulletproof,' he said, pointing the gun back at Fitz. 'It might have caused me a nasty accident.'

'Wait,' Fitz rushed. 'There's only ten thousand euro in it. But I know a way you can recoup ten times what you lost.'

He told the King about the footballers in the hotel, and the videos he'd made of them with his girls.

The King tilted his head. He wasn't interested in match-fixing. That could take months. He wanted his money or his drugs. Now.

Grinning, he slid on the silencer and squeezed the trigger. The tracker he'd put with the drugs would tell him exactly where they were. He didn't need Fitz any more. It was more important to send out a message: *if you try to double-cross the King, you pay with your life.*

56

After they left the hotel, Jo drove in silence through the bus lanes, negotiating the city's traffic. She'd attached the flashing Special Branch blue light to the roof of the car, to weave in and out of lanes when buses and taxis blocked her path. She didn't talk for a while, either. There was too much to think about. Kevin Mooney had confirmed that Blaise Stanley had been in Marrakesh the night Tara was raped. It was all starting to come together.

'You should give Sexton the Barry Roberts case,' she said eventually, checking Dan's reaction.

'Absolutely no way,' he answered.

'He needs to get his teeth stuck into something,' Jo said. 'Gangland is his speciality. It's the sort of case he'd be really good at.'

Gangland murders accounted, on average, for a third of the annual violent death rate, but in the last year Barry Roberts had been responsible for increasing that percentage to half. Also, he had to have intimidated at least one judge, and several gardaí, to get around charges in the past. A prison officer who'd fallen foul of him had been shot dead on his doorstep. There was no question about who was responsible, but there was no evidence, either. He was one of those people who made Jo reconsider her views on the death penalty. He'd hurt so many others that he was like a cancer on society. In her view he needed to be removed.

But Dan's face had hardened. 'You don't have to tell me anything about Sexton's needs.'

Jo recalled Sexton had once had a soft spot for Jeanie, and wondered at Dan's tone now. She decided not to pursue it. Every time they talked about Jeanie, she felt a surge of jealousy, and they ended up fighting.

She pulled out her phone at a traffic light and dialled Rory's school, to discover he'd headed home alone. 'I cannot believe there was no escort for the Roberts prison trip,' she complained, dialling Rory's mobile, and screwing up her face as she listened to the sound that meant it was dead.

'That would have been Blaise Stanley's decision, too,' Dan said.

Jo didn't want to think about how they were going to deal with Stanley, or what they were going to have to do next. Her head was already spinning from all the new developments in the case.

She phoned the mum who'd collected Harry and sighed heavily when voicemail cut in. She left a message saying they were on their way.

She tried Rory's number again, but got the same sound. Rory's phone rarely had any credit. She dialled the home number again, which rang out.

Dan switched on the two-way radio, to pick up any dispatches between stations.

'Listen,' he said, tweaking up the volume as Jo disconnected her call.

In-between the static, Jo heard a discussion about Barry 'King Krud' Roberts, who'd been seen in Molloy's pub that evening – the same pub she and Dan had been drinking in.

'What time did they say?' Jo asked Dan.

'About half an hour ago,' he replied, glancing over. 'Must have been in only minutes after we left.'

She felt a jolt of fear and tried her phone again, one-handed.

She noticed Dan was checking his wing mirror. Dan was normally unflappable. If he was worried, so was she.

'The old man in the pub said Roberts was from that area,' she said, trying to be logical. 'Maybe that's why he was there.'

The sound of an urgent message from Donnybrook Station radioing a squad car made Dan glance over at her in concern. There'd just been a double shooting in the Triton.

Jo's fingers tightened on the steering-wheel. She had no doubt that 'King Krud' was on the rampage, and she and Dan were now on his hit-list. They had to get home and find Rory – fast.

57

Foxy was trying to lip-read what the RTÉ news presenter was saying as Sal giggled and repeated her mother's words.

'Do me a cheesy quaver . . . favour. Dad, cheesy quaver means favour, doesn't it?'

'Yes.' Foxy smiled.

Dorothy was fussing, topping up the tea he didn't want after the three-course meal she'd made, and offering more cake. He couldn't make himself comfortable on the chair, but nothing needed doing. The milk jug was full, there were spoons for the sugar – Dorothy had ordered him to sit down, and then seen to everything.

'Sal, maybe you could go to your Irish dancing class this evening, now you're feeling better,' he said.

'Will you collect me, Mum?'

Foxy shook his head and opened his mouth to object, but Dorothy had already agreed. He looked back at the TV. That bastard Barry Roberts had escaped.

Sal was looking at him expectantly, like she was waiting for his answer.

'Sorry, love, what did you say?'

'I asked: do you want to come, too?' she said.

'We'll see,' he answered.

The image on the screen was of a reporter good-looking enough to have been a Hollywood actress, talking to the camera while intermittently gesturing back to a cordoned-off section of the M50. Foxy leaned forward. He reached for the remote and turned the telly up.

A ticker-tape headline flashed across the bottom of the screen, filling him in as the reporter started to interview some shocked hotel guests. Two people had just been gunned down at the Triton Hotel.

'Jesus,' Foxy muttered.

'Do. You. Like. Mickey. Mouse?' Dorothy was asking Sal.

'Sal has the most fantastic hearing,' Foxy remarked, still staring at the box.

'Mickey Mouse is for babies,' Sal answered. 'My favourite band is Westlife. My favourite TV show is *Hannah Montana*. My favourite film star is Robert Pattinson. He's drop-dead gorgeous.'

'Ahem,' Foxy said.

'Oh, except I'm not allowed to watch any of his

scary things.' Sal giggled again and put a finger to her lips. 'But I have, Mum. Don't tell Dad.'

Dorothy's face lit up.

'What do you like, Mum?' Sal asked.

'Well, I suppose I like singing most. I used to want to be a singer years back.'

'What stopped you?' Foxy asked, standing, and looking around for the phone.

'There was no *X Factor* back then.' Dorothy sighed.

'That's my all-time favourite programme,' Sal said, contradicting herself excitedly. 'After *Dancing On Ice*, and *Deal or No Deal*.'

Foxy blocked his daughter's hand with his, mid-air. 'That's enough cake, missy,' he said. 'You won't be able to manage your Irish dancing if you keep that up.'

'Last bit,' she promised.

The TV camera flicked to the sight of the coroner arriving at the scene.

'What's up?' Dorothy asked.

'There's been a development in the case I'm working on,' he answered, lifting up the couch cushions. 'I need to ring Jo. Has anyone seen the phone?'

Dorothy walked over to the mantelpiece and lifted it up. 'This it?'

He reached over and took it off her.

'If you need to head off, I can bring Sal to Irish dancing if you like,' she said.

Sal beamed. 'Please, Dad, please, please, please . . .'

Foxy was holding the phone to his ear, having dialled Jo's number, but it was engaged. 'Actually, that would be a great help. Thanks.'

Dorothy smiled, and picked at something on the neck of his jumper. 'You've put it on inside out, you big ninny,' she said.

Sal laughed.

After kissing his daughter on the forehead, Foxy reached for his coat and held his arms out stiffly in protest as Dorothy hugged him.

58

Even though they found Rory safe at home, and getting through his homework in his room, Jo's stomach still churned with anxiety. They had collected Harry, who was nodding off on Dan's chest as he pushed back a corner of the curtain and peered out at the street. Every now and then Dan would glance at the news on the TV, which he had on in the background, the volume turned down low. Barry Roberts's prison mugshot was in the top right hand of the screen as images – of the smashed-up prison van, the spent cartridges still on the road from the gunfire, and the courthouse – played on the screen. One of Dan's hands was spread across most of Harry's back. Jo held her breath. She felt as if she was looking at what life could have been like if she hadn't spent the last two years alone. She walked over, bent down, and touched Dan's back gently.

'Give him here,' she said, reaching for Harry. Dan stood up to help the transfer, and stretched his arms over his head when it was complete.

'Have you packed what you need?' he asked quietly. 'We have to get the boys out of here.'

Jo held Harry tightly in her arms. They knew from a phone call Dan had made in the car who the victims in the Triton were – Charles Fitzmaurice and a security man called Johnny, the same one they'd seen in the reception area of the hotel. She needed time to think, but there wasn't any.

'Can we have dinner first?' she asked. 'It is eight o'clock.'

'No,' Dan answered, firmly.

Jo continued down the hall, and laid Harry out on his back in his bed, flicking the night light on as she pulled off his clothes as gently as she could to change him into his pyjamas. He was wiped out, and didn't stir. She looked around for his overnight bag, spotted it on the floor, and lifted it on to the bed to check its contents. Hearing Dan's voice in Rory's room, Jo lifted Harry as she headed back out, and stuck her head in to see Rory packing up his books.

'How about you take Becky for that dinner tonight, and we'll collect you later?' Jo asked quietly.

Rory looked over to check Dan's reaction.

Dan nodded. 'That's a good idea, son. We need you out of the house for a few hours, just as a precaution. It's probably nothing.'

As Rory left the room to ring Becky, Jo sat down

on the bed, rocking Harry gently. 'I don't know why Barry Roberts was in Molloy's so soon after us,' she said. 'But there are any number of reasons why he targeted Charles Fitzmaurice.'

'Yes,' Dan said, taking the overnight bag from her arm, hooking it over his own shoulder, and transferring a bulky folder from his pocket into the bag, before kneeling down beside her. 'Of course.'

Jo closed her eyes as Dan reached for her hands. She rolled her neck.

'What if we could turn back the clock?' he asked. 'Would you have done anything differently?'

She kept her eyes closed. 'I'd have tried harder to make it work between us. What about you?'

'I'd have insisted you take pole dancing classes,' he said, making her smile.

A loud bang outside made her heart skip a beat.

'What the hell was that?' Dan said, jumping up and letting the bag slip to the floor.

As he headed to the front door, Jo picked up the bag, and reached for the item he'd just put in, which was sticking out of the top. Curious, she pulled it out. It was a Manila folder with 'Barry Roberts Case' written across it. She opened it. Inside were a few printouts – and the evidence bag she'd given him that morning, with the tracking device still sealed inside.

59

Five minutes felt like five hours as Jo called for Rory to get in the car. Harry wasn't impressed at being woken, and though she tried to soothe him on the move, he seemed to pick up on her own anxiety – rubbing his eyes and wailing. Jo ran down the hall, grabbing the car keys and her mobile. She opened the front door a fraction, and called Dan's name over the sound of Harry's irate cries, but got no answer.

'What's the matter, Mum?' Rory demanded.

'Get in the car. Now,' Jo ordered.

'Where's Dad? What about Dad?'

Jo didn't answer. It was pitch dark outside and the floodlight that normally came on didn't. She handed Harry to Rory and put the car into reverse the second his door closed. He barely had time to click a belt on.

Dialling Sexton's number, Jo pressed the phone to her ear as she started to drive. If she could get the tracking device out of here, maybe she could lure whoever was around away from Dan.

'I'm glad you rang, I need to brief you about what Murray Lawlor's been up to,' Sexton said.

'Not now,' Jo answered, panic-stricken, as she shifted the car into first gear.

'We can't leave Dad,' Rory shouted.

'What's the matter?' Sexton asked.

'Dan's in trouble,' Jo said.

'I'm on my way,' Sexton answered.

'No! Get a unit over. I'm driving the boys out of here. Dan may be hurt.'

'Why do you say that?' Sexton asked, sounding alarmed.

'He went outside, and he hasn't come back.' Jo said. 'I think Barry Roberts has got him.'

60

Jo was about five miles from home, waiting for a red light at the junction of Foster's Avenue on the N11 to change, when she heard the first faint hint of a siren in the distance.

Rory was giving her the silent treatment, still furious about leaving Dan behind, but at least he and Harry were safe.

As soon as the flashing lights came into view, she flicked on the indicator, locked hard on the steering, and crossed the lanes to U-turn over to the far side of the road, pulling up outside the Radisson Hotel. She waited for the squad car to pass, keeping her car in gear, her right foot pressed to the clutch. She opened the window and half-turned, catching sight of Harry fast asleep in the back as she dropped the tracker on the street. Then she sped off in hot pursuit.

Twelve minutes later she parked up behind the squad car in her own drive to find Sexton already there, standing in her front door, shining a torch out. Every light in the house was on.

'Have you found Dan?' she called, as Rory jumped out and ran up to Sexton, who shook his head in response.

Rory flapped his arms in frustration, and tried to head into the house.

'Stay where I can see you,' Jo told him.

Rory grunted something inaudible back. Goose-bumps spread up her back. If anything bad had happened to Dan, he was never going to forgive her.

Oakley climbed out of the squad car she'd just followed. Jo lowered her window a fraction to let some fresh air in for Harry – still asleep in the back – and locked the car doors.

She held her hair off her face as she walked up to join Oakley and Sexton, noticing that the front door looked like it had been kicked in.

'Don't worry, I did that,' Sexton said.

Oakley pulled out his notebook, checked his watch, and noted the time. 'What happened?' he asked, still studying the pad.

Jo felt herself choke up. She took a deep breath and talked through the wobble in her voice. 'Barry Roberts followed us to Molloy's, the Triton, and then here,' Jo said. 'We heard a noise and Dan went outside and Roberts did something to him, I know he did. We've got to set up road blocks, get the air-support unit out, try and find him.'

'One thing at a time,' Oakley said, pen cocked. 'Did you see Roberts?'

'She didn't see anyone,' Rory complained.

Jo shook her head. 'We're wasting time here . . .'

'Sorry, was that a "no" you didn't see him?' Oakley asked Jo officiously. 'We have to be completely clear about what you're saying here.'

'Why? So you can lie about it later?' Jo snapped.

'No. Because you rate instinct too highly. Police work's about facts,' Oakley said.

Jo gritted her teeth. 'The fact is, no, I did not see Roberts, but yes, he was there.'

Sexton put his arm around her.

'How do you know?' Oakley asked.

'Because there was a tracking device in my car,' Jo said. 'And he was following it.' She hadn't wanted to mention the tracking device, because doing so might get Dan into trouble. But there was no help for it now. She knew he'd had a lot on his mind, but he should have handed it in to forensics.

'So where is this device now, then?' Oakley said.

'I threw it out of my car outside the Radisson Hotel.'

'So we've just got to take your word for it?' Oakley said.

'Use your noggin,' Sexton told Oakley, frowning.

'Where do you think Dan is? I'll call in the request for road blocks. Jo. You get yourself inside and I'll get you a cup of tea.'

Jo looked towards the car. 'I have to get Harry,' she said.

Jo took the sofa, blocking Harry from rolling off it, while Sexton carried in a mug of tea which he handed to her before sitting on the arm of a chair opposite.

'No thanks,' Jo said.

'Drink it,' he insisted.

Jo took it from him and put it on a side table. The room was shadowy, the only light falling in from the kitchen. She wanted it that way so Harry could sleep.

'The main thing is not to panic,' he said. 'We think Roberts may have been on a motorcycle, and if he was he couldn't have taken Dan anywhere. Describe the noise you heard outside for me.'

'It was like a . . . gunshot,' Jo said. 'We have to get out there and look for him! He could be lying out there now, injured, or worse.'

'You're jumping to conclusions, Jo.'

'Please, Gavin, if that moron Oakley is allowed to handle this he'll make a balls of it. Please.'

'Don't worry, there are two ERUs on their way.' Sexton was referring to the emergency response unit, an elite squad of trained marksmen.

'But Oakley . . . ?'

Foxy arrived, breathing hard, before Sexton could answer. 'I just heard. What's going on?'

Jo burst into tears.

'They've hurt Dan, I know they have. He wouldn't have left me and the boys alone in the house.'

Oakley came into the room and cleared his throat. 'Has Dan ever gone missing before?'

'No . . . Yes . . . Dan would never have left his boys like that, no matter what was going on between us,' Jo said.

Oakley flicked on the light, and Harry whimpered. 'Turn it off,' Jo said.

'Where did he go the last time?' Oakley asked, moving to the mantelpiece where he picked up a picture of Rory and Harry, angled it into the light coming through the door, and studied it.

Jo felt a stab of anger. She looked at Foxy but knew from his expression she'd have to answer.

'Some hotel,' she said reluctantly.

'For how long?' Oakley asked, making a note.

'Three nights,' Jo said.

Oakley tucked his pen and pad in his pocket. 'When was this?'

'Look, how is it relevant?' Jo demanded.

'He has been under a lot of pressure lately with the report about to come out,' Oakley said.

'How do you know about that?' she snapped.

'Easy, Jo,' Foxy said. He turned to Oakley. 'Why don't you make a start on the neighbours?' he suggested.

The gravel outside the house crunched as another car approached. Oakley moved to the window and drew back the blind. 'It's the dog unit,' he said.

Jo drew a breath. The dogs were trained to pick up the scent of death. 'We need to get Harry out of here,' Foxy said. 'You can bring him to my house, and let him sleep there. Sal's great with him, and Dorothy's there. You can come back later, if you like.'

'Roberts could still be around,' Jo said.

'How do you know that?' Foxy asked. 'He could be anywhere by now. He's probably followed the tracker.'

The sound of the dogs barking excitedly made Oakley raise his eyebrows. He and Sexton hurried outside.

Jo stood, but Foxy stopped her from following. 'It mightn't be anything.'

Dazed, she headed down the hallway towards the kitchen, then stopped as Oakley reappeared.

'Do you know what blood type Dan is?' he asked.

61

Foxy put on a brave face for Jo's sake, but secretly feared the worst. The blood the dogs had found a few hundred yards down the road was AB, which was Dan's. A DNA analysis could confirm whether or not it was Dan's, but would take days to process.

Rory reacted to the news like the young man he now was. He took Foxy aside and told him that the main thing was to keep his mother busy. He was his father's son, Foxy thought, promising him he'd keep an eye on her.

Jo looked washed out. Foxy didn't try to patronize her by telling her everything would be all right. Jo had been on too many doorsteps herself to know that the only thing worse than coping with sudden loss was being given false hope.

Because she had the boys with her, Foxy was able to persuade her to leave the scene and come back to his place. He wanted her to stay the night, but he only had two bedrooms, and Jo wasn't willing to accept a bed if it meant putting someone else on the floor. She needed her own space, she assured him, and left to go to a hotel several hours later, with the boys.

Foxy looked at Dot with changed eyes after they were gone. She had been a rock during the commotion, keeping the tea on tap, and even though nobody had been able to eat, the smell of her bacon sandwiches had been comforting. Sal had slept through all of it, allaying his main concern, which was that he'd have to explain the concept of evil to an innocent like her. He'd always tried to tell her the truth.

'Come here,' Dot said as he waved Jo off and closed the front door. She patted the seat on the couch beside him. He noticed a bright throw had appeared on the worn green velvet cushions. There was a new picture on the wall, too, he realized.

'They'll find Dan,' Dot promised, rubbing his back. 'I know they will, I can feel it in my waters.'

Foxy pressed his hands to his face. They'd find Dan all right, but if Barry Roberts was involved, he wouldn't be alive.

'I blame this King chap's parents,' Dot said.

Foxy had had too long a day to explain how ridiculous this remark was, especially coming from her.

'We've got ASBOs in England to nip any delinquency in the bud before it takes hold,' she continued.

He knew she was trying to make him feel better, but he just wanted to sleep, and the couch was his only option now that she was going to stay in his bed.

He sighed. 'We've got them here, too.'

'Where did it go wrong, then? For someone like Roberts, I mean? Bet you'll find he was abused as a kid. It desensitizes them. Makes hurting other people easy. Do you think he's mad or bad?'

'Who knows?' Foxy said. He didn't care. He just wanted to stretch out on his side and sleep. Come first light the search would begin again.

'Anyway, cocaine has had its heyday,' Dot said. 'It's all head-shops now, that's why the drug dealers are burning them out. Too much competition.'

Foxy stood up. 'Look, I need to get some bedding for in here.' He hoped she'd take the hint, and leave him to sleep.

'No need to do that,' Dot said.

'I told you you could have a bed tonight, and a bed you will have,' he said.

'That's not what I meant,' Dot said, putting her hand on his. 'I know you've still got a double. There's more than enough room for the two of us. And you might not need a cuddle tonight, but I certainly want reminding that the world's not all bad.'

62

Deeply shocked by Dan's disappearance, Sexton went back to collect Murray Lawlor from his office. It was tearing him up that someone he cared about, a good, decent person like Jo, should be targeted by the very criminals she was protecting the public against. His emotions hardened to anger as he entered the building, using the set of keys he'd taken with him earlier.

What he saw there made his knees go from under him.

Murray was still in his chair, but now a black circle on his forehead showed exactly how close the gun had been. His jaw hung slack, and his lifeless eyes stared upwards.

Sexton drove to Charles Fitzmaurice's home like a man possessed. Tara had told him that Fitz was in this up to his eyes, and even though Fitz was dead, his family might still be worth talking to.

Hugo Fitzmaurice opened the door.

Sexton burst in, taking him by surprise, and twisted his arm high behind his back, slamming him up against a woodpanelled wall and squashing his face sideways.

'Let me go. I want to find Barry Roberts as much as you do,' Hugo grunted. 'I know exactly where that toe-rag will surface.'

Wednesday

63

Jo didn't sleep, although she longed to. Staying awake was like a living nightmare. Her thoughts were so dark that her heart felt permanently lodged in her throat. What had they done to Dan? Was he alive and suffering? Was he dead? They must have hurt him, he'd never have gone without a fight. What if he needed urgent medical attention? What if he was somewhere within reach but unable to call out? What if Roberts came back to get the boys? How would she protect them? She couldn't watch over them twenty-four seven, and even if she did, she would be powerless against the King and his cronies.

She sat up in her hotel bed. She couldn't switch on the light, because the boys were asleep beside her, but she couldn't keep still, either. She went into the en suite, shut the door, and sat on the edge of the bath. Something about the sparkling glass and blue tiles in there made happy memories of her life with Dan suddenly flood into her mind. She remembered a dazzlingly hot day on holiday by the sea, and Dan splashing in the water with Rory; lying in bed on a Sunday, a shaft of sunlight across the sheets, her body wrapped in Dan's arms; the warm, intoxicating scent of Dan's skin. She started weeping, wiped the tears angrily from her cheeks, and ran herself a glass of water from the tap. But she was too tense to swallow.

The questions came so thick and fast that she felt as if she'd run a marathon. The 'what ifs' were eating her up inside, and she paced up and down the little room, her emotions ranging from complete terror, to anger, to paralysis. She wanted to curl up and wait for everything to end so she could cope. What if it was already too late? What was she going to do without Dan?

64

Jo pulled in at the Triton just after eight, having dropped Harry off at his crèche and Rory at school, in spite of his protests. He was taking it as an affront that life should go on when his father was still missing, but Jo needed to be able to concentrate solely on finding Dan, without having to look after her children. Her head was not in a good place. The more time passed without him making contact, the worse her fears.

The hotel was sealed off, but Foxy was standing at a mobile chip van handing a fiver over.

'Jo, how are you?' he asked.

She gave him a nod.

He took a coffee and offered it to her. She shook her head.

'Now that's what I call enterprise,' Foxy said about the chip van, talking through the awkward silence between them, as if he hoped it would lift her spirits. 'The driver heard the news and headed here in anticipation of gathering press.' He pointed to the far side of the road. 'There's quite a few already, should be more as the day progresses, I presume. Look, there's something you should know . . .'

Jo glanced over at the reporters. She could make out Ryan Freeman, the crime reporter whose daughter's kidnap had played a part in Jo's last big case. She hadn't seen Ryan since, but she waved back when he saluted her. He was a short, overweight man, his hair in permanent need of a cut. His donkey jacket pockets were always overflowing with rolled-up newspapers and spiral notebooks. 'Oh shit, he's coming over,' Jo said. 'That's all I need.'

'Come on,' Foxy said, pointing the way along a series of gangplanks that had been set up around the hotel so as not to disturb potential evidence.

'I'll just ask him how his daughter, Katie, is. You go ahead. If he sees you, he'll try and get a line out of you.'

'Jo, how are you?' Ryan asked. He took her hand and kissed her cheek.

Foxy turned his back and carried on into the hotel.

'I'm good,' Jo answered. 'How's Katie?'

'She's a different child now, you wouldn't recognize her.'

'I'm glad. And Angie. How's your wife doing?'

Ryan scratched his chin. 'Angie and I . . . we're not together any more. We couldn't get over what happened with Anto Crawley.'

'I'm sorry. Well, tell Katie I was asking for her.' Jo turned to follow Foxy.

'So how come you're involved in this one anyway?' Ryan asked after her.

'I was just passing,' Jo said over her shoulder.

'You'll have heard the rumours about what was going on in the hotel Fitz owned?'

Jo stopped in her tracks and turned around.

'Gangland's not your area,' Ryan continued. He sounded like he was still working it out. 'You and I both know this is connected to another of your investigations. Tara Parker Trench. Is there anything else going on I should know about?'

Jo shrugged. 'You tell me.'

Ryan walked up to her. 'For old times' sake, you'd better watch your back, Jo. It's more than my job's worth to tell you this, but I owe you a hell of a lot more than my job.'

'What do you mean?'

'I mean Charles Fitzmaurice was a big fund-raiser for the justice minister during his election campaign. Blaise Stanley wouldn't have weathered any association.'

'Christ!' Jo said, unnerved. She was going to need Stanley to approve any dragnet to find Dan.

'I thought you might have guessed something was going on – you know, what with Fred Oakley succeeding Dan.'

Jo took a deep breath to steady herself, then, nodding goodbye to Ryan, walked quickly towards the hotel.

Foxy was in the lobby, waiting for the lift. 'So when were you going to tell me about Oakley?' she asked.

Foxy checked to see how she was taking it. 'I'm sorry,' he said. 'He's been made acting head.'

'Don't,' Jo said. 'Blaise Stanley is the only one who's going to regret it.'

The crime scene was heavily taped, with pools of dark blood on the carpet where Fitz and his security man had been murdered.

'Johnny Nash,' Foxy said. 'He worked at the Triton.'

'Yeah,' Jo answered. 'I met him.'

'He had a few convictions for GBH,' Foxy said.

Jo walked round Fitz's outline and out into the corridor. Two detectives were there, their backs to her.

'You heard about Oakley?' one asked.

'Yeah – and the chief,' said the other.

'I heard his days were numbered even if Roberts hadn't seen him off,' said the first.

When they realized who was behind them, their embarrassment was palpable.

Jo tapped the nearest on the chest. 'You use Chief Superintendent Dan Mason's name and title if you ever mention him again, or I'll have you up before a disciplinary committee,' she said. 'Neither of you was fit to shine his boots.'

What scared her more than her anger – she could have happily swung for them – was her own use of the past tense.

65

Back in her office, Jo put the sex tape safely into her bag, aware that a man's suit jacket was draped over the back of her chair. She sat down in front of the computer and clicked on Jeanie's email logo. She was guessing that if Oakley was now acting head, she wouldn't have this office for much longer.

The computer clock read 10 a.m. Glancing up regularly to make sure no one was coming, Jo used the arrow key to bring the cursor down through the subject lines in Jeanie's email box until she found something she hoped might help her. It had been sent from Dan's email on Monday and was entitled 'Tom Burke complaint'.

A rap on the door made her look up. *Speak of the devil*, Jo thought. Oakley filled the doorway. He was seriously running to fat.

'Great,' Jo muttered, double-clicking the email open. When the computer didn't react, she double-clicked again, aware that the whirring noise it was making as it tried to catch up with her command was not a good sign.

'How many men are you allocating for the search party to find Dan?' she asked, staring at the frozen screen. The bloody cursor wouldn't move, and the little egg-timer logo had stopped spilling grains of sand. *Do not crash on me now*, she willed it, clicking furiously.

'I'm going to have a meeting shortly, to decide just that,' he said, clapping his hands together and looking around.

'Not another meeting!' Jo objected.

'I wanted a word, actually,' he said, shifting uncomfortably. 'I can't put you on the case. You know how it is.'

'Have you lost your mind?' Jo flared, about to put her left thumb and two fingers on the CTRL, SHIFT and Escape buttons, just as the email opened. She scanned the contents.

'You're too conflicted to work on it,' he said. 'You could always apply for compassionate leave, if you're too upset to work, of course.'

The email was addressed to Fred Oakley from Dan, and Jeanie had been cc'd into it. It read:

Further to the complaint to the garda ombudsman by a member of the public about your failure to investigate vital information, I am informing you that it is claimed that you were told a week ago that a paedophile who'd failed to adhere to the terms of his release and register as per the Sex Offenders Act was living beside a local national school, and that you did not immediately act on this information. Please be advised that no evidence could be found to support this allegation. The complaint therefore has not been upheld.

Oakley was unplugging the DVD player so he could take it from the office. He seemed more concerned with rearranging the furniture than finding Dan, as far as Jo could see. She was about to object again, but the contents of the screen reeled her in. She read:

PS For your information, Fred, you're only off the hook because I called someone in the ombudsman's office to tell them about last night, and they agreed to make it look like you did initiate an investigation and found Burke as a result. But let this be a note of caution for the future. Any sightings of criminals, or information on criminal activity that's supplied to any individual officer, must be acted upon or passed on at once to avoid cock-ups. Dan.

'Problem with the computer?' Oakley asked, moving towards Jo's side of the desk.

'Nope,' she answered, reaching round to the wall for the flex, and pulling it out.

Nothing happened for a couple of seconds, but as Oakley leaned over her to have a look at the screen it finally went blank.

Jo stood up and put her finger on his chest. 'I know all about the complaint against you – about your failure to investigate that paedophile, Tom Burke. You may have got away with pretending it was my fault Gabriella Parker Trench wasn't interviewed on Monday, but this time I've proof of your incompetence. If you even suggest taking me off Dan's case, Fred, I promise you, I'll get in touch with the garda ombudsman myself, with my own complaint. Don't get too attached to your new office, I've a feeling it's about to bring you as much luck as mine did.'

Sexton bumped into her as she was leaving the station.

'Jo, I think I know where Roberts could be hiding,' he said urgently. 'I'm going to go and check it out.'

'I'm coming with you,' she answered.

'No, I'll ring you if anything turns up. You need to talk to Tara. She's recovered consciousness.'

66

Tara had been transferred from intensive care to the special observation unit of the hospital. Jo had tried not to cry since Dan had disappeared, but the smell of disinfectant being sluiced along the corridor by a cleaner made her eyes brim. She brushed the tears away. Buried memories of her father's death were never far from the surface. The thought that Dan might end up recovering somewhere like this, because someone had set out to hurt him, chilled her more than any accident ever could. He was a good, decent man and if she got the chance to have the honour of having him back in her life, she was never going to let him go again.

She looked into each room as she continued down the ward. After a couple of passers-by glanced at her curiously she realized she'd been whispering, 'Please let Dan be all right,' to herself as she walked.

Tara was in a private room, propped up in bed wearing a light-green hospital robe, the wires of a heart monitor running underneath it to a machine.

She looked much older and very frail, as if the slightest movement now required every ounce of her concentration. Her hair was dank, and her dull, hollowed eyes watched Jo listlessly as she rubbed her hands together under a hospital superbug disinfectant dispenser. Jo sat down on the chair beside the bed just as a monitor started beeping.

A nurse did a double-take from the corridor as she spotted Jo and headed over.

'Didn't you see the signs about the winter vomiting bug?' she demanded. 'No visitors allowed.'

'I'm not a visitor,' Jo replied, standing to show her ID.

'Make it quick,' the nurse said, unimpressed, pressing a button on the monitor to stop the beep. 'She's due a feed.'

'Isn't there supposed to be a guard keeping an eye on her?' Jo said, lowering her voice.

'There was one here, briefly,' the nurse answered. 'He said something about being taken off the case by higher powers.'

Jo leaned over Tara as the nurse left. 'How are you feeling?' she asked.

Tara gave a tiny nod. 'Presley?' she asked, feebly.

'Safe with your mum,' Jo replied.

'I want to see him,' Tara croaked, trying to hoist herself up in the bed.

'You'll have to get yourself clean first,' Jo said. 'You need professional help. You may have survived this time, but what's going to happen when you have to cope with the stress of prison life? They're awash with drugs in there. It'll only be a matter of time before you OD in prison, too, the way you're going.'

Tara's eyes widened. 'Prison! What have I done to deserve that?'

'Take your pick. You went to the garage to pick up a haul of drugs, for starters,' Jo said.

'I didn't know about the drugs,' Tara said. 'I swear it on Presley's life.'

'Can you say the same about Imogen's murder?' Jo probed.

A different machine started to beep angrily. Jo realized it was the one monitoring Tara's blood pressure. The equipment used for lie detectors wasn't dissimilar. Stress testing was all based on monitoring heart rate and perspiration levels. Jo knew she was on the right track.

'Jeff told me everything when we arrested him,' she said. 'You thought Imogen had taken Presley, didn't you? That's why you killed her.'

'I want to see Presley,' Tara said stubbornly. 'When are you going to bring him in to see me? Mick won't. Mum won't. Please.'

'I'll have him here this afternoon, if you tell me the

truth about what was going on in the garage, and if you promise to get yourself clean. You're going to have to prove to everyone you're fit to be his mother. Presley doesn't need all the expensive, fancy stuff you get him. He needs you.'

Tears rolled down Tara's face, and then she started to talk.

67

'Fitz was disappointed with the escort business,' Tara said quietly. 'He was giving Imogen a lot of stick about it. He said she'd duped him, lied about how much money there was to be made. He said he was the one taking all the risks, and there wasn't much of a return.'

'Go on,' Jo encouraged, taking her hand and giving it a squeeze. She felt like shaking Tara, though. She also wanted to get a move on, so she could hook up with Sexton and join in the search for Dan.

Tara gave Jo a look. 'Fitz said if Imogen didn't supply him with more girls, he would count her out as a partner. But Imogen couldn't find any Irish girls willing to work at the new rates. She tried, believe you me. She put so much pressure on us all; well, she got me to go to Marrakesh, didn't she . . .?'

Jo knew she was holding back. 'There must have been something else going on in Marrakesh, other than the footballers' party. Why did Imogen go, too?'

Tara turned away to look at the wall. 'I told you, she wanted to get more girls.'

'From Morocco? Who was the contact?' Jo asked.

'Fitz has this guy working for him – Murray Lawlor – he looks after the door at the Blizzard, makes sure everything ticks over with no trouble. Used to be a cop.'

'I know him,' Jo said.

'Murray is a middleman for a big gangster supplying drugs to the club. This gangster provides protection for the club, protection from his own cronies, mainly, if you want to look at it like that.'

'Go on,' Jo said, drawing her out.

'Murray offered to hook Imogen up with someone who could get her some girls from north Africa. But in return, she had to bring a haul of drugs back from Morocco for his boss, the gangster. Fitz couldn't do it. He'd been caught in his helicopter before, and customs were watching out for him. It was a problem, because the gangster was in prison, and didn't trust any of his own men to do it. He was afraid they'd try and rip him off. But Fitz said that as long as Murray got the drugs over, he'd buy them from him. Fitz was branching out into a lot of other areas because of the way the hotel trade was going. He'd even invested in a lock-up, so as to have somewhere to store the drugs when they came in.'

'You know the location?' Jo asked.

'Somewhere in North Wall.'

'And who's the gangster?' Jo demanded.

Tara shrugged weakly.

'It's Barry Roberts, isn't it?' Jo pushed.

Tara nodded reluctantly.

'So Murray Lawlor wanted Imogen to bring a haul of cocaine back from north Africa for Barry Roberts?' Jo said slowly. 'And in return he was going to front up a few females to work at the Triton?'

Tara sniffed in reply.

'But how was Imogen going to transport the drugs?' Jo asked. 'There's no way she could have got them through on a chartered flight.'

'She arranged for someone to take them on a ferry to the south of Spain in a camper van,' Tara whispered. 'With the girls . . . And just in case anything went wrong, she brought one of the Triton's VIP clients over for the party with her. A politician. He didn't know what was going on, but he would have been extremely useful to Imogen if anything had gone wrong.'

Blaise Stanley, Jo realized, letting out a long hard sigh. And there'd been a camper van in the garage the night Presley vanished. It was the only vehicle she'd taken no notice of, precisely because it was designed to avert suspicion. She was furious with herself for being so stupid.

'How many girls were involved?' she asked impatiently.

'Two,' Tara said. 'There should have been three, but there was a problem. Imogen went berserk. She said the deal was three girls or it was all off. So they snatched a kid off the street rather than risk Imogen pulling out – just a kid. They couldn't control her, she kept trying to escape. They drugged her, and I didn't see her again after that.'

'Where's she now?' Jo asked, worried.

Tara shook her head. 'Only two girls made it back to Dublin. Murray wouldn't tell me what happened.'

'And finally there was an incident in the garage on the night the drugs arrived,' Jo prompted. 'Something unexpected. A fight. The cops were called. Marcus had been sent to collect the drugs. But they needed to be stashed somewhere in a hurry. Your car.'

'And just in case I got any bright ideas, Presley was taken,' Tara said.

'What was Jeff paying you for?' Jo asked.

'What do you think?' Tara asked. 'He wanted me to visit him after Morocco. I think in his head he thought we had a future. I suppose I used that. I thought he could help me get out of Imogen's clutches. But he was too weak.'

'And the film of you being raped in the pool – how did your mother get hold of it?'

Tara sighed deeply. She was visibly growing weaker,

but Jo needed to keep her talking. 'Jeff owed me money. He couldn't come up with the readies. Imogen controlled everything in his life, even the amount of cash in his pocket. He gave me a memory stick and told me to consider it a gift. I didn't know what was on it when I took it. He told me it was the one thing I could use against Imogen if the time came.' She paused, and took a few shaky breaths.

'My mum must have watched it the night Presley was taken, and downloaded it on to a DVD. She's the one who told me about you and what you had done to save that other kid.'

'Did she kill Imogen?' Jo asked.

But Tara was gazing at the door of her room. Gabriella was standing there with Presley. Tara tried to hold her arms out, but she barely had the strength.

Jo gripped her hand. 'Come on, Tara. Give me this last piece of the puzzle and I'll leave you with Presley.'

Tara gave a sob. 'No, I killed Imogen. Early on Monday morning, I went to see her. I told her I wanted my boy back. She said I could have him if I gave her the DVD. I didn't know what she was talking about. I picked up a rock and hit her. If anyone had the right to kill her, it was me, and maybe that missing girl from Morocco.' She turned to Jo, her eyes wide with fear. 'I killed Imogen. Are you satisfied now?'

68

A steady stream of press flowed between Abra-kebabra, the kebab shop on the corner, and the road block sealing off the street where Barry Roberts's mother lived in Crumlin.

Sexton had phoned Jo at the hospital with the news.

'Roberts has got a hostage,' he'd explained. 'The ERU SWAT team are here now.'

Jo processed what that meant. 'Roberts is armed, isn't he?' she asked, gripping the phone so tightly her knuckles went white. 'Why am I only hearing this now?'

'Because it's only just happened,' Sexton answered softly. 'Are you going to come over?'

'Come over?' Jo said. 'I want to do the hostage negotiation.'

Half an hour later, Jo was at the road block in Crumlin. She showed her ID to the officer keeping the cordon.

'Inspector, you do know who we believe Roberts has taken hostage in there?' the officer asked.

'Yes,' Jo said.

'You can't go in without a bulletproof vest.'

Jo carried on, ducking under the tape. 'Try stopping me,' she muttered.

The officer pressed a button on his radio and left an urgent message.

As Jo arrived on the scene seconds later, she heard Oakley say, 'Roger that.' He watched Jo walk up to Roberts's front door. 'Officer, I'm warning you to stop now, before you endanger life,' he boomed through a megaphone.

Jo gave him the finger over her shoulder and stayed put.

A shot rang out.

Jo couldn't tell which direction it had come from, but she could hear a commotion behind the front door.

She bent and shouted through the letterbox. 'Two cops are better than one, Roberts. Here I am – yours for the taking.'

Seconds later the door opened and, ignoring Oakley's voice on the megaphone demanding she turn back, Jo stepped inside the house.

69

Dan sat on a kitchen chair, his head slumped on his chest, a length of blue washing-line rope binding his wrists and ankles, and strung to a noose around his neck so that if he struggled it would tighten. A plastic carrier bag covered his face, and the handles were knotted under his jaw. If the bag hadn't made a tiny movement as air passed in and out through a small hole in front of his mouth, Jo would have believed him already gone, there was so much blood on his shirt. Roberts was standing directly behind him with a lighter in one hand, the handle of a Glock poking up from the waistband of his jeans, and a sawn-off shotgun pointed at Dan's head.

'Sit down,' he told Jo.

'Aren't you in enough trouble?' she asked, pulling the chair out.

She thought Dan's back straightened a fraction at the sound of her voice. Jo drew a breath. The smell of petrol was overpowering. She'd sensed it first in the hall, which had one of those clear plastic runners down the middle to protect the carpet from stains. Jo had slipped more than once on the way in from all the fluid sluiced there.

There was a bark of laughter from Roberts. 'She's got spunk,' he said, nudging Dan's shoulder with the sawn-off. 'Bet she's feisty in bed.'

Jo could hear muffled crying from another room. Roberts's eyes darted to the door then moved back.

'That your old mum?' Jo asked.

Roberts didn't answer.

Jo looked around the room. 'She did her best for you, I can tell. You should see the hovels some of the scrotes we deal with grew up in. This is a nice place, clean and warm. What are you going to say to the judge when the time comes, if you can't blame your crimes on your start in life, like the rest of them?'

Roberts puffed out his chest. 'I ain't going back inside, not for no one.'

'You didn't give school much of a chance, either, did you?'

The sound of padded footsteps made her turn, and she saw a grey-haired woman shuffle into the room in a pair of fluffy pink slippers. 'It's not his fault,' she said.

Roberts sighed. 'I'll handle this, Mam,' he said.

Jo crossed her arms and spoke directly to the woman. 'Let me guess, his father was an alcoholic who used to beat you. He's the one to blame. Is that it?'

Roberts's face tightened. 'Don't you dare speak to her like that.' Spit turned to shiny strings at the corners of his mouth.

'It's all right, Barry,' the old woman answered, in a strong Dublin accent. 'I want to tell this one, who thinks she knows everything, what was done to you. Barry was a good boy. He was taken off me, and put into care. One of the staff in the home used to abuse him, my son, who was taken from me.'

'Shut it, Mam,' Roberts reacted.

Jo turned to him. 'How many civilians have you killed? Nine, plus Murray Lawlor, Big Johnny and Fitz? Ten? Well, if you count those young addicts you poisoned it's even more, isn't it? You arranged for three prison officers to be killed yesterday, too. They didn't abuse you, did they? Where's this going to end, Barry? Do you think they're going to let you walk out of here, maybe catch a flight to some Costa, after all that? Use your loaf.'

The sheen of sweat that had broken out across Roberts's face told Jo that whatever drugs had been in his system were now wearing off.

'He dies next,' Roberts answered, gesturing towards Dan. 'One for the road.'

'They don't care about him,' Jo said. 'He's been working on a case to bring down the justice minister, the same one who'll decide how long your life sentence lasts.'

'You're lying,' Roberts answered.

'It's all on tape. I'm surprised your lawyer didn't mention it. George Hannah, isn't it? He's got a lot of friends in high places. How do you think Fitz managed to evade a sentence? Why do you think they let me come in here to talk to you? They'd be delighted if you did away with me, too. If you torch this place you'll be doing exactly what they want.'

'He's not going to set light to his own home,' Roberts's mother said. 'He's just trying to buy time to think.'

'Shut it!' Roberts yelled. 'I can't . . .'

There was a screeching noise as Dan suddenly shunted the chair back into Roberts's groin, trapping him against the sink. Dan coughed for air as Roberts hauled on the noose.

Jo dived towards the old lady and twisted her arm up behind her back. The old woman yelped in pain as Jo put her neck into the crook of her arm and held fast.

'Let her go!' Roberts yelled.

'I will if you take the bag off his head, cut off his ropes, and let him go.'

Roberts looked at his mother and ripped the plastic bag off Dan.

The state of Dan's face made Jo gasp. His eyes were

black, his lip split, and bruises had puffed out every-where into shades of brown, red and purple. The rope was too tight around his neck: the skin above it was swollen and glossy.

Roberts pulled a drawer open behind him and took a kitchen knife out of it, which he put to Dan's throat.

Jo squeezed the old woman's neck, making her moan. 'Now the rope,' she said.

Roberts started to saw through the rope with the knife, so close to Dan's neck that Dan closed his eyes. After a couple of minutes and several superficial nicks that drew a lot of blood, the noose snapped. Dan took deep gulps of air.

'Now,' Roberts said, 'like I said, let her go.'

But the room had filled with thick, choking, blinding smoke before Jo had a chance to answer.

70

Foxy was making his way through a council estate, which was a maze of cul-de-sacs not mapped by logic, street names, or numbers, to get to Hassan's house. He'd been there before, when he'd managed to recover the sex tape for Jo from Hassan's excuse of a wife.

Foxy wanted to be in Crumlin, where the hostage negotiation was unfolding, but Jo had told him to track down Hassan at all costs, and get a statement to back up what she'd discovered from Tara.

Foxy had just arrived at Hassan's home when the man himself emerged from his front door and climbed into a waiting HiAce transit van – which Foxy could see belonged to Marcus Rankin, the pool-cleaning specialist, because his name and mobile number were written on the side.

Maintaining a safe distance, Foxy decided to follow, cursing the anti-joyriding ramps, which were going to play havoc with the squad car's sump. He allowed the van to drive past, watching it from his rear-view mirror, so Hassan wouldn't spot him behind the wheel. Based on the number of scorched-earth patches and cider cans strewn on the open ground opposite, though, he didn't think the squad car in itself would be enough to arouse much suspicion.

It had been years since he'd done any active policing, and he was glad of it. The country had changed. The days when the priests and politicians held any moral authority were over. Now, kids growing up with nothing thought that following in the footsteps of the likes of Barry Roberts was a real career option.

Aware that the HiAce had just turned right with a bleed arrow, he tried to switch lanes without using the siren, but the motorists streaming around the corner stubbornly ignored his attempts to cut in. Foxy stuck his hand out of the window and managed to edge in just as the lights changed, leaving him with another quandary. If he jumped them, his cover would definitely be blown – Rankin and Hassan would spot him and change their plans.

He waited, and by some miracle, when he finally rounded the turn he could still see the HiAce ahead. He followed it to a lock-up in North Wall. There he watched as Rankin jumped out of the driver's seat and walked around to the side of the van, sliding the door open.

Two young girls, squinting against the light, stepped out. One was a Filipina, and the other looked Moroccan. Foxy sprinted across, grabbing Rankin and Hassan, and snapping cuffs on their wrists. 'You have the right to remain silent,' he said. 'Anything you do say will be taken down, and may be used against you in a court of law . . .'

71

Jo pulled her shirt up over her nose and mouth, but she still couldn't stop spluttering and spitting at the noxious fumes given off by the tear gas.

The SWAT team were screaming for everyone to lie down on the floor, but that didn't stop Roberts discharging his weapon, or the team firing back.

Jo crawled towards Dan and desperately tugged at the feet of his chair to pull him down to safety. He fell with a thud.

She couldn't see anything, but she knew the slippery substance covering him wasn't petrol. She kissed his face, and whispered the things she'd needed to say to him for a long time directly in his ear. No matter what happened, they were going to be together from now on.

Thursday

72

Sexton sat in his car, parked outside Jo's home, staring at the dog-eared envelope on his lap – Maura's suicide note. Now that there was something he was dreading even more than opening it – calling on Jo to see how she, Dan and their family were doing – reading it didn't seem such a big deal. Sexton banged his head against the headrest and stared straight ahead. He wound down his window and let in some cool air as he broke the seal and pulled the note out. No matter what it said, it couldn't be any worse than the pain he knew was waiting for him inside Jo's house. He'd sat with her since they'd recaptured Roberts, listened to her pour her heart out, struggling to contain his own feelings of regret. He didn't think he'd seen anything more heartbreaking than the sight of little Harry, oblivious to everything, holding his big brother's hand as Jo broke the news of Dan's injuries to them. Rory's face was red from crying, but he hadn't shed a tear in front of Sexton; he was his father's son all right.

He did his best to keep Jo's spirits up, but he knew only too well how hollow words could sound when you needed them most. He'd promised Jo that if he could get out of bed every morning, so could she. He'd told her she might never get over what had happened, but for her boys' sakes she would have to keep going, and that, for them, she'd find a way to make her peace with it. Dan would need her now, more than ever.

Sexton rubbed his face in his hands. He was exhausted. The irony was, it was probably the biggest case the station had ever cracked – a human trafficking and drugs ring, Barry Roberts locked up for good by ballistics that linked him to the murder of Fitz, Big Johnny and Murray Lawlor. Some of the most famous footballers in the world were due to stand trial, and even Justice Minister Blaise Stanley had been exposed. He, Sexton, was in the clear now, too, his investigative work cancelling out the cock-up he'd made earlier, when he'd been found in the Triton Hotel bedroom with Tara. But, by Christ, the price had been high. He didn't know if they'd ever be able to persuade Jo to come back.

He bowed his head and read the note. It consisted of one line. 'I love you, but I can't go on. Patricia.'

Sexton felt the hackles on the back of his neck rise.

Why would Maura have signed off a note using the wrong name?

She didn't write it, he said to himself.

He looked at the note again. It was definitely Maura's handwriting, but there wasn't a single tear-stain on it. Maura couldn't manage to sit through an episode of *EastEnders* without bawling her heart out. She'd never have written a suicide note without sobbing. String herself up with the flex of a vacuum cleaner? Take their baby's life while she was at it? His wife hadn't topped herself at all.

Sexton shoved the note in the dash. It was for another day, when Jo didn't need him as much as she did now.

Epilogue

Jo had been given special leave while Dan recovered in rehabilitation. She lost all sense of time in the months away from work. There weren't weeks any more, only good days and bad days. The good days were the ones when he tried to talk to her, and she saw signs of the fighter she knew he was. On the bad days, he'd try to force her away, saying terrible things to try to make her believe he didn't love her; sometimes briefly succeeding, and making her storm away. She'd only ever get as far as the car park, a blast of cold air always bringing her back to her senses. There were worse days – when he could say nothing at all because he was so consumed by his own overwhelming sense of powerlessness and rage at the prospect that he might never walk again.

Then, Jo would grip his hand and tell him that she was not going anywhere, and that she loved him, and that he was going to do everything again, but that it would take time. She would prattle on with meaningless news, just talking for the sake of it, to try and ignore the faraway look in his eyes as he battled to come to terms with his condition.

But hardest on her was the fact that not once since his kidnap had he told her he loved her. That was what scared her the most. She could reason away most of her doubts by remembering the man he used to be. *He hated pity, and didn't want to make me feel fettered to him*, she told herself. That was why he'd begged Jo, sobbing like a child, not to bring the boys in to see him until he knew what his chances were. Until then, he wanted them to remember their father as a man who was strong, and could protect them if they needed it.

Rory had put his fist through a door when Jo had told him Dan wouldn't see him. Her friends had been a godsend. She'd had to accept help, and they'd thrown her a lifeline. Dorothy was living with Foxy and Sal again, and her regular offers to babysit Harry, and the home-made meals she had brought over, had freed Jo up to spend even more time trying to bring Dan around.

But alone in bed at night, she could sometimes feel so lost that the practicalities of what needed to happen next seemed insurmountable. But Jo couldn't leave Dan, not when she'd had a taste of what it might be like to have to live in a world without him.

* * *

She parked the car, and walked round to the passenger side. Dan was sitting there, hunched up and tense. He frowned at her as she opened the door and tried to guide his legs on to the pavement.

'I said I'd do it,' he said angrily.

She stepped back.

The front door opened and Rory came out, holding Harry's hand. He froze when he saw his father. Dan had planted his own legs on the pavement and was clutching at the doorframe, trying to heave himself out of the car. Jo knew he didn't want her to help, but it was agonizing watching him struggle.

Finally he made it. He straightened, let go of the car, and took two shaky steps forward.

'Well, aren't you going to give me a proper welcome?' he asked his sons.

Rory smiled widely, and ran towards him with Harry, and Jo thought her heart would burst as Dan clasped them both tightly in his arms.

Acknowledgements

As ever, thanks to the inspirational crime editor Selina Walker for all the guidance and encouragement, and for not letting even several feet of snow, which managed to cut off the power and the post, close down the roads and schools, and shut down the entire month of December, get between us and the finish. Thanks, too, to the rest of the Transworld team – Eoin McHugh, Brian Langan, Madeline Toy, Stephen Mulcahey, Kate Tolley, Helen Gleed O'Connor and Declan Heeney. And to Alison Barrow for the amazing night in Belfast with the fabulous Tess Gerritsen and David Torrans. I also have to thank fellow author and journalist Lucy Pinney for giving me a great idea for the next book, Jenni Murray for going easy on me, and Lisanne Radice and Claire Rourke for helping me think things through.

I owe a major thank-you to my agent, Jane Gregory, for taking me into her fold with some of my all-time favourite crime authors, and also to my

Sunday World editors and friends. Thanks to all my girlfriends, Vanessa O'Loughlin, Carmel Wallace, Sarah Hamilton, and Maria Duffy.

Lastly, but most importantly, my husband Brian, and Peter and Johnny who make everything worth it, my parents Eamonn and Sheila, and all my family who allow me to talk about unsavoury things over dinner.

Too Close For Comfort

Niamh O'Connor

BEHIND THE FAÇADE of Nun's Cross, an exclusive gated development in South Dublin, lurks a dark secret. The body of one of its residents, Amanda Wells, is found in a shallow grave in the Dublin mountains, a plastic bag stuffed in her mouth. When her neighbour Derek Carpenter disappears, he becomes the prime suspect: he was questioned about the disappearance of his sister-in-law, Sarah, many years earlier. It seems like an open and shut case.

DI Jo Birmingham is not so sure, and she has her own personal reasons to prove Derek innocent: it was her husband Dan who had cleared Derek of Sarah's disappearance. But when Jo starts digging, she unearths more than she bargained for, and her own fragile domestic peace comes under threat. And the one person who could help Jo crack the case, Derek's wife Liz, is so desperate to protect her family that she is going out of her way to thwart all efforts to establish the truth. Can both women emerge unscathed?

The gripping new thriller from Niamh O'Connor –
available June 2012.

If I Never See You Again

Niamh O'Connor

The Detective

Meet Jo Birmingham. Single mum, streetwise detective, and spiky as hell. Recently promoted, she is one of the few female detective superintendents on the Dublin police force. But with a failed marriage behind her and two young sons at home, trying to strike the right work-life balance has run her ragged.

The Serial Killer

When Jo identifies the missing link in a chain of brutal killings, she comes under fierce scrutiny from her male colleagues in the force, especially her boss and ex-husband Dan Mason. But as the body count rises, so do the body parts. As fear stalks the city, it soon becomes obvious both to the police and to the media that a serial killer is at large.

A Terrifying Game of Cat and Mouse

And so Jo embarks on a terrifying psychological journey to find out who the killer is, and how he is choosing his victims. Soon she is involved in a deadly game in which there are no rules. Because the killer is waiting for her . . .

Headstone

Ken Bruen

Some people help the less fortunate. Others kill them.

EVIL HAS MANY guises. Jack Taylor has encountered most of them but nothing before has ever truly terrified him until a group called Headstone rears its ugly head. An elderly priest is viciously beaten until nearly dead. A special needs boy is brutally attacked. A series of seemingly random, insane, violent events even has the Guards shaken.

Most would see a headstone as a marker of the dead, but this coterie of evil intends to act as a death knell to every aspect of Jack's life as an act of appalling violence alerts him to the horror enveloping Galway.

Accepting the power of Headstone, Jack realizes that in order to fight back he must relinquish the remaining shreds of what has made him human – knowledge that may have come too late to prevent an act of such ferocious evil that the whole country would be changed forever – and in the worst way.

The Devil

Ken Bruen

WHEN PI JACK TAYLOR is called to investigate the frenzied murder of a student, he remembers a recent encounter with an over-friendly stranger in an airport bar. A stranger who seemed to know rather more than he should about Jack.

After several more murders and too many encounters to be coincidental, Jack believes he may have met his nemesis.

But why has he been chosen? And could he really be dealing with the Devil himself?